"If you love to shop 'til you drop, watch out for Josie Belle's first entry in a new mystery series—because murder's no bargain."

—Leann Sweeney, author of
The Cat, the Wife and the Weapon

Killer Deals

The women took their places. A crowd of fifty or so had gathered, but Maggie and her crew had arrived at five this morning to stake out their turf. Stegner's was a premier outlet in southern Virginia that specialized in shoes, handbags and belts. Twice a year, they had a sale that could blow the doors off a woman's closet.

Maggie and the Good Buy Girls had yet to miss a sale at Stegner's. Their system was honed to perfection. They arrived early, they took the spot in front of the doors on the side of the store where they were headed, and they let nothing get in their way.

Maggie glanced at her watch and began the countdown. "Seven, six, five . . ." She could feel her crew take its mark.

"Three, two, one!"

The automatic doors slid open, and the crowd pressed forward. The professionals walked swiftly, but in an orderly fashion. Shoulder to shoulder, the Good Buy Girls veered to the left as planned.

The amateurs bolted into the store, throwing elbows and body slamming people out of the way until what had been a fine day of shopping had turned into an Ultimate Fighting cage match.

"Focus!" Maggie ordered

50% off Murder

Josie Belle

BERKLEY PRIME CRIME, NEW YORK

THE BERKLEY PUBLISHING GROUP
Published by the Penguin Group
Penguin Group (USA) Inc.
375 Hudson Street, New York, New York 10014, USA

Penguin Group (Canada), 90 Eglinton Avenue East, Suite 700, Toronto, Ontario M4P 2Y3, Canada
(a division of Pearson Penguin Canada Inc.) • Penguin Books Ltd., 80 Strand, London WC2R 0RL,
England • Penguin Group Ireland, 25 St. Stephen's Green, Dublin 2, Ireland (a division of Penguin
Books Ltd.) • Penguin Group (Australia), 250 Camberwell Road, Camberwell, Victoria 3124, Australia
(a division of Pearson Australia Group Pty. Ltd.) • Penguin Books India Pvt. Ltd., 11 Community
Centre, Panchsheel Park, New Delhi—110 017, India • Penguin Group (NZ), 67 Apollo Drive,
Rosedale, Auckland 0632, New Zealand (a division of Pearson New Zealand Ltd.) • Penguin Books
(South Africa) (Pty.) Ltd., 24 Sturdee Avenue, Rosebank, Johannesburg 2196, South Africa

Penguin Books Ltd., Registered Offices: 80 Strand, London WC2R 0RL, England

This is a work of fiction. Names, characters, places, and incidents either are the product of the author's
imagination or are used fictitiously, and any resemblance to actual persons, living or dead, business
establishments, events, or locales is entirely coincidental. The publisher does not have any control over
and does not assume any responsibility for author or third-party websites or their content.

50% OFF MURDER

A Berkley Prime Crime Book / published by arrangement with the author

PUBLISHING HISTORY
Berkley Prime Crime mass-market edition / April 2012

Copyright © 2012 by Jennifer McKinlay Orf.
Cover illustration by Mary Ann Lasher.
Cover design by Sarah Oberrender.
Interior text design by Laura K. Corless.

ISBN: 978-0-425-24702-0

BERKLEY® PRIME CRIME
Berkley Prime Crime Books are published by The Berkley Publishing Group,
a division of Penguin Group (USA) Inc.,
375 Hudson Street, New York, New York 10014.
BERKLEY® PRIME CRIME and the PRIME CRIME logo are trademarks of
Penguin Group (USA) Inc.

PRINTED IN THE UNITED STATES OF AMERICA

10 9 8 7 6 5 4 3 2 1

ALWAYS LEARNING   **PEARSON**

For my mom, Susan McKinlay, and my aunt Nancy Gould, the best shoppers I know. I love you two more than a smoking-hot bargain. And in loving memory of my aunt Joan Seybold, whose gifts always had the "wow" factor.

Acknowledgments

A big thank-you to my wonderful editor, Michelle Vega—you really made this book sparkle. A very grateful high five to copyeditor Andy Ball—you're brilliant. Also, I have to give a knuckle bump to my agent, Jessica Faust, for her unwavering confidence that I could write yet another series. And, as always, high fives and hugs to my dudes, Beckett, Wyatt and Chris.

Chapter 1

"Okay, is everyone clear on what they're supposed to do?" Maggie Gerber asked.

"Head straight for shoes, do not get distracted by handbags," Ginger Lancaster said. It appeared she was reminding herself.

"What do you do when you get there?" Maggie asked.

"Sizes eight and nine, leather only," Joanne Claramotta answered. She had her best running shoes on and was jogging in place, her usual warm-up routine for storming a store.

"What is our primary target?" Maggie asked.

"Designer only, preferably Italian," Claire Freemont answered. "No knockoffs."

"Excellent." Maggie said.

She took a moment to study the reflection of her crew in the store's glass door. They all wore track suits of varying colors and running shoes, and carried canvas shopping bags on their arms.

Claire had her blonde bob pulled back by a wide, neon pink headband, which matched her sweat suit and also helped to keep her glasses in place. She looked determined.

Joanne, in navy blue, wore her long dark hair in a pony-tail on top of her head. She stopped jogging and was stretching, looking prepared to run over anybody who got in her way.

Ginger, who kept her black hair cut close to her head, was in a baby blue track suit, which enhanced the rich brown of her skin. She was muttering, "No handbags," under her breath like a mantra. Her eyes were narrowed in concentration. She had her game face on.

Finally, Maggie took a cursory glance at herself. She was in her favorite green workout suit, and her shoulder-length auburn hair was pulled back and clipped at the nape of her neck. She had her shopping tote on her arm. She was good to go. She could feel the surge of adrenaline coursing through her body as the rush of scoring a good deal was just minutes away.

She consulted her watch. "We're in the sixty-second range. Remember, when the doors open, go to the left."

The women took their places. A crowd of fifty or so had gathered, but Maggie and her crew had arrived at five this morning to stake out their turf. Stegner's was a premier outlet in southern Virginia that specialized in shoes, handbags and belts. Twice a year they had a sale that could literally blow the doors off a woman's closet.

Maggie and the Good Buy Girls, as they called themselves, had yet to miss a sale at Stegner's. Their system was honed to perfection. They arrived early, they took the spot in front of the doors on the side of the store where they were headed, and they let nothing get in their way.

"Thirty seconds," Maggie said.

The crowd behind them shifted restlessly. The lure of ridiculously marked down Manolo, Weitzman and Prada shoes, as well as Coach and Michael Kors handbags, was drawing them all like bees to pollen.

Abruptly, a platinum blonde, wearing black leather stiletto boots with black leggings and a zebra striped halter top, elbowed her way to the front of the crowd until she was standing beside Maggie.

"You're going down, Gerber," the woman hissed.

Maggie turned and saw her nemesis, Summer Phillips, standing there.

"Are you actually trash-talking me?" she asked.

"Trash, is that how you see yourself?" Summer asked. "So you are more self-aware than I thought."

Maggie felt her temples contract as her temper flared.

"Why are you here, Summer?" she asked. "Didn't your fourth husband pay enough to get rid of you when he divorced you? I wouldn't think outlet sales were your thing."

Summer's bloodred lip curled back, and she looked like she wanted to bite Maggie.

"Countdown, Maggie," Ginger said.

When Maggie didn't respond, Ginger leaned forward and saw Summer Phillips on the other side of her.

"Uh-oh," she said. "This is bad."

Maggie was breathing in through her nose and out through her mouth. Summer Phillips had been the bane of her existence since they were kids.

For some reason that Maggie had never fully understood, Summer lived to make her life a misery. She had made sure that Maggie was mocked, picked on and ridiculed at every possible turn. She had even tried to befriend Ginger, but Ginger had refused, seeing Summer for the devil in spandex that she was.

Maggie hadn't seen much of Summer over the past few years, but now here she was, horning in on one of Maggie's ultimate joys, a sale. Well, she was darned if she was going to let this big-busted, bleached blonde bubblehead ruin one of the highlights of her summer.

Shaking Summer's presence off like a bad case of fleas, Maggie glanced at her watch and began the count down: "Seven, six, five . . ."

She could feel her crew take their mark.

"Three, two, one!"

The automatic doors slid open, and the crowd pressed forward. The professionals walked swiftly, but in an orderly fashion. Shoulder to shoulder, the Good Buy Girls veered to the left as planned and headed straight for the eights and nines.

The amateurs, like Summer, bolted into the store, throwing elbows and body slamming people out of the way until what would have been a fine day of shopping turned into an Ultimate Fighting cage match.

"Focus!" Maggie ordered. "Eyes on the prize."

The four of them strode to the shoes. They fanned out by size, Claire and Joanne in the eights and Maggie and Ginger in the nines. Working in teams, they started on the end of the row and worked their way to the middle, stuffing their canvas bags full of the shoes that met their criteria.

Maggie was a third of the way in when Summer, looking disheveled, stumbled into her row. As Maggie went to pick up a pair of Jimmy Choo ankle boots, Summer snatched them from her hand.

"Hey!" Maggie snapped. "That's rude!"

"I got them first," Summer argued.

"Maggie, focus!" Ginger's voice ordered from behind her. Maggie glanced up. Other shoppers were beginning to crowd into the aisle. She had to work fast.

"Fine," she said and turned her back on Summer. She reached for a pair of Alberto Fermani's, and Summer snatched those, too. "What is your problem?"

"I don't have a problem!" Summer said. "What's yours?"

"What are you, twelve?" Maggie asked. The crowd was pressing inward. She reached blindly for a pair of plastic pumps, thinking she might hit Summer over the head with them, but Summer grabbed those, too.

It was obvious that Summer's sole purpose was to ruin Maggie's shopping expedition. Well, Maggie had played this game with other amateurs. Summer was going to lose.

Maggie reached for a pair of cheap knockoffs, but Summer snatched them away. While she juggled the four pairs of shoes in her arms, Maggie grabbed a pair of Seychelles. And so it went, Maggie faking out Summer with lousy shoes and using her distraction to grab the good ones, until she met Ginger in the middle.

"We're good?" Maggie asked.

"Good," Ginger confirmed. "Let's meet the others."

They wound their way past the throng—through a sea of handbags, during which Ginger kept her eyes on the floor— to the corner where they always met up.

Now, it was time to unload their bags and finalize their decisions.

They each had managed to snag seven to ten pairs of shoes in the correct sizes. Now they would try them on, check the prices and figure out which ones they would actually buy. If the deal was good enough and no one wanted the shoes, Maggie would buy them anyway and sell them online. She had discovered she could make a tidy monthly income selling items she picked up at sales.

She and Ginger went through the size nines. They each picked two pairs of shoes to buy for themselves and then debated the rest. When you were looking at a three-hundred-dollar pair of shoes that had been marked down to thirty, many things had to be taken into consideration.

Fit, practicality and style were of the utmost consideration. But then this was why they came here. There was no substitute for quality. A good pair of Weitzmans could last ten to fifteen years, wear well and never look out of date. Poorly made shoes would cost the same and last one season. Not only that, but they'd probably cause foot damage before they ended up in a landfill.

"There she is! I demand that you throw her out!"

The Good Buy Girls glanced up from their pile of shoes as one.

There, looking indignant and pointing a bony, red talon–tipped finger at Maggie, stood Summer Phillips. Beside her was Stegners' manager, Barney Comstock.

He broke into a grin at the sight of them. "Hey, it's the GBGs. Great to see you!"

"Hi, Barney," they all said together.

"GBGs?" Summer asked, looking disgusted.

"Good Buy Girls," Barney said. "Get it? Good *buy* girls! I didn't see you come in. We had a bit of a ruckus at the opening today."

He cast Summer an unhappy look, and Maggie was pleased that he knew exactly whose fault that was.

Summer's face flushed. She did not like the way this was going. Maggie had to duck her head to keep from laughing. She and Barney went back more than twenty years. He'd helped her pick her wedding shoes, for Pete's sake.

"So, Ms. Philbrick here says you have some shoes of hers," Barney said.

"The name is Phillips," Summer snapped.

"Oh, oops, sorry," he said, not looking at all repentant.

Barney had managed Stegner's for over forty years. His gray hair was just a fringe around his bald head, and both his jowls and his belly sagged as if gravity had a hold and wasn't about to let go. Summer could throw whatever she wanted at him, but Maggie knew Barney had been dealing with obnoxious customers since the pillbox hat had gone the way of the dinosaur. Surely, he could handle Summer.

Summer stomped her stiletto into the industrial carpeting. "I want my shoes back."

"Maggie." Barney put his hand on the back of his neck and blew out a breath, as if he really hated this part of his job. "She seems to think you've got some of her shoes."

Maggie gritted her teeth. "Really? Because she followed me into the aisle and snatched every pair I touched."

Summer turned up her nose as if she smelled something bad, and said, "I never."

"That's obvious," Joanne snapped. Joanne was Brooklyn born and bred, and she did not take insults to herself or her friends well. She moved to stand behind Maggie in a show of support. Both Ginger and Claire moved in as well.

After all those years of being cornered in the locker room by Summer and her posse of chesty cheerleaders, Maggie had to acknowledge that she liked having her peeps at her back.

"Let's all calm down," she said. "Now, Summer, which shoes do you think I took from you?"

It was admittedly a trick question. Since they had all dumped their shoes into a pile, taking out only the ones for themselves so far, Summer had no way of knowing what shoes Maggie had gathered, nor could she tell which pairs Maggie had put aside for herself.

"Why, those!" Summer said, and she reached into the pile and pulled out a pink pair of pumps by Via Spiga.

Maggie almost laughed at the absurdity of it all.

The pumps were size eights, and had been picked up by Claire or Joanne. A quick glance at Summer's stilettos and Maggie frowned.

"Really? You fit into size eights? Barney, don't her boots look to be elevens?" Maggie asked.

"Hmm, I'd say twelves—wide," he said. He rubbed his chin with the back of his hand. "You have some sturdy feet there, ma'am."

Summer sucked in a breath as if she'd been slapped. The Via Spigas dropped from her hand and she growled, "How dare you?"

"Oh, we dare," Joanne said. "Care to make it a double dare?"

Like any bully who finds herself outnumbered, Summer spun on her pointy heel and fled the store. Joanne led the group in knuckle pounds and the women went back to their in-depth shoe analysis.

"Here you go, ladies," Gwen Morgan said. She carried a tray with four coffees on it: two lattes, one espresso and a chai tea. "Your punch card is full, Maggie, so next time you get a freebie."

"Excellent," Maggie said. She took the card from Gwen and put it in her wallet.

The ladies were basking in their post-sale success, sitting on the front patio of the Perk Up, surrounded by their bags from Stegner's. The drive back from the store had taken an hour. It was midday now, and they had a nice view of the goings-on in town from their spot on Main Street.

Gwen and her husband, Jay Morgan, owned the Perk Up, which they had opened five years before, during the coffee boom. They had a small bakery case in there as well and offered an assortment of baked goods to go with the coffee. A glance at the mostly empty coffeehouse made Maggie wonder how business was going. It was so close to lunch, she would have expected the tables to be full. Then again, it was the end of summer and people were trying to get in the last of their vacations and prepare for back-to-school, so maybe the slowness was just temporary.

Gwen served their coffee and tea, and said, "If you need anything else, let me know."

"Think she knows where we can hire a hit on Summer Phillips?" Joanne whispered.

"I'm pretty sure husband number two tried that," Ginger said. "The woman is like a cat with nine lives."

"A feral cat," Maggie said.

"Still, you got her good with the size eights," Claire said. "She outed herself. That was classic."

"Yeah, but what I can't figure is why she was even at Stegner's," Maggie said. "I mean she's loaded. Why is she bargain hunting, and why do I get the feeling it was mostly to mess with me?"

"I don't know, but if I were you, I'd watch my back," Ginger said. "And we'll help."

"Absolutely," Claire said.

Joanne lifted her espresso and said, "To the Good Buy Girls. We came, we saw, we scored."

Chapter 2

"Maggie!" Ginger Lancaster burst through Maggie Gerber's front door like a bargain hunter on Black Friday. "Maggie, did you hear the news?"

Maggie met Ginger in the living room and stared at her wild-eyed friend. She held up her hand and said, "Don't tell me, let me guess."

Ginger looked like she would burst with the news, but she nodded for Maggie to go ahead while she caught her breath.

"Summer Phillips's Spanx gave out from exhaustion, and she busted out all over the country club?" Maggie asked.

"No! Did they?" Ginger asked, her eyes getting even wider.

"Nah, but that would be great, wouldn't it?" Maggie asked.

"Oh, girlfriend, you had me going!" Ginger waved a hand at her.

"Sorry," Maggie said. "I have a rich fantasy life."

Ginger shook her head, and said, "If Summer packs on much more baggage in her caboose, you may be forecasting the future."

"Well, then I hope they send out a warning to all low-lying areas," Maggie said.

Maggie hadn't seen Summer since the incident at Stegner's the week before. Still, it did not change the fact that Summer seemed to have decided to don her mean-girl mantle and go out of her way to make Maggie's life difficult—again.

Ginger chuckled. She had a contagious *heh-heh-heh* sort of laugh that reached out and tickled Maggie's ribs, making it impossible not to laugh in return.

"Nice shoes," Maggie said, stepping around her longtime friend to close the front door behind her.

"I saw them in the window of My Sister's Closet, you know, the thrift store on Main Street, and had to have them," Ginger said. "Eight dollars, and I got Trudi to throw in the matching handbag."

Maggie tucked her shoulder-length auburn hair, inherited along with her pale skin and freckles from the strong O'Brien gene pool of her father's side of the family, behind her ears as she bent down to get a closer look. The short heeled, brown Ferragamo pumps were exquisite. "Eight dollars and the handbag? You managed to score a handbag? Are you kidding me?"

"Excuse me, I am one of the original Good Buy Girls," Ginger said with her hands on her hips. "If there is one thing I do not kid about, it's a bargain."

Maggie grinned and hugged her oldest friend. The two women had grown up over on Hardy Street near the center of St. Stanley, a small town in southern Virginia. Both had come from large families in which getting by meant doing without or being creative with the spending. Now that they were older and had families of their own to care for, being creative had become their social outlet as well as a method of survival.

They had formed the Good Buy Girls, a club that shared coupons, discounts and bargain tips, twenty years before, when they were both newly married with babies on board.

The club membership had shifted and changed over the years except for Ginger and Maggie. Maggie liked to think they were lifers in the Good Buy Girls.

Ginger was the same age as Maggie, and they shared the same dress and shoe sizes, both being on the tall side of medium in height, but somehow Maggie always felt washed out when she stood next to Ginger, with her latte-colored skin, velvet brown eyes and boisterous laugh. Ginger was outspoken and funny and never engaged in a conversation in which she did not have the last word.

But then, maybe that was why they'd remained close friends all these years. Maggie was more of a watcher, quietly studying the world around her, while Ginger was more a doer. They balanced each other.

"So, what's your news?" Maggie asked.

"Oh, you got me so distracted, I forgot," Ginger said. "You may want to sit down."

"Why? Is it bad?" Maggie settled onto the armrest of the couch, feeling a nervous flutter in her chest. She hated—absolutely *hated*—bad news.

"Well, I suppose that depends upon your perspective," Ginger said. She watched Maggie's face closely when she added, "Sam Collins is back in town."

"What?" Maggie slid off of the armrest onto the couch with a thump.

"I thought that might get your attention," Ginger said. "They've hired him for the vacant sheriff post."

"He's the sheriff?" Maggie felt her chest get tight, and the room lurched a bit to the side. She wasn't positive, but she feared either her head or her heart might implode.

"Well, he retired from the Richmond force as a detective," Ginger said. "The mayor and the town council thought, given that he grew up here in St. Stanley, he'd be a good fit."

If a meteor had landed in the center of the town square and little green men had climbed out of it, Maggie could not have been more shocked.

"When does he start?" she asked.

"He already has," Ginger said. "As of yesterday."

Maggie could feel her pulse pound in her ears. This meant she could be in Santana's grocery store buying rhubarb or she could be at the Perk Up grabbing a cappuccino or at the library returning books and smack right into him. *Oh, horror!*

"Are you all right?" Ginger asked.

"Me? Yeah, I'm fine," Maggie lied. "It's just a surprise, that's all. I mean, I never thought Sam Collins would come back to St. Stanley. He's been gone for a long time."

"Twenty-four years," Ginger said. "Can you believe it?"

"Have you seen him?" Maggie asked. "Please tell me he is bald and fat."

Ginger laughed. "Okay, he's bald and fat."

Maggie grinned, and then Ginger shook her head.

"I'm just kidding," Ginger said. "I haven't seen him."

"Way to dash my hopes," Maggie said. She felt as if her equilibrium was returning. "So, we don't know for sure, but he could be bald and fat."

"Cling to that life raft," Ginger said. "Nice to know you still hate him as much as you did when we were kids."

Maggie glowered. "He deserved it. He nicknamed me 'Carrots'—I hated that!"

"Because of your hair," Ginger said. "Well, it doesn't look like that anymore. It's a much darker shade of red now. Who knows? Maybe you two will even become friends."

"I seriously doubt it," Maggie said.

Ginger tipped her head to the side, and Maggie realized she was giving away too much. Ginger knew her too well and would guess that it was more than just childhood teasing that made her dislike Sam Collins.

Maggie forced her mouth into a smile that felt more like a grimace as she rose from the couch. She would have to shove aside all thought of the new sheriff and wait to process this information later when she was alone, with no one to bear witness to the panic coursing through her.

"So, what did you bring for coupons?" she asked.

She looped her arm through Ginger's and steered her toward the kitchen. It was their weekly GBG meeting, where they coupon-swapped and shared bargain info. Because Maggie's house wasn't overrun by men like Ginger's, it had become their base of operations years ago, and no one had ever thought to change it.

"I brought the circulars from Sunday's paper," Ginger said. "Is Sandy here? There are a bunch of diaper coupons in this pile that, thank heavens, I no longer need."

Ginger was the mother of four teenage boys. Even with her husband's corporate sales job and her own private accounting business, the enormity of the Lancaster family grocery bill was mythic.

"She's in the kitchen, giving Josh a snack," Maggie said. "I have some diaper coupons for her, too."

The two women passed through the cozy living room and into the kitchen. Sandy, Maggie's niece, who had her same auburn hair, fair skin and pale green eyes, and Josh, Sandy's two-year-old son, were seated at the tiny table Maggie had picked up at a yard sale just for him. He was snacking on Cheerios and banana chunks and clutching his favorite Thomas the Tank Engine toy in his chubby little fist.

"Well, hi there, handsome," Ginger said as she buzzed the boy's blond head with a smacking kiss. He looked up at her with merry blue eyes and cheeks stuffed with bananas.

"Auntie Gingy," the boy said. "Nanas?"

Ginger grinned and said, "Thanks anyway, pumpkin, I think those 'nanas' are for you." Then she sighed. "I miss the days when I could make my boys happy with cereal and fruit. Do you know I made four trays of corn bread yesterday and a Crock-Pot full of beans, and it was gone in half an hour? Not even a crumb was left."

"Oh my." Sandy's eyes went wide. Obviously, the thought of growing boys and their appetites was the stuff of nightmares for the young mother.

Maggie put a reassuring hand on Sandy's head. She reminded her so much of herself. Maggie's husband, Charlie, had been a deputy for the St. Stanley Sheriff's Department. He'd been killed in the line of duty when she was just twenty-five years old and their daughter, Laura, had not been much older than young Josh. Maggie had survived, but it had been a struggle. Now Laura was a sophomore at Penn State, and Maggie couldn't be more proud, even though the tuition made her go a little lightheaded and see spots.

Sandy's husband had shipped out to fight in Afghanistan two years ago, barely getting to meet his young son before he was gone. When Laura left for college, Maggie had been afraid she'd be lonely, so she invited Sandy and Josh to move in while they waited for her husband to return. It worked for both of them as Sandy didn't want to relocate to Florida to live with her mother but wanted to stay in St. Stanley to finish nursing school. While Sandy studied, Maggie helped watch Josh.

"When Jake finally gets deployed home, I'd like one more baby," Sandy said. "But then I think I'm done. Two hands, two kids."

"You're a wise young woman," Ginger said. "I'd take a bullet for any one of my boys; I love them so, but ooh, if someone had shown me my future grocery bill back then, well, let's just say it would be unlikely that Roger would ever have seen me naked again after baby number one."

The women laughed and Joanne poked her head in from the sun porch at the back of the house.

"What did I miss?" Joanne asked.

"Naked Ginger," Sandy teased.

"Do tell," Joanne said with a grin. Her long dark hair was in its usual ponytail, making her look younger than she was.

Joanne was the newest member of the Good Buy Girls. Maggie had invited Joanne to join the club when they had gotten into a tussle over a pair of half-price bed sheets at the linen shop in the mall over in Dumontville. Maggie had won, naturally, but a friendship had been forged.

Joanne was married to Michael Claramotta, and together they owned the butcher shop–deli More than Meats in the center of town that was *the* place to buy lunch. They had relocated to St. Stanley from Brooklyn ten years before, and although they had opened the deli and invested their money in several apartment buildings in town, they had both grown up poor, and thrift was a way of life for them. No one in the Good Buy Girls club got a bigger charge out of getting a good deal than Joanne.

"I was just saying that if I had known what my grocery bill would be, it would be unlikely that Roger would have had the opportunity to make any more babies with me," Ginger said softly.

It was well known in the group that the one thing thirty-seven-year-old Joanne wanted more than even a good deal was a baby, but so far she and Michael hadn't gotten lucky.

"As if!" Joanne busted out with a laugh, reassuring them that she was fine. "I've seen you two together. You are the most lovey-dovey couple on the planet. It's positively disgusting. Now, come on, I've got the tables ready."

The ladies filed out through the French doors to the sun porch on the back of the house. The glassed-in room with its hanging plants and cushy wicker furniture and freestanding air conditioner was their weekly base of operations. This week was particularly important, as Labor Day was rapidly approaching, and they needed to finalize their battle plans.

Fliers, mailers and circulars littered the card table that had been set up, and they each took a seat in a folding chair.

"Wait, where's Claire?" Ginger asked. "She's bringing the eats, isn't she?"

"She'll be here," Maggie said. "She may have gotten held up at the library."

"All right then, do we all have our diaper coupons for Sandy?"

Maggie pulled out her coupon pouch, blue and mauve paisley; it had been her constant companion since starting her own household when she was newly married twenty-two years before. She called it "Old Blue" and its well-thumbed tabs were as familiar to her as her own smile. Old Blue was divided by sections, and Maggie went right to the baby products one and pulled out the clippings she had gathered for her niece.

The others all pulled out their coupon pouches as well, and a small pile accumulated in the center for Sandy. Being a solo parent and a full-time student, she didn't have the time to be an official member of the Good Buy Girls, but they considered her one of their own and always kept an eye out for bargains for her.

"Aunt Maggie, I'm taking Josh to the park. Back in an hour," Sandy called, poking her head into the room.

"I go park!" Josh cried, and he waddled into the sun room to Maggie to give her a banana-scented hug.

"Have fun, sweetie," Maggie said, and she squeezed him back, enjoying the petal-soft feel of his mop of blond hair against her cheek.

Sandy held out her hand, and Josh grabbed it. As they

left the room, the doorbell rang and Sandy called, "I'll get it."

They heard the door open and the murmur of voices. Then the door shut and Claire raced into the room with her coupon pouch in one hand and a boxed cake in the other.

"Sorry, I'm late," she cried. "It was murder getting here."

Chapter 3

"How so?" Maggie asked, taking in Claire's disheveled appearance.

"I hit every red light going across town," Claire said. She shook her short blonde bob, and drew in a long breath before continuing. "Then I stopped in at the Perk Up to see what they had on sale, but their bakery case was wiped out. Gwen had just taken all the day-old baked goods down to Spring Gardens, the assisted-care living facility for seniors."

"Well, it looks like you brought us something yummy." Ginger sat up straighter in her chair, trying to peek inside the mangled box that Claire still clutched.

"Oh yeah, so then I ran over to Santana's to see if the grocery store had anything in their bakery worth buying." Claire set the box down on the table. "And look what I got for half off."

The rest of the Good Buy Girls peered into the box. It

was a quarter sheet cake with "Happy Birthday Ralph" written on it, circled by big blue roses.

"Who is Ralph?" Joanne asked.

"I don't know, but he never picked up his cake," Claire said. "So we get to have it."

"Why is there a piece missing?" Ginger asked. "Did you feel the need to taste test it for us?"

Her brown eyes were teasing, and Claire gave an unsteady laugh. "Yeah, that's it." She glanced around her as if looking for something. "Oh, shoot, I forgot my cake knife!"

"No worries," Maggie said. "I have one."

She studied Claire's flushed face. Her small, rectangular glasses were askew, and she must have fastened her jacket in a hurry, because the buttons and holes were misaligned, leaving one corner of the front of her jacket hanging lower than the other.

She handed Claire some plates and forks with the knife and asked, "Are you sure you're okay?"

"I'm fine," Claire said, not meeting her gaze. "It was just a very busy morning."

"I'll go get some iced tea," Maggie said. She watched as Claire held the cake knife with shaky fingers.

Maggie frowned. She didn't think for one second that Claire was fine. But she had to respect the other woman's privacy. If Claire wanted to talk, she would.

"Wait, stop!" Joanne ordered.

Claire hovered over the cake and looked at her with wide eyes. "What?"

"Shouldn't we sing 'Happy Birthday' to Ralph?" Joanne asked, and then her lips parted in a teasing grin.

"Oh, you." Ginger tossed a napkin at Joanne and they dissolved into giggles.

Claire gave them a small smile and started to serve up the cake. It was a chocolate cake with a raspberry mousse filling and vanilla buttercream frosting.

"Hmm-mm," Ginger said. "Ralph has good taste."

Once they finished their cake, Maggie cleared the box away, and they straightened the table and settled down to business.

"Now, who needs housewares?" Maggie asked. She held up a flier for the local appliance store.

"I need a new range," Joanne said. "But I'm waiting until Spencer's has the one I want in an already opened box."

"Smart," Ginger said. "Roger picked up a digital camera that was in an opened box, and they took off twenty-five percent."

"I do love the open-box policy. Too bad more people don't return their stuff," Maggie said. "Okay, moving on. Who is going clothes shopping over the Labor Day weekend?"

All of the ladies nodded, but Ginger looked pained. "All four boys need back-to-school sneakers."

The group groaned in sympathy. Ginger's boys were not small, and their shoe requirements would cost more than the entire group's clothing bills put together.

"Wait! I saw something in here," Joanne said as she thumbed through her stack of fliers and pulled out one for a store in the Dumontville Shopping Mall. "Yes, here it is. Two-for-one Nikes at the sporting goods store."

Ginger took the flier and scanned the ad to make sure there were no loopholes. No, it was a straight up two-fer.

She pumped her fist. "Excellent. Thanks, Joanne. Now I just need to get my hands on another one of these."

They all scanned their circulars until they found another coupon for the sporting goods store.

On went their strategy session until they had matched everyone's needs with the sales that were happening and figured out their schedules to hit all of the stores at optimum supply-and-demand times.

When they finished Ralph's cake with a second serving for all of them and washed it down with the last of the iced tea, they were ready to call it a day.

Maggie walked them to the door, each clutching their burgeoning coupon books. They would meet at the same time next week to finalize their plans.

Claire was the last to go, and Maggie put her hand on her arm before she slipped out the door. "Call me if you need me, okay?"

Claire gave her an uncertain look. "Okay."

"Anytime," Maggie insisted.

Claire nodded and hurried down the walk, as if trying to put some distance between them. Maggie couldn't help but wonder why. She watched curiously as Claire climbed into her car and drove away.

Maggie had known Claire since she came to St. Stanley five years ago. They had met at the library's annual book sale, one of Maggie's favorite events of the year, where they had both been eyeing a vintage Betty Crocker cookbook.

Maggie had let Claire take it, since she already had one, but they had struck up a conversation and found they had a mutual love of books and bargains. Maggie had invited Claire to join their group, but she had demurred.

Over the next few months, Maggie noticed that Claire was a bit of a loner who liked to keep to herself. Given that she was only in her mid-thirties, this seemed like a waste to Maggie, so she and Ginger decided they needed to have an intervention.

They began having their Good Buy Girl meetings in a study room at the library. Claire took to dropping by the meetings with her own coupon book and, before she realized it, they had recruited her for membership into the GBGs. Once she'd caught on, Claire laughed loud and long. It was the first time Maggie had heard her laugh, and she thought it a shame that she didn't do it more often.

As they got to know her, they discovered that Claire had a dry sense of humor, she never dated and her biggest extravagance was gourmet pet food for her cat, Mr. Tumnus.

Maggie went back to her kitchen and glanced at her calendar. She was watching Josh tomorrow for Sandy, and it just happened to be a story-time morning at the library. Perfect. That would give her a chance to check on Claire without her becoming too suspicious. Not that she was a busybody, Maggie told herself as she folded up the card table and stored it in the closet off the porch. It was just that she cared about her friends, and she had learned in her forty-one years of living that it was better to ask questions and annoy someone than to not ask and watch them suffer.

Chapter 4

Maggie strapped Josh into his covered bicycle trailer, which was attached to her mountain bike. Both she and Sandy used it to cart him around, as it was cheaper and healthier than driving.

"Go, Auntie Maggie!" Josh ordered and held up the green Percy train clutched in his chubby fist like it was a drum major's baton.

Maggie clicked the chinstrap on her helmet and pushed off toward the center of town. Her small house on Society Road was nestled in the historic district of St. Stanley, just a half mile from the town center.

She stayed in the bike lane, waving when a friend or neighbor honked as they passed her. She turned onto Main Street and headed for the town green. The library and town hall sat on one end of the green. A narrow road between the two historic red brick buildings led to the large parking lot that they shared. Because Maggie was on her bike, she pedaled up the walk and stopped at the bike rack in front of the library.

She unzipped the cover over Josh and unbuckled him. She stored her helmet in the back and grabbed her bag of books to return. Josh, knowing it was story day, shot ahead of her, and Maggie was forced to jog to keep up with him.

"Josh," she said as she caught his hand in hers. "What are our two library rules?"

"No yelling and no running," he said in his little-boy lisp.

"Good. Let's go see who is telling stories today."

They made their way into the children's room. The entrance was designed to look like a castle, with a real wooden drawbridge over blue carpet and big gray stacked blocks painted to look like castle walls. At each end of the castle walls were small, round rooms, decorated to look like turrets that the kids could climb into to read.

As always, Josh was very emphatic that Maggie must walk on the wooden bridge and not the blue carpet, otherwise the alligators in the moat might eat her.

Maggie pretended to almost fall onto the blue carpet, leaving Josh shaking his finger at her and telling her she had to be more careful. Maggie ruffled his head as she chuckled. She did love this little man so.

Once in the story-time room, Josh toddled over to his best pal, Freddy, who was there with his mom.

"Hi, Maggie." Freddy's mom, a pretty woman named Linda who was expecting her second baby any day, greeted her.

"Hi, Linda, how are you?" Maggie knelt beside the young woman.

"More than ready, that's how I am," she said with a tired smile as she rubbed her extended belly. "Is Sandy at class today?"

"Yes, she's got microbiology." They both shuddered.

"Will you tell her I said hi?" Linda asked.

"Absolutely," Maggie said. "Would you mind keeping an eye on Josh for me? I just want to run and say hello to Claire."

"Oh sure," Linda said. "You know he and Freddy are as thick as thieves. Hmm, maybe that's not such a good choice of words."

They both laughed, and Maggie said, "I'll be right back."

"Take your time."

Maggie closed the story room door behind her, knowing Josh was in excellent hands. She just wanted to pop in and make sure Claire was all right.

She found Claire in her office sorting through two boxes of books. She looked more put together today; at least her jacket buttons were lined up.

"Knock knock," Maggie said in the open doorway.

Claire looked up, and a smile lit her features.

"Where's your barnacle?" Claire asked.

"He's in story time," Maggie said. She took it as a good sign that Claire was back to being her teasing self. Everyone called Josh Maggie's barnacle because he liked to be wherever she was.

"Well, don't leave without letting me see him," Claire said. "I barely got to give him a squeeze yesterday since he was headed out when I came in."

"I promise. What have you got here?"

"Donations," Claire said with a sigh. "You know I love

books more than anyone, but when they smell like the bottom of someone's compost heap and start growing mushrooms, really, it's time to throw them out."

"Mrs. Shoemaker?" Maggie guessed. She was an elderly lady who lived down the street from Maggie, who was known for being loath to part with anything, and in fact had some hoarding tendencies that were alarming.

"Yeah, I have to put these in the basement so that Preston, our handyman, can sneak them to the dump on his next run. Then I can tell her that they're in storage."

"Well, it is storage of a sort," Maggie said.

Claire grinned at her, obviously pleased that Maggie understood her dilemma.

"You seem better today," Maggie said.

"Hmm, yesterday was . . . well, it was a bit of a rough day," Claire said. She looked like she wanted to say more, but then she shook her head. Her blonde bob brushed against her cheeks, and she pushed her glasses up on her nose.

"Here, let me help you carry these down to the basement," Maggie said. She hefted up a box before Claire could protest.

"Thanks," Claire said. She picked up the other one and led the way out of her office and into the narrow hallway.

Maggie wrinkled her nose at the moldy smell of the box in her arms. Good grief, it smelled like damp, dirty socks that had been dragged through a cow pasture. Bleck!

Claire rested her box on her hip as she unlocked the door that led to the basement. She hefted it up again as she stepped on the creaky stairs that led below.

The library's basement was dark and almost as dank as the boxes they carried. It wasn't accessible to the public and was used mainly for housing broken furniture or other items that needed to be hauled to Claire's special storage.

A lone light bulb was the only defense against the gloom. It had a hanging chain for an on switch, which could only be reached from the basement floor.

Maggie inched her way down the steps behind Claire, relieved when they were on the floor and Claire was able to reach the light. With a click, the light flared on, illuminating the area.

Maggie blinked to adjust her eyes, but nothing prepared her for the sound of Claire's scream, which rent the quiet of the basement like the sharp edge of a knife.

Chapter 5

"Claire, what is it?" Maggie cried. "Did you see a rat?"

She stood on tiptoe, as if this would help, and scanned the area around her feet, dreading the thought of some beady-eyed critter staring back up at her.

"B . . . b . . . body," Claire said. The box of books she clutched in her arms slid from her grasp and she began to wilt. Maggie dropped her box of books and grabbed Claire just before she slammed her head into the stairs.

"Claire!" she called her friend's name. "Claire!"

There was no response. Claire's limp body was too heavy for her to hold, and Maggie was forced to prop her against the steps before she dropped her. She studied Claire's face. Even in the dim light it looked gray. What was wrong? Had she fainted?

Maggie gently patted Claire's cheek. "Claire, wake up!"

There was no response. The sound of footsteps pounding

down the hall brought Maggie's attention up to the door above.

"Down here!" she yelled. "We're down here."

Preston Turner, the town handyman, came running down the stairs. His work boots thumped on the steps, jarring Claire's body. As soon as he saw her, he slowed his pace.

"What happened?" he asked as he stopped beside Maggie. "I heard a scream."

"I'm not sure, but Claire fainted," she said. "Can you help me get her out of here?"

Preston crouched down beside Claire. He ran a hand through his short brown hair, which was just beginning to sprout some gray. "She didn't bang her head, did she?"

"No, I caught her," Maggie said.

"What made her scream like that?" he asked. "It sounded like someone was being tortured."

"I don't know," Maggie said.

She glanced over her shoulder and leaned forward a bit so that she was closer to where Claire had been standing when she screamed. That's when she saw a pair of men's shoes, toes pointing up at the ceiling, poking out from behind an old file cabinet.

"Oh no," she said. Curiosity propelled her forward even as a nervous flutter in her gut told her to run.

She moved farther into the circle of light cast by the lone bulb. The body of a man lay on the floor in a pool of his own blood. A large knife stuck out of his chest, and a book lay on the floor next to his hand.

"What is it, Maggie?" Preston asked as he carried Claire toward her.

"A body," Maggie said. She went over to check the man

for a pulse. His skin was cold, colder than the cement floor he lay on. His eyes were open and staring up at the ceiling. There was no pulse in his wrist or his neck. "He's dead."

Preston's eyes went wide, and he said, "Come on, up you go. Let's get Miss Claire upstairs and call Sheriff Collins."

Maggie studied the dead man. He was tall. He wore an impeccable charcoal suit—Armani, Maggie guessed, judging by the cut and the cloth. His shoes were soft leather loafers, the kind one wore in a carpeted boardroom, not in a musty old library basement. His features, pale and slack with death, were still strong and handsome. This was a man who was comfortable with power, or at least, he had been. His thick silver hair put his age somewhere in his fifties.

Maggie studied his face. She didn't know him. She'd lived in St. Stanley all her life and knew most everyone by reputation if not personally, and she found it disturbing that this strange man had been stabbed and bled to death in her town library, and she had no idea who he was.

"Come on, Maggie, there's nothing you can do for him."

"Should we just leave him here?"

"Well, I don't suppose he's going anywhere," Preston said.

Maggie shook her head. "You're right. Let's go."

She paused, her attention caught by the book lying beside the man. She noticed the cover of the book was well worn with age and use, but the title was printed in large letters and read, *The House of Mirth*. Yeah, not so much.

She led the way back up the stairs to Claire's office. She called the sheriff's office, proud that her fingers only shook a little and her voice only quavered on the word *body*. When the deputy was done taking the information, she hung up, feeling a little sick to her stomach.

"Miss Claire, are you all right?" Preston asked. He had placed her on the old brown couch that ran the length of her office wall.

She made a whimpering noise, and he turned a helpless gaze toward Maggie. Preston was a whiz at fixing all things mechanical, but give him a person hurt or in tears and he was rendered helpless.

"Claire, can you hear me?" Maggie moved to stand beside the couch. "Claire."

She gently patted Claire's cheek, and her eyelids fluttered open. Behind her glasses her hazel eyes looked unfocused but, as Maggie watched, Claire slowly took in her surroundings and remembered what she'd seen.

"What happened . . . wait, is he dead?" she asked. Her voice sounded hoarse, as if her scream had done some damage on its way out of her mouth. She sat up, looking pale and shaky but determined.

Preston handed her the metal water bottle she kept on her desk, and Claire twisted off the top and took a small sip. She swallowed carefully as if afraid it might hurt or refuse to go down.

"Yes, he's dead," Maggie said.

Claire looked as if she might faint again, so Maggie gripped her hand and squeezed it hard. Claire squeezed back, whether in gratitude or to make her stop, Maggie wasn't sure, so she eased her grip.

"We called it in to the sheriff's office," Maggie said. "They should be here any minute. Preston, would you mind blocking the hall so that no one gets through until the sheriff gets here?"

"Sure," he said. He gave Claire a concerned look, but left without questioning her.

Claire got up on unsteady feet and began to pace the room. She looked as if she was trying to stay in motion so she could outrun the bad images that were dogging her in her mind.

Maggie watched her friend with concern. She didn't know what she could say that could make the grisly scene in the basement any better. A man was dead, obviously stabbed here in the library. This sort of thing just didn't happen in St. Stanley.

But when Claire passed by her for the fifteenth time, Maggie thought she ought to at least try to talk her down.

"It's all right, Claire, really. The sheriff will be here any second, and he'll take care of this. I know that Carlton is on vacation, and as acting library director, this is something you're going to have to sort out, but really it's the sheriff's problem not yours. Everything will be all right. You'll see."

"It's not all right," Claire moaned as she sat down. "It's never going to be all right."

"Oh, honey, I know this was a bit of a shock . . ." Maggie began, but Claire interrupted her.

"No, you don't understand. The man, the dead man, I know him. I used to date him."

Chapter 6

"You used to—" Maggie began, but Claire hushed her as Sheriff Sam Collins strode into the room.

Maggie felt the air catch on her inhale in a hiccupy gasp that was impossible to turn into a fake cough or even a sneeze. Sam Collins stopped halfway across the room, looking as surprised to see her as she was to see him.

In spite of herself, Maggie took in the sight of Sam, noting that the years since she had seen him last had hardly left a mark on him. He was as tall as she remembered, with the football-player shoulders that had left most of her high school classmates panting after him like a pack of rabid dogs. His wavy brown hair was still thick and full, with just traces of gray in it.

He wore the sheriff's uniform well, the starched white shirt with his badge pinned above the left pocket with a narrow dark tie over dark pants. He looked every inch the head of the sheriff's department, and Maggie wondered how the deputies were adjusting to having a new boss.

Sam still had the stubborn jaw and sharp blue eyes that when he was younger had given him a rough-edged masculinity beyond his years. She wondered if his tough-guy look had helped his career over the years. She imagined it had, but this wasn't Richmond, this was St. Stanley. Memories, particularly hers, were less impressed with appearances than with substance, which if she remembered correctly he had little of.

"Maggie." He said her name in his familiar low drawl, and she felt it reverberate right through her chest.

Dang it! How had she forgotten about his voice? And why hadn't he gotten fat or bald? Why was he even better looking than she remembered? It wasn't fair.

"Sam," she said. She was pleased that her voice didn't betray the emotion she felt at seeing him again.

"I have some questions for you, ladies," he said.

Claire turned her head so that only Maggie could see her. "Don't tell," she whispered. "Please."

Maggie looked at her friend, and then at Sam, and then back at Claire. Oh, she really didn't like this. She studied Claire's face. Behind the narrow glasses, she looked dead scared. There had to be a reason she was asking Maggie to keep her secret.

Maggie nodded. She would keep quiet until Claire could tell her what was going on. She owed her friend that.

Claire had been the one who'd found the best tutor in St. Stanley for Laura when she needed to bring up her math grades to get into Penn State. And Claire was the one who had helped Joanne and Michael find the best doctor to assist them in their quest for a baby. Claire was always there to help others. If there was history between her and the dead man in the basement, Maggie could wait to hear what she had to say.

Of course, the fact that Maggie detested Sam Collins helped, because no matter how good-looking he still was, she was pretty sure she'd rather Zumba in bare feet over hot coals than talk to him.

Claire rose slowly and extended her hand to Sam, shaking off her fainting spell like a duck flapping water off its wings.

"Good morning, Sheriff Collins," she said. "I'm Claire Freemont. Thanks for getting here so quickly."

"Are you all right?" he asked. "Preston said you fainted."

"I'm fine now," she said. "Luckily, Maggie broke my fall, so no damage was done."

Sam looked past her to Maggie as if verifying what she said was true. Maggie gave him a curt nod but found she couldn't maintain eye contact.

Maggie had known Sam since they were both Josh's age. Even as a kid, Sam had been the smartest kid in the class, the fastest runner and the quickest with a joke. Every girl in St. Stanley had worshipped Sam Collins from afar, and some from not so far. Every girl, that is, except for Maggie. Maggie couldn't stand him.

Mostly, it went back to their elementary school days. As Ginger had reminded her, her hair back then had been the unfortunate shade of orange found mostly on carrots, and Sam Collins had teased her mercilessly about it. Maggie had never forgiven him for that, among other things.

"How have you been, Maggie?" he asked, forcing her to look at him.

"Fine, thanks," she said with a sniff, refusing to acknowledge that he affected her in any way.

"Can you wait here while I go check out the basement?" he asked. His gaze fastened on Maggie as if he knew she was the flight risk. "Both of you."

"Yes," they agreed.

He left the room, pulling a pair of blue latex gloves out of his back pocket as he went. As his footsteps faded away, the only sound in the room was the steady ticking of the clock on the wall.

Claire sat back down next to Maggie and rested her elbows on her knees, then she lowered her head and blew out a breath.

"Thanks for not saying anything," she said.

"No problem," Maggie said. "You will explain it, though, won't you?"

"Yes, just not right now," Claire said with a worried glance at the door. "Correct me if I'm wrong, but I get the feeling you don't like Sheriff Collins."

"What makes you say that?" Maggie asked.

"Please, if looks could kill, there'd be more than one dead body in the library," Claire said.

"Huh," Maggie grunted, opting to remain noncommittal. She glanced at the clock and realized story time would be ending shortly.

"I have to go collect Josh," she said. "If Sam returns before I do, tell him I'll be right back."

"All right," Claire said.

"Are you sure you'll be okay by yourself?" Maggie asked.

"Oh, yeah, sure," Claire said.

Maggie could tell she was trying to look brave. "I'll be just a minute."

Maggie hurried down the hall and back into the main part of the building. She slipped into the story-time room right as the kids were getting their hands stamped. Josh toddled over to show her the train stamp he had on the back of his hand.

She crouched down next to Linda, who was rolling to her side in order to get to her feet. Maggie hurriedly gave her a hand.

"Thanks," Linda said. "I swear this baby grows a pound a minute."

"Thanks for minding Josh for me," Maggie said. "I was unexpectedly delayed."

"No problem," Linda said. She held her hand out to Freddy, who slipped his small hand into his mother's. "Say, bye to your friend."

"Bye," Freddy said and reached out to hug Josh.

"Bye-bye," Josh answered and hugged him in return.

Maggie watched Linda and Freddy go, and said, "Let's go say hi to Auntie Claire, Josh."

"Okay," he agreed.

They had to work their way across the wooden bridge again. Josh held on to Maggie so as to make sure she didn't fall into the water. They crossed the large open space of the main library and made their way to Claire's office in the back.

In the few minutes Maggie had been gone, several more officers had arrived. The hallway to the basement was now crowded with people, including Sam and what looked to be several of the state's crime lab personnel.

Maggie scooted around them and slipped into Claire's office. Claire was still sitting on the couch looking lost amidst the flurry of activity happening around her.

Maggie sat beside Claire and pulled Josh up into her lap. "How's it going?"

"It looks like it's going to be a long day," Claire said.

"Will you have to stay here for all of it?" Maggie asked.

"I don't know," she said. "I'm thinking we should close the library, but I don't know how Carlton would feel about that. He doesn't even like to close on Sundays or holidays."

"Well, this is a little more serious than that. I'm sure the investigators can make a recommendation if you think Carlton would need justification to close."

"I don't want to interrupt," Claire said. "They're going to block off the hallway to the basement. Maybe that will be enough."

"Bill, I'm warning you!" a stern voice shouted in the hallway.

Maggie looked at Claire and she explained, "Bill Waters from the *St. Stanley Gazette* is out there asking questions, and I heard Sheriff Collins threaten to toss him if he tried to get into the basement one more time."

"Auntie Claire sad?" Josh asked, and he reached out and patted her cheek.

"A little," Claire said, and she pressed his plump hand to her face and gave him a small smile. "Would you like to color, Josh?"

His eyes lit up and he hopped off of Maggie's lap and

followed Claire to her desk, where she always kept a stash of crayons and coloring paper for him. He set busily to work, completely disregarding the lines and blithely coloring every inch of the paper in black, his most favorite color.

Claire sat back down with Maggie, and she said, "I don't know how long this is going to take."

"Have they asked you any questions?"

"Not yet," she said. "I think the sheriff has been too busy directing the crime scene investigators. He doesn't seem particularly happy with them."

"Yeah, he's so conceited he probably doesn't think anyone's ever been able to solve a crime in St. Stanley before he became sheriff," Maggie scoffed. "And I'm sure he's probably afraid the state's investigators are going to steal all of his glory."

Claire blanched, and Maggie felt her scalp prickle.

"He's standing right behind me, isn't he?" she asked.

Claire gave a tiny nod of her head. Maggie felt her face get warm, but then she refused to feel ashamed. Her grandmother always said that eavesdroppers seldom hear anything good about themselves, so it served Sam right—or so she tried to convince herself.

She glanced over her shoulder at Sam. His face read *not happy* and was doing a quick slide into *really irritated.*

"That probably came out harsher than intended," she said.

"Really?" he asked. He didn't look like he believed her.

"Yes, really," she said. She sounded impatient, and she glanced away before she made a bad situation even worse. Oh, this man just rubbed her the wrong way. She was normally such a nice person. How, after all these years, did

Sam Collins still manage to bring out the absolute worst in her?

"I find that hard to imagine," he said. "Don't hold back, Maggie. Why don't you clear the air and say what you really feel?"

Chapter 7

"Did you have questions for us?" Maggie countered. She was not about to be intimidated by Sam. "Because my nephew is rapidly approaching his nap time, and it won't go well for anyone if he misses it."

Sam glanced at Josh, happily drawing at the desk. "He looks fine to me."

Maggie narrowed her gaze at him. Oh, she'd give almost anything for Josh to pitch a fit right now, if for no other reason than to prove her right. But of course, he didn't, making Sam think he was right. How very annoying.

"Don't say I didn't warn you," she said.

"In fact, I do need to ask you ladies some questions," Sam said, ignoring her dire tone.

"Certainly," Claire said.

He asked them each to recount the details of finding the body in the basement. They took turns. Claire went first and described what happened up until she fainted, then Maggie finished the tale. Sam said nothing but made notes on a small pad that he took out of his shirt pocket.

"Do either of you know the identity of the man in the basement?"

"No," Maggie said. She looked at Claire, whose face had gone white.

"Actually, yes, I know him," Claire said.

It sounded as if every word was being dragged out of her by force. Sam's gaze sharpened on her face.

"Who is he?" he asked.

"His name is John Templeton," Claire said. "I knew him when I lived in Baltimore."

"How well did you know him?" Sam asked.

"He was an acquaintance," she said.

Sam looked at Maggie. He gave her a look that told her he hadn't missed the lack of surprise on her face. She stared back. She had only found out that Claire knew the man a few minutes before he did; surely, he couldn't blame her for that.

She crossed her arms over her chest. He frowned at her, then he turned to Claire, and said, "Ms. Freemont, I'm going to need you to come down to the station."

"She'd be happy to," Maggie said before Claire could respond. "We'll just call her attorney and meet you there, shall we?"

Claire reared back and stared at Maggie in surprise. Sam glowered and looked like he wanted to slap handcuffs on Maggie just for kicks and giggles, but she didn't care. She'd watched enough episodes of *Law & Order* to know that you never let the police question you without an attorney present, whether you'd done anything wrong or not.

"Fine," Sam snapped. "Have your attorney meet us there in fifteen minutes. Ms. Freemont, however, will ride to the station with me."

As he stomped away, Claire said, "I don't have an attorney."

"You will," Maggie said. "Ready, buddy?"

She hustled over to the desk and gathered up Josh, who wrapped his arms about her neck with a whoop of delight.

"I have to get Josh back to his mother, but I'll meet you at the station with representation. Do not say a word without an attorney present. Clear?"

"But doesn't that make me look guilty of something?" Claire asked.

"No, it makes you look smart," Maggie said. "Remember, not one word."

"But where are you going to find an attorney?" Claire asked.

"The Frosty Freeze," Maggie said. "Where else?"

Chapter 8

Maggie pedaled as fast as possible. She was relieved to see Sandy's car in the driveway, and she hustled Josh into the house as fast as she could.

"I have to go," she said as soon as she handed Josh to his mother. "Claire. Jail. Attorney. Back later."

"What?" Sandy asked. She had her school books open on the kitchen table. and she hugged her son close while she stared at Maggie with her head to one side like a dog hearing a high-pitched whistle.

Maggie was out of breath from the bike ride, however, and couldn't explain any more than that. She tossed her helmet aside and grabbed her keys. She hustled out to her Volvo station wagon and started it up.

The Frosty Freeze sat on the edge of the center of town, just off of the town square on a small side street. When the local veteran's organization put on their summer band concerts in the gazebo on the square, the Frosty Freeze did a bang-up business. Maggie was pretty sure it was the profits from the concert series that kept it afloat for the rest of the year.

The Freeze, as it was called, was a vintage building from the fifties, which boasted the classic long front windows and squared-off edges popular at the time. Maggie remembered what a special treat it had been when she was a kid to go and get a cone at the Freeze. She had always ordered a soft vanilla ice cream dipped in cherry coating, a candy-like liquid that hardened around the cold ice cream, while her older sister had gotten soft chocolate dipped in chocolate. To this day the taste of candied cherry on vanilla reminded her of summer.

Now that it was late August and the hot summer was departing like a going-out-of-business sale, the Freeze wasn't as busy as usual, so she only had to wait for the man ahead of her to get his double-dip cone and get out of her way.

"Welcome to the Freeze, what can I get you?"

Maggie hunkered down to peer through the small window used for placing orders. Most of the large windows on the front of the building were taken up by huge faded posters of ice cream sundaes, cones and milk shakes. In order to be seen, she had to practically stick her head inside.

"I need an attorney, Max."

The young man, who hadn't been looking out the window, raised his head up so fast that he smacked it on the glass partition.

"Ouch! Maggie!" he said, rubbing the spot on his head that had connected with the glass. "Way to scare a guy."

"Sorry, but this is an emergency," she said. "I need a lawyer who specializes in criminal law."

"Did you try the phone book?" he asked. "How about a Martindale-Hubbell directory? I hear they put out a fine list of attorneys."

"Maxwell Button," Maggie said in her most threatening, scary-mom voice. "Don't you get smart with me."

"Aw, Maggie, you know I don't practice law for real," he said. "I only sat for the bar exam because it was something to do that summer."

"Well, you didn't spend those years studying at the T. C. Williams School of Law for nothing. The time to use that degree is now," she said. "This is an emergency. Now come on."

"I can't just close up the Frosty Freeze," he said. "Hugh will kill me."

"Claire is in trouble. Big trouble."

Max blew out a breath. "I'll get fired."

"Good," she said. "You're wasting your potential in there. Now lock up and let's go."

To the grating soundtrack of a lot of male muttering, which Maggie pretended not to hear, the window slammed shut and the open sign was flipped to closed.

In a few minutes, Max came around the building and Maggie took in the sight of the knock-kneed, greasy-haired, pimple-ridden, twenty-year-old boy genius who had tutored Laura to outstanding grades in math, all while studying for the Virginia State bar exam in his spare time.

"So, how is Claire in trouble?" he asked. His voice cracked when he said her name, letting Maggie know he still had a powerful crush on the librarian.

She led the way to her car and said, "A man was found murdered in the basement of the library."

Max's eyebrows shot up. "Seriously?"

"It gets worse," Maggie said as they climbed into her Volvo station wagon. "Claire used to date him when she lived in Baltimore."

Max let out a low whistle. "That's bad."

"Get your game face on," Maggie said. "She needs you."

Max ran a hand through his long hair as if trying to give it some sort of order. Maggie would have told him not to bother, that it was his mind that they needed, but she knew he was trying to get himself into lawyer mode.

Maxwell Button was a wunderkind. In addition to his law degree, he also had an advanced degree in physics and was currently studying for his doctorate in art history. If it was true that human beings only used 10 percent of their brains, Maggie was pretty sure that Max was the exception to the rule and was operating at 80 percent capacity at least.

The problem with Max was that he while he loved acquiring knowledge, he wasn't much for applying his smarts for useful purposes. He was happy working the cone-dipping machine at the Frosty Freeze and felt no compunction to actually utilize his education. Maggie found this to be maddening, but she'd discovered that no amount of encouragement heaped upon him motivated Max enough to leave the ice cream stand behind.

"You know, I've been immersed in my dissertation on Botticelli," he said. "I'll need some time to recall my Juris Doctor."

"You have five minutes," Maggie said. "Get busy."

Max closed his eyes and tipped his head back. Maggie

turned onto Main Street, stopping at the light and trying not to give in to the anxious feelings that were swamping her.

She wondered where Claire was now and if Sam was being nice to her. Having not seen Sam in over twenty years, she really didn't know what sort of person he had become.

The Sam she once knew represented everything she disliked in a man. He was far too good-looking and self-assured. He'd never had to work hard at anything in his life. He'd pretty much charmed his way through high school and into a full college scholarship. He'd gotten lucky with a job on the Richmond PD and swiftly scored a sweet gig as a detective on the force, not that she had paid any attention to the constant stories of the former St. Stanley hometown football hero. Nope, not her.

Now Sam was back in St. Stanley and had taken the job that should have been Maggie's late husband's, had he lived and continued to pursue a career in law enforcement.

Okay, that wasn't fair. She knew it. She could even admit it. But even after more than fifteen years, she had a hard time letting go of Charlie and what their life could have been together. Charlie had been killed in the line of duty, while he was a newly minted deputy on the St. Stanley force. He had never gotten the opportunities that Sam Collins had and, whether it was fair or not, Maggie couldn't help but resent Sam for it.

She put on her signal and turned into the parking lot for the police station. The lot was packed, and she was forced to park at the back. That was fine. The walk would give Max a chance to get his plan together.

"Max," she said. "We're here."

Max blinked his eyes open and blew out a breath.

Chapter 9

"Surely you jest," Sam said.

"Nope, 'fraid not," Maggie said. She stared him straight in the eye, willing him to look away first.

"Kid, you cannot be serious," he said. "Are you even old enough to drink?"

"No," Max said. "But alcohol consumption is not a requirement when offering legal representation."

"Your parents are Daisy and Cooter Button?" Sam asked, as if trying to wrap his brain around the scenario before him.

Maggie supposed she couldn't blame him. St. Stanley wasn't Richmond. It had been a long time since he'd lived here. It was undoubtedly going to be an adjustment to get back to small-town living.

"Yes, sir, they are my parents," Max said.

He didn't flinch at the question like he used to. Maggie was proud of him for that. It had taken Max a long time to understand that where he came from didn't make him the person that he was. Claire had been one of the first people in town to help him see that.

Max had spent most of his formative years by himself in the town library, reading everything he could get his hands on. Small wonder—his parents only had half a brain between them, and it was usually pickled.

Daisy and Cooter lived in a beaten-down trailer on the outskirts of town and, while their son studied the writings of Copernicus, they spent their days trying to figure out where their next shot of whiskey with a beer chaser would come from.

Sensing things were not good at Max's home, Claire had helped him get his part-time job at the Freeze. When he was old enough to leave his parents, she found him an apartment on the top of the town garage. The garage was walking distance to the bus stop, which took him to the University of Richmond for his studies.

Without Claire providing constant support and guidance, Maggie shuddered to think what might have happened to Max. Of course, as a result, Max had carried a torch for Claire from the day she discovered him trying to sleep in between the stacks in the library. Maggie was pretty sure there was nothing he wouldn't do for the kind librarian.

"I didn't know they had any children," Sam said.

"A lot has changed since you've been gone," Maggie said.

Sam met her gaze, and said, "And a lot hasn't."

Maggie felt her face grow warm. What did he mean? Was he talking about her hostility toward him? Yeah, well, small wonder. She shook her head. It didn't matter. The only reason she was here was Claire.

They were in a small interview room at the back of the station. Claire sat at the scarred wooden table, looking the picture of misery while the sheriff stood across from her. When Maggie and Max had arrived, Sam had risen from his seat.

"Well, now that Claire's attorney is present, we can get on with this," Maggie said.

"Was there a reason you felt you needed an attorney, Ms. Freemont?" Sam asked. His voice was deceptively mild, but Maggie could sense a trap.

"Don't answer that, Claire," she said. "He's baiting you."

"Why are you here?" Sam asked her. A muscle was beginning to throb in his jaw, and Maggie got the feeling he was about to lose his temper.

"To make sure you don't railroad my friend," Maggie said, knowing full well this was the equivalent to waving a red flag in front of an angry bull.

"I am not the enemy. Why is everyone treating me like I'm the enemy?" Sam asked. His voice rose in volume, and his eyebrows lowered in a full-on frown.

Maggie just shook her head and took the seat to Claire's right and signaled for Max to take the other.

"Ms. Freemont, are you really going to let some teenager be your first line of defense?" Sam asked. He was holding a pencil in his hand, and he tapped the eraser against the top of the table.

"Yes," she said. She gave Max a fond smile. "It's really nice of you to be here. Thank you, Max."

Max's face flushed red, and he glanced down at his beat-up Converse sneakers. "Have they questioned you at all?"

"No, I told them I wanted my attorney present," Claire said. "Are you sure you're willing to represent me, Max?"

"Absolutely," he said. His voice cracked again, and Maggie fervently hoped that this thing went no further. She could not imagine Max in a trial situation. Yes, his mind was brilliant, but what would a jury make of him? She didn't want to know.

"Fine, then, your attorney can be present, but not her," Sam said. He took the seat across the table from them and pointed his pencil at Maggie.

Maggie opened her mouth to argue, but Max held up his hand. "It's fine, Maggie, I've got it."

"You've got it?" she asked. She looked at him like he'd recently fallen off his skateboard and sustained a head injury.

"Yeah," he said, and he tipped his head to the door. He leaned behind Claire and motioned for Maggie to do the same. In a low voice, he said, "You and Sheriff Collins don't get along. You'll only antagonize him if you stay, which will not help Claire at all."

"Are you kicking me out?" she asked.

"Yes," Max said. His tone made it clear that he thought he couldn't be any more obvious.

"I'm just going to ask Ms. Freemont some questions," Sam said. "I'm not arresting her. You don't need to be here."

Maggie narrowed her eyes at him, and then she put her hand on Claire's shoulder. "You'll be okay?"

Claire nodded. "I'll be fine."

"I'll be right outside," Maggie said. She gave Sam one more glower, and then she turned and left the room.

Out in the hall, the police station was abuzz. Several reporters were cooling their heels, texting away on their smartphones, while waiting to interview the sheriff. Several deputies manned the front desk, and the station hummed with the frenetic energy of something really bad happening that they were all still trying to process.

St. Stanley was a sleepy little town tucked away in the rolling hills of southern Virginia, about an hour west of the ocean. Not much happened in the pleasant little burg to cause such a stir—certainly not murder.

Maggie wondered how the questioning was going. She wondered if she'd be able to hear if she put her ear to the door, but then she knew Sam would probably catch her, and that wouldn't go well for any of them.

She took a seat on a hard wooden bench that did not invite lingering and resigned herself to wait. She needed to give Max a ride back to the ice cream stand, and she didn't want Claire to be alone after such an ordeal.

Her mind drifted back to the body in the library basement. Where was he now? Had the state's crime scene investigators taken him for an autopsy? Surely, no one in St. Stanley was qualified to deal with a man found stabbed.

Maggie felt herself suddenly sit up straighter. The knife sticking out of the man's chest, she could see it in her mind. It had been a cake knife. Claire had arrived at her house yesterday looking harried, and she said she had forgotten her cake knife. Had the one protruding from the man's chest been Claire's?

Maggie glanced warily from side to side as if someone might have overheard her thoughts. The knife wasn't

Claire's. She was sure of that . . . Well, even if it *was* Claire's, she was sure that Claire had not been the one to shove it into the man's chest.

She took her phone out of her purse and dialed Ginger's number. Ginger answered on the third ring.

"Lancaster Accounting, how can I help you?"

"Ginger, it's Maggie," she said. "What's your schedule for today?"

"Light," she said. "Why? Does this involve a sale? Did you find a better deal on sneakers than two for one?"

"Sadly, no, on all counts." Maggie took a deep breath. "There was a dead body found in the library this morning, and Sam Collins is questioning Claire right now."

"A what in the where?" Ginger's voice was shrill. "Questioning Claire? Why? What does she have to do with it other than working at the library?"

"Apparently, she used to know the man," Maggie said.

"She needs an attorney," Ginger said. "Immediately."

"I've got Max Button in with her."

"Good call, he's a genius. He got my oldest through calculus. So, what are you doing now?"

"Waiting," Maggie said. "Sam wouldn't let me stay in the room with them."

"Sam, huh," Ginger said. "Is he as cute as ever?"

"If you consider rattlesnakes cute."

"Well, if he's a rattlesnake, he can slither onto my porch any old time."

"Ginger!" Maggie gasped. "What would Roger say?"

"Oh, honey, I'm married, not dead," Ginger said. "I'm allowed to look at eye candy, and so is Roger. We're just not allowed to have any of it."

"Sam Collins is not eye candy, at least not to me."

"Are you ever going to forgive him for teasing you when you were kids?"

"That would be a no," Maggie said.

What she didn't add was that it wasn't just Sam teasing her when they were kids that made her dislike him so. What no one knew, not even Ginger, was that well before she'd met Charlie there had been a few crazy weeks during the summer after her junior year of high school where Maggie had been sure that she was in love with Sam Collins and he with her. What she would ultimately never forgive him for was breaking her heart.

Chapter 10

Maggie agreed to stop by Ginger's office with more information as soon as she had any, and Ginger said she would call Joanne and fill her in on what was happening. They decided an emergency meeting of the GBGs was in order for that evening.

The door to the interview room opened, and Sam stepped out. He gave Maggie an aggravated look, and said, "The attorney needs a minute to confer with his client."

Maggie raised her eyebrows.

Sam opened his mouth as if wanted to say something, but then closed it and shook his head. Maggie thought she should say something, but she found the words wouldn't come.

This was the first time she'd been alone with Sam Collins in twenty-four years. So many times she had fantasized about what she would say to him if the opportunity ever presented itself. It had always involved a lovely worded tirade that would leave him feeling like a pile of dung, followed by her tossing her auburn hair and slamming a door.

Yeah, and here she was rendered mute, not a door available to slam, and she was suffering from a seriously advanced case of bike helmet hair from this morning's jaunt to the library.

"Coffee," Sam growled. "You want any?"

Maggie shook her head. At least she could manage that. He disappeared down the hall, returning a few minutes later with a steaming mug in his hand. He knocked on the door twice and then entered, shutting it behind him before Maggie could manage a peek inside. Darn it.

And so she sat on the bench until her butt was completely numb. Finally, the door opened and Claire came out, followed by Max.

"Thank you, Max. You were great," Claire said to him as they joined Maggie.

She rose stiffly, feeling the cramps flee her legs as the blood rushed back into them.

"So, you're free to go?" she asked.

Sam appeared from behind them. "For now."

With that, he strode off, and Maggie looked at the other two with wide eyes.

"What's up with him?"

"The crime scene investigators have called him back to the library," Max said. "Looks like they're wrapping up over there."

"So, what were you able to tell him about the situation?" Maggie asked.

"The truth. I told him the truth." Maggie just stared at

her until Claire added, "Yes, I told him I used to date the victim, John Templeton, five years ago and that I haven't seen him since I left Baltimore."

"That must have gone over well," Maggie said.

Claire and Max exchanged a look, and Maggie knew they were shutting her out of something. Had Claire confided in Max? Well, of course, she had. He was her attorney. Maggie wasn't sure how she felt about this, even if she was the one who had put the two of them together.

A reporter was talking to a deputy who pointed toward them.

"Come on," Max said. "We need to git while the gittin' is good."

He took both of their elbows and led them down the hall toward the exit. The reporter looked as if she was about to call out to them, but Max pulled them in close and started whispering nonsense.

"Fudge ripple with hot caramel sauce covered in whipped cream with chopped walnuts on the side," he said.

"Sounds good to me," Maggie said. "Are you buying?"

"I think this one is on me," Claire said.

They cleared the doors with no cameras or mics jammed into their faces. So no one yet knew of the connection between Claire and the dead man. Maggie fervently hoped it stayed that way. They made a beeline for Maggie's car. Max opened the door for Claire and then climbed in back.

Maggie hit the gas hard, leaving the station behind, and headed back to the Frosty Freeze. Not surprisingly, at least to Maggie, they found Max's boss standing in front of the closed window, looking particularly irritated.

"Uh-oh," Max said from the back seat.

"Don't worry, I've got this," Maggie said. It was the least she could do, since she had dragged him out of there to begin with.

"Button!" His boss glared at the back seat of Maggie's station wagon. "Button, are you in there? What's the big idea, closing during the middle of the day right before the lunch crush?"

Maggie looked around at the empty lot and then at Hugh Simpson, the owner. He was short and fat with a bad comb-over and favored plaid pants with silk shirts, unbuttoned low and topped off with a big, fat chain around his neck. Seriously, thirty plus years had passed since the era of the Hustle, and the man still hadn't gotten the word that disco was dead.

"It's my fault, Hugh," Maggie said. "There was a small emergency and we needed Max's legal expertise."

"Oh, really?" Hugh asked. "I'm sorry, but show me where it says the Frosty Freeze offers free legal advice?"

"Sorry, Mr. Simpson," Max said.

He climbed out of the backseat, only stopping to mutter something low to Claire. She nodded, and then he scooted through the side door of the building, back into the ice cream stand, where he pulled up the window shade and flipped the sign to OPEN.

"Sorry?" Hugh barked, smoothing a stray strand of hair back across his dome. "Sorry doesn't get me my lost revenue. You are fired!"

Max poked his head out the window, rolled his eyes and shook his head. Hugh had fired him at least once a week since he'd taken the job here five years ago.

"We're here to order sundaes," Maggie said to Hugh. "Will that help?"

"If you're paying fifty bucks a piece for them, maybe," he snapped.

Maggie gasped. Her thrifty soul felt violated by the mere suggestion.

Claire came to stand beside her. She looked wan and subdued, and a spat with Hugh Simpson wasn't going to help her in the least.

"Tell you what," Maggie said. "If I can get twenty people to come here in the next hour, will you let Max keep his job?"

"Twenty, huh?" Hugh studied her from beneath heavy lidded eyes. "No tricks?"

"From me?" Maggie asked. She opened her eyes wide, the picture of innocence.

"You're sly," he said. "Always with the coupons and the price matching, I want twenty individual paying customers with no special deals."

Maggie nodded and held out her hand. Hugh studied it as if looking for a toy buzzer. Reluctantly, he took her hand in his and pumped it up and down.

"I hope this works out for you," Hugh said to Max. "When you don't have your nose jammed in a book, you're a good employee."

"Thanks, Mr. Simpson," Max said. He pushed two fudge ripple sundaes with hot caramel sauce through the open window. Claire paid their tab and Maggie smiled at Hugh and said, "Eighteen to go."

Hugh grunted and strode around to the side door and disappeared into the small office he had there.

Maggie and Claire approached the window.

"Sorry about that," Maggie said to Max. "I didn't mean to get you in trouble."

"I think he enjoys firing me," Max said. "You really don't have to go get eighteen more customers. He'll get over it. He always does. Remember when I had my physics final, and I forgot to come into work for a week? He got over it. Good ice cream dippers are hard to find, you know."

"Thanks, but a deal is a deal," Maggie said. She scooped some of her sundae into her mouth. "He'll get his customers. Don't you worry."

"How are you planning on doing that, anyway?" Max asked. "I mean, it's August, and everyone is gearing up to go back to school. We'll be closing for the season at the end of September."

"I have a plan," Maggie said.

She devoured more of her sundae. She was feeling the pressure to get going, but didn't want to waste her ice cream by tossing it out. She made a concentrated effort to finish it, wincing through a bout of brain freeze. When she tossed the empty paper cup out, she noticed that Claire had been busily pushing her own sundae around, helping it melt but not tasting it.

"I need to go back to the library to see what sort of damage control needs to be done," she said.

"I'll drop you off," Maggie said. "Thanks again, Max, we'll see you later."

Claire tossed her ice cream out, and they climbed back into Maggie's car.

"Are you sure you want to go back there?" she asked Claire. "I mean, the body . . . er . . . the investigators may not be done yet and it could be disturbing."

"I need to be there," Claire said. "With my boss on vacation, I'm supposed to be in charge. I had to leave Hannah, our children's librarian, to supervise while I was at the police station. Supervising is not her strength. I have to get back."

"All right, but I'm coming in with you," Maggie said. "Just to make sure everything is okay."

"Thanks," Claire said.

They parked in the library lot and noticed that only one sheriff's car remained. When they approached the door, they found it locked, and Claire looked worriedly at Maggie.

She used her key to let them in, and they found the library quieter than Maggie had ever seen it. A lone woman, Hannah Teague, sat at the circulation desk. When she saw them, her shoulders sagged in relief.

"Oh, Claire, thank goodness," she said. She was a petite woman with medium-length brown hair and glasses. She came around the desk and gave Claire a big hug, which Claire stiffly returned. Claire wasn't a hugger by nature.

"Are you all right?" Hannah asked. "That must have been awful, finding a body like that."

Claire nodded and quickly changed the subject, asking, "Hannah, why is the door locked?"

Hannah blew out a breath as if she wasn't sure what Claire would think of what she had to say.

"Well, I didn't know what else to do. They told me they were going to wheel the body right through the middle of the library, and I had just finished toddler time and there were tons of kids here. All I could think was that we had to get everyone out of here. So I closed the library for the day."

Claire nodded. "That was a good call. I should have done it before I left, but things were . . ."

"Yeah," Hannah agreed. "Crazy. Are you going to call Carlton and tell him what's going on?"

"I suppose I have to," Claire said. She glanced down the hall where her office was located. "Is anyone still here?"

"Sam Collins," Hannah said. "He's taking one last look around the basement before he seals it."

Claire nodded. "Okay, then. Well, I'd best go call Carlton. You can go, Hannah. There's no need for you to stay."

"I'm not leaving you alone in the building," Hannah said. "I'll be in the children's area, weeding the board books. You let me know when you're ready, and we'll leave together."

Claire gave her a small smile. "Thanks."

They watched as Hannah walked back to her area. Maggie went with Claire to her office. She didn't know what she'd been expecting, but it certainly wasn't the mess they found.

"What is this stuff?" Maggie asked, finding a black, filmy dust on her fingers from the door.

"Looks like they checked my office for fingerprints," Claire said. "Probably to see if John was in here before he was killed."

"Well, that's just . . ."

Maggie began to wind up into a tirade when a voice from the door said, "Thorough."

They spun around to see Sam Collins standing there. He looked harried, but Maggie didn't care. She didn't like that he was questioning her friend, and she had no problem letting him know.

"They don't teach cleanup at the police academy?" she asked. "Pretty sloppy if you ask me."

"No one asked you," he said. He turned to Claire, "Will the library remain closed?"

"For the day," she said.

He nodded. "I've sealed off the basement. No one is to go down there under any circumstances."

"Understood," she said.

"I'll need you to collect the keys to the basement from anyone who has one," he said.

Claire reached into her drawer and pulled out a key ring. With shaky fingers, she pulled off a key and handed it to him. "The only other person who has a key besides me and Preston, the maintenance man, is Carlton, our director, but he's on vacation until next week."

"I'll get Preston's key, then, and lock it up," he said. He turned to leave the room and then turned back. "You're not planning any vacations in the near future, are you?"

"No," Claire said. She looked frightened, and Maggie had to squelch the urge to go over and kick Sam in the shins.

"Good," he said. He turned and left the room.

Maggie studied Claire. "Are you all right?"

Claire nodded, but they both knew she was lying.

"I'm going to call Carlton and tell him what's happening," she said. "Then I think I'll go home for the day."

"I think that's an excellent plan," Maggie said. Even though Claire wasn't a hugger, Maggie stepped across the room and gave her a big one. To her surprise, Claire hugged her back hard.

"Do you want me to stay?" Maggie offered.

Claire gave her a small smile. "Don't you have eighteen ice cream eaters to gather?"

"That can wait," Maggie said.

"Thanks, but I'll be all right," she said. "I have Hannah here, and I'll be leaving shortly. You go on."

"If you're sure," Maggie said. Claire nodded. "Call me if you need anything."

Claire nodded again.

Maggie left the library in a hurry. Claire was right. She had to get eighteen people to the Frosty Freeze, and she wanted to get the Good Buy Girls together, because if Claire thought she was going to sit at home alone tonight and brood, she was seriously mistaken.

Maggie was just getting into her car when she felt someone step up behind her. Years of self-defense classes whirled through her brain. She spun around, assuming a fighting stance ready to do some damage, but it was just Sam.

"Ah! You scared me!" she snapped. She inched away from him, not liking having him in her personal space bubble. Bad things happened when this man got into her bubble.

His eyes narrowed as if he was offended that she felt the need to move away from him. Too bad.

"Maggie, you look like you want to punch me," he said. "Any particular reason?"

Oh, she had a whole list; instead, she said, "You're awfully oversensitive for a sheriff. Surely, you must know most people aren't happy to see you."

"When I save their lives, they are," he said.

"Yeah, but I bet you write more tickets than save lives, so really, small wonder your popularity isn't all that," she said. She knew she was being mean, but it was nothing compared to what he'd done to her. She refused to feel badly for being snippy.

"Why are you so angry with me?" he asked, stepping closer and looking thoroughly exasperated.

"I'm not angry," she said, stepping back. She shrugged and glanced away. "I couldn't care less about you."

"In the police academy, they teach the five signs that someone is lying," he said. "You just gave me two of them by shrugging and looking away. I can tell you're lying, Maggie."

"Huh," she scoffed.

"That would be another sign," he said.

The fact that he was right only made Maggie even madder at him. But when all else failed, she went with her first line of defense: deny, deny, deny.

"Oh, please, what's the matter? Is the return of the football hero to St. Stanley not all you thought it would be?" she asked. "What did you think? The town was going to fill the football bleachers and drive you around the field in a convertible and cheer your homecoming?"

Sam stared at her. His blue eyes were blazing, and she was surprised she didn't catch fire under his glare. His jaw was clamped, and she could see the knot of muscles in his cheek clench and unclench. He looked close to losing his temper, and she wondered if she had pushed him too far.

"For your information, the only thing I remember about the football bleachers is being under them . . . with you," he said. He looked like he wanted to take a step closer to her, but instead he spun on his heel and stalked away.

Chapter 11

Maggie opened the driver's-side door with hands that shook and fell into her seat with legs the consistency of jelly. He remembered. All this time she had thought she was just a summer conquest for him, a postscript to his senior year that was forgotten in the glory of his college days, and in one sentence he had stripped her of that angry, protective coating.

She punched her steering wheel, feeling hot tears well up behind her eyes. How did he do that? How did he reach past twenty-four years of her shoving aside his memory with an angry huff and make her feel that stupid, ridiculous flicker of longing again?

And with that longing, she felt swamped by guilt. She had loved her husband, Charlie Gerber. He had come into her life in the wake of her heartbreak over Sam, and he had been handsome and funny and kind, a perfect husband and father, and she felt so lucky that he had chosen to spend his life with her. But even the deep love she felt for Charlie had not erased the crazy passionate feelings she'd had for Sam Collins, and that made her feel guilty, which made her even more annoyed with Sam and his ability to bring back those old feelings.

She rested her head on the steering wheel and forced herself to think about happy things, like her daughter, Laura, a pretty redhead who, like her father, was as kind as she was smart. One of Maggie's favorite memories was of Laura catching ladybugs in their small garden. One ladybug had climbed under her pretty yellow dress and tickled its way across her belly, making Laura laugh her contagious little-girl giggle.

Maggie remembered that day so vividly. She could feel Laura's small hand in hers, hear the birds twittering and smell the summer roses in bloom. It was one of her go-to memories in times of stress, and it always grounded her. She let out a sigh. She was okay.

Once her emotions were under control, Maggie started up her car and headed to the office where she did medical billing for Dr. Franklin. It had been a full-time job when she was younger, but now that Dr. Franklin was semiretired, Maggie worked just part-time for him.

As she turned onto Main Street and passed the library, she refused to look at the building. She didn't even want to catch a glance of Sam Collins, for fear that he'd manage to get past her defenses again.

She inhaled a deep breath through her nose, held it and slowly let it out through her mouth. There was no point in dwelling on the past, no point in even thinking about it. Her life had worked out the way it was supposed to, for if she hadn't fallen in love with and married Charlie, she wouldn't have Laura. She couldn't imagine her life without her bright, beautiful girl. So there it was.

There was no point in looking over her shoulder at the shadows of her youth—it served no purpose. Of course, if she followed that line of thought, there wasn't much point in being so angry with Sam Collins either. She didn't think she was quite ready to let go of that, however.

She drove across St. Stanley to Spring Gardens, the assisted-care facility that was built into one of the historic homes in the center of town. Dr. Franklin had left his busy practice and kept a small office in the facility, figuring that the patients who needed him the most were the elderly who resided at Spring Gardens.

Maggie turned in past the large, wrought-iron gate that framed the gravel drive leading to the tall, three-story red brick building. A fountain bubbled in the middle of the circular drive, which she turned off of toward the small lot at the side of the building.

She parked in the staff section of the lot and found her ID badge.

As she headed toward the building, she saw Ray Roberson seated in the facility's bus with his feet up on the dash while he scanned the newspaper. An older black man, heavyset with graying hair and dentures that he liked to move around in his mouth when he was cogitating on a problem, Ray had been a school bus driver back in the day. In fact, Maggie had ridden his bus when she went to St. Stanley Elementary. When Ray had retired, he'd bought one of the old school buses that was about to be retired as well.

Now he lived at Spring Gardens, rent free, in return for being the facility's on-call bus driver.

Maggie stopped by the open door of the bus and called, "Hi, Mr. Ray."

"Well, hello, Miss Maggie," he said as he lowered the paper. "I didn't think you worked today."

"I don't," she said. "But I thought I'd pop on over. I have a bit of a dilemma, you see."

"Do tell," he said as he shuffled his dentures from side to side.

"I promised Hugh Simpson that eighteen people would come by the Frosty for ice cream, or he's going to fire Max Button," she said.

"Might be good for the boy," Ray said. "He's too smart to stay there."

"Agreed, but since I'm the one who got him in trouble for abandoning his post, I don't want him fired on my account."

"Now where could you find eighteen ice cream eaters?" Ray asked. "I'm betting the bingo hall might offer supply to your demand."

"That is an excellent suggestion, Mr. Ray," she said. "Are you feeling up for a drive, by any chance?"

"I could be persuaded."

"Bus driver gets a freebie," she said.

"A cone or a sundae?" he asked.

"Sundae, for sure," she said.

"With whipped cream and sprinkles?"

"And a cherry."

"I don't like cherries," he said.

"No cherry, then," she said.

"Mmm, I guess I could go for a sundae."

"Excellent," Maggie said. "Prep the bus. They'll be out in five."

Maggie entered the side door to the building and headed over to the recreation room. There was an intense game of bingo going on.

As Paula Duwalter called out, "B1," Jerry and Dennis Applebaum looked like they were about to come to blows. Paula did not look particularly fazed by this, as the two brothers came to blows over every competition that the seniors had.

Maggie worked her way over to the table where the two men were sitting with teeth bared, hunched over their boards waiting for the next number to be called.

"Hurry up!" Jerry barked. "A man could die waiting for you to get to the next number."

"If we're lucky," Dennis snapped.

Maggie peeked at their bingo cards. They only had a few spaces to go. Someone was going to win soon. Paula called out three more numbers, and Jerry shot up from the table, yelling, "Bingo!"

In his tank top with his gray chest hair poking out over the neckband, plaid shorts and loafers with black socks, Jerry was the epitome of old-man chic.

Wearing similar attire, except with striped shorts, Dennis popped out of his seat to look at his brother's bingo card.

"He cheated!" Dennis shouted. "I challenge that bingo."

Paula let out a put-upon sigh. Maggie suspected it was because she was forced to do this for every game. The rest of the seniors in the room looked like they couldn't give two hoots who had won the bingo. This was just the opening Maggie needed.

"You know, Dennis," she said. "If Jerry won this bingo round, that would be good for you."

"How do you figure?" he asked. "I don't see how his cheating is doing me any good."

"I didn't cheat," Jerry argued. He cracked his knuckles, and Maggie was afraid he'd get himself sedated before her plan was in motion.

"It's just that I saw the Spring Gardens bus out front, and it looked to me like it was headed to the Frosty Freeze, so if Jerry here is busy picking out his bingo prize, you would score the front seat, Dennis."

The two brothers stared at each other for a heartbeat, and then they both scrambled for the door, throwing elbows and shoving each other.

"Misters Applebaum!" Paula hollered after them. "What is the meaning of this?"

"A trip to the Frosty Freeze," Maggie said. "I heard the bus driver say they were going."

Moving as one, the rest of the seniors hustled up from their tables and hurried to the door. There was a little bit of a jam-up, but Dennis gave Jerry a wet willy by licking his index finger and sticking it in his brother's ear. *Ew!*

As Jerry jumped back, all of the seniors stampeded past him on their way to the front door.

"What the heck was that all about?" Paula asked.

"Ice cream at the Frosty Freeze," Maggie said.

"We don't have a trip planned for today," she said. "At least I don't think so."

This was the beauty of Paula Duwalter. She was a former Miss Virginia, by about thirty years, but she still walked the walk and talked the talk, meaning she wasn't the sharpest tack on the bulletin board.

"Really? I saw Ray getting the bus ready," Maggie said.

"Huh, imagine that," Paula said. "Hey, is Dr. Franklin in today?"

"No, why?" Maggie asked. She was itching to get on her way, but she knew Paula, and if she didn't stop and listen, Paula would get all huffy, and that never boded well for anyone.

"I've got this twinge in my neck," Paula said. "Whenever I sleep on my right side, I wake up all tight."

Maggie glanced down the corridor. The seniors were almost at the front. Oh dear, she really didn't have time for Paula's hypochondria right now.

"I know how to fix that," she said.

"Really?" Paula asked. "Because I don't want any pills. One of the contestants in the Miss America pageant with me was addicted to diet pills. I won't take pills."

Somehow, Paula always managed to work her Miss America–contender status into every conversation. It was a gift, truly.

"There are no pills. It's very simple," Maggie said. She was losing sight of the oldsters. Time to go. "If sleeping on your right side hurts, then don't sleep on your right side."

She left the room with Paula frowning after her. Well, what did she expect when she asked the person in charge of billing for medical advice? It was like the old joke, "Doc, it hurts when I bend my elbow like this." And the doc says, "Then don't bend your elbow like that."

She hustled down the corridor to the front of the building.

Ray was holding up his arms, trying to wave off the incoming tide of seniors that was headed for the bus. They plowed right over him in their orthopedic shoes.

Maggie took a quick head count as they climbed in: eighteen seniors, plus Ray. Excellent.

"Thanks, Mr. Ray," Maggie smiled. "You're really doing me a solid here."

"Huh," he said. "At least with ice cream, there won't be any runners, not like at the mall."

Maggie nodded. Ice cream would keep the oldsters subdued. One of the many reasons the facility liked Ray for their driver was that he had a knack for keeping tabs on the seniors, especially the runners, the ones who tried to make a break for it and go home.

"The things I do for free ice cream." He glanced over his shoulder at the rowdy group. "Pipe down, or we're not going."

"Come on, everyone, let's sing," Dotty, a former cruise ship director, ordered.

There were resistant grunts and groans, but she ignored them and, with her platinum wig bouncing on her head and her fake eyelashes all aflutter, she sang in a high, clear soprano, "One hundred bottles of Ensure on the wall, one hundred bottles of Ensure, you take one down and pass it around, ninety-nine . . ."

Her voice trailed off as Ray pulled the doors shut and punched the gas. The bus bounced its way out of the parking lot toward the Frosty Freeze.

Maggie pulled out her cell phone and called Max. She had to give him a heads-up that Ray got a freebie. Now Hugh would have his eighteen, Max's job would be secure, and the seniors would be happy. Now she could go over to Ginger's office and catch her up on what was happening.

Max sounded impressed when she told him to expect the bus. Then they agreed to meet at Claire's later in the day to discuss their strategy, should Claire get called in by the sheriff again.

Maggie hopped into her car and drove to Ginger's house. She lived in one of the historic houses on the town green. It had been a fixer-upper when she and Roger had bought it twenty years ago, and it had come a long way since, but with four teenage boys living in it, it had an air of frat house that could not be denied.

Ginger had converted the stand-alone garage into an office for her accounting business. It worked perfectly, except for when her boys were home and started to play basketball, using the hoop attached to her office, which was why she stuck primarily to morning hours.

Maggie parked in the drive and hurried to the side door. It was unlocked, so she popped her head in and found Ginger working on her computer. She waved and waited for Ginger to stop typing before she spoke.

"Okay, I'm saved and good," Ginger said. "Now what the heck is going on? How's Claire?"

"She's been better," Maggie said.

"Did Sam arrest her?" Ginger asked.

"No, but I'm worried that he will," Maggie said.

"But why would he?" Ginger asked. "So what if she knew the man five years ago? It doesn't make her the killer. I mean, why would she kill him?"

Maggie shrugged. She had been kicked out of the interview room, so she was left not knowing very much.

"That's what we'll have to ask her," Maggie said.

"So, what's the plan?" Ginger asked.

"I'm going to stop by More than Meats to see Joanne and get her up to speed, and then we'll have an emergency meeting of the Good Buy Girls tonight and see what we can do to help Claire."

"Does she want our help?" Ginger asked.

"What do you mean?"

"Maggie," Ginger began, and then paused as if choosing her words carefully. "Not everyone is like you."

"What's that supposed to mean?" Maggie asked, wondering if she should start feeling offended.

"Simply that you are not one for secrets," Ginger said. "You are very open about your life and your feelings. Claire isn't like that. Claire is very private. She may not want the rest of us mucking around in her business."

"If Claire ever needed her friends, it's now," Maggie said. "I say we have the meeting, and if she wants us to back off, we will, but we'll offer her our support first."

Ginger nodded. "I guess that would be okay."

Maggie studied her hands. She found it amazing that the person who knew her better than anyone else on the planet thought she wore her heart on her sleeve and had no secrets. She wondered if she should tell Ginger about her romance-gone-wrong with Sam Collins. She opened her mouth to begin, but then found she couldn't say a word.

Somehow, talking about it would bring it all back, even more than having him here in St. Stanley again, if that was possible, and she was having a hard enough time with that. If anyone knew that they had once been a couple, she feared it would make dealing with him even worse.

"So, seven o'clock. I'll pick you up," Maggie said.

"I'll be ready," Ginger said.

"Bye." Maggie rose and headed for the door. She always said good-bye first, so that Ginger could have the last word.

"Bye," Ginger called after her, and Maggie smiled.

Since Maggie was already in the center of town, it was a short drive from the residential section of old, historic homes, around the town square, to the shops that lined Main Street. More than Meats, a combination deli and butcher shop perched on Main Street near First Street, was nestled between the Perk Up and the Enchanted Florist.

Maggie parked on First Street and walked back around the corner, pausing to admire the bucket of blossoms outside the florist, before heading into the deli. Thankfully, they were in the middle of the afternoon lull. Joanne was wearing her usual bright yellow apron while she hustled around the tables refilling the sugar bowls and wiping down any crumbs left from the lunch crush.

"Hi, Joanne," Maggie called as the door shut behind her.

"Maggie, how's Claire?" Joanne asked, dropping her cloth and reaching out to take Maggie's hands in hers. "Ginger said she was taken in for questioning. Is she all right? I texted her, but she hasn't gotten back to me."

"Hi, Maggie!" Michael Claramotta, Joanne's husband, waved to her from behind the deli counter at the back of the small restaurant.

If there was such a thing as a perfect couple, Maggie thought Michael and Joanne Claramotta were it. They'd been childhood sweethearts since the second grade, when Michael had given Joanne a cheesy paper valentine with a honeybee on it that asked, "Will you bee mine?" Joanne said she knew when she opened it that she was going to marry him.

Michael was the perfect other half for Joanne. He complimented her slender build with a muscular physique, and he stood a half foot taller than she was. Ginger often joked that they could be models for the bride and groom statues on the tops of wedding cakes, they were such a perfect-looking couple.

"Hi!" She waved back and turned to Joanne, "Yes, it's true, and she's okay, but I don't have much more information than that."

Michael came around the deli counter with a frosty glass of sweet tea that he handed to Maggie. Michael was always the perfect host; it was exactly what she needed.

"Thank you," she said, and took a long drink.

"The rumors have been flying fast and furious all afternoon," he said. "Was the man really naked except for a pair of women's high heels?"

Maggie almost had tea come out her nose.

"Ew, no!" she said as she coughed.

"Oh." Michael looked disappointed.

"I told you that you can't trust anything Summer Phillips has to say," Joanne chided her husband in a gentle tone.

"I know," he said. "Still, you have to admit . . ."

"No, I don't. That is a disturbing mental picture that only someone as vile as Summer could think up," Joanne said.

"Well, in all fairness, she's not the only one," he said. "How about Tyler Fawkes saying that the body had been dismembered with a rusty hacksaw?"

"Oh, ick," Maggie said.

"Oh, yeah, and Jamie Singleton said the body was decapitated, and the head was missing," Joanne said.

"Oh, double ick," Maggie said.

"Yeah, it's been a long day," Joanne said.

"Well, I saw the body, and I can tell you, it was clothed, no high heels, all body parts were attached, including the head," she said.

Joanne reached out and put an arm around Maggie's shoulders. "That must have been rough."

"I thought I'd seen some gnarly things while working for Dr. Franklin," Maggie said. "You know, we get the occasional goiter or festering chancre, but this was . . . well, I'm good with never seeing a dead man with a knife through his chest ever again."

The bells chimed on the door, and Michael left them, giving Maggie's shoulder a squeeze as he went to wait on the deli customer.

"So, Ginger said we're having an emergency meeting of the GBGs," Joanne said. "I'm in."

"Seven o'clock at Claire's," Maggie confirmed.

"I'll meet you there, and I'll bring a deli platter," Joanne said. "We have to make sure she keeps up her strength, and nothing says you care like a plate full of cold cuts."

Maggie had to agree.

Chapter 12

Maggie knocked on Claire's front door. She lived in a small bungalow in an older neighborhood that surrounded the town's abandoned wire factory. The factory had been closed long before Maggie was born, and the small houses in the neighborhood that surrounded it, which had once been the factory workers' homes, had become an artists' haven.

In her non-library spare time, Claire painted small still lifes in oil, so she fit right in with her glass-blowing, steel-sculpting neighbors. Twice a year the artists had a weekend-long art show on the town green. Maggie loved it because she always found new and unusual gifts for people at the show, and she had noticed that if she waited until the last day, the prices dropped dramatically because the artists were looking to unload some inventory.

A movement in the window caught Maggie's attention,

and she glanced over to see Claire's cat, Mr. Tumnus, watching her from his bay window perch.

"Maybe she's not home," Ginger said. She was carrying an orange pound cake with vanilla glaze that she had made that afternoon, while Maggie had two bottles of wine tucked in the crook of her arm.

"She has to be home," Maggie said. "Where else could she be? On a hot date?"

The door was yanked open, and Claire poked her head out. "Who's on a hot date?"

"We were wondering if you were," Ginger said. "Open up. We come bearing food."

"Is that your famous pound cake?" Claire asked.

"The one and only blue ribbon–winning pound cake in all of St. Stanley, yes, it is," Ginger said.

Claire stepped back, opening the door wide.

Pound cake will get you in every time, Maggie thought.

She trooped in, with Ginger bringing up the rear. Just before Claire shut the door, Joanne arrived with her tray of deli goodies.

"Wait for me!" she cried, and followed them into the small house.

"Have you eaten?" Ginger asked, looking Claire over with her best "don't even try to lie to me" mother look.

"I forgot," Claire admitted. She gestured to the shirt she was wearing, an oversize blue T-shirt covered in paint splotches in a rainbow of colors. "I was trying to do some art therapy to see if it would help."

"And?" Maggie asked.

"It didn't," Claire said.

The house consisted of one large front room, which Claire used as a living room. It was cozy with wood floors, overstuffed bookcases, a fireplace and a large TV in the corner. They trooped through the arched door at the end of it into the kitchen, which had been recently renovated.

A large granite breakfast counter that seated four separated the eating area from the rest of the kitchen, and the ladies placed their food on the counter and each took a stool, while Claire passed out plates and glasses.

"This is so nice of you," she said to the others. She looked a little misty, and Maggie suspected she wasn't used to having others do for her.

"Nah, this is nothing," Ginger said, making light of it. "It's just what GBGs do when one of us needs a boost."

"I need more than a boost," Claire said. "I need an alibi."

"You don't have one?" Joanne asked. Two worry lines formed a V between her eyebrows, and she nibbled on a piece of Swiss cheese with tiny little bites. Joanne was an emotional eater.

"Not unless you count Mr. Tumnus," Claire said. They all turned to look at the chubby gray tabby, who began to lick his chest hair as if priming himself to be the center of attention.

"That's ridiculous," Ginger said. "Anyone who knows you knows that you're not capable of murder. The whole thing is just silly."

"Well, that's the problem," Claire said. "Sheriff Collins doesn't know me. The only thing he knows is that I used to date John Templeton, the deceased, and the sheriff thinks it's mighty suspicious that he was found dead in my library with my cake knife sticking out of his chest and with one of the books from my personal library lying beside him."

Maggie, Ginger and Joanne sat staring at her, utterly gobsmacked.

"Oh, you didn't know all that?" Claire asked faintly. "I just assumed with St. Stanley being so small—well, if it makes any difference, I loaned that book out so long ago, I can't even remember who I lent it to . . ."

"No, we didn't know all of that," Maggie said. "In fact, the St. Stanley rumor machine is such that we've heard all sorts of things, but not that."

"Like what?" Claire asked, looking worried. "What are people saying about me?"

"No, no, not about you," Joanne assured her. "More about the body."

Claire, looking in need of fortification, handed Maggie the corkscrew. "Explain."

"Well, I heard that the body was dressed in a clown suit," Ginger said. "But that came from one of my boys, so I didn't believe it."

Claire's mouth formed a small O, and she blinked, obviously dumbfounded. Maggie took pity on her and gave her the first glass of wine.

"Oh, that's the mildest of the rumors," Joanne said. "You let Summer Phillips loose with some gossip, and it goes all kinds of sideways, like the body was naked . . ."

"Except for a pair of high heels," Maggie added.

Claire cringed at the distasteful mental picture. "What is wrong with people?"

Maggie filled the rest of the glasses and passed them out.

The ladies filled their plates and nibbled at their food while they talked.

"Speaking of Summer Phillips," Joanne said. "Did you know she used to date the new sheriff, Sam Collins, back when he lived here?"

"We knew," Ginger said. She waved a hand to indicate herself and Maggie.

Maggie felt her fingers tighten on the stem of her wineglass, but she bit into a slice of salami in an attempt to seem nonchalant.

"Well, it seems Summer is eager to revisit their former relationship," Joanne said. "At least, that's what it looked like when we saw her draping herself all over his car this afternoon."

"Do tell," Ginger said. "I know Maggie would love to hear all about her favorite law enforcement officer."

Maggie gave her a scorching blast of stink eye, but Ginger had known her for so many years that she had built up a powerful immunity. Unfortunately.

"That's sarcasm, right?" Claire asked. "Because I've seen how you two look at each other, and Sheriff Collins doesn't seem overly fond of you either."

"Let's just say that the sheriff and I have known each other since we were in diapers, and we get on about as well as a baby's butt and a vicious case of diaper rash," Maggie said. "I'll leave it to you to figure out who is the butt in this scenario and who is the rash."

Ginger hooted with laughter. "You just called Sam Collins a butt!"

The others laughed as well, and Maggie was pleased to

see Claire's shoulders drop from their anxious perch around her ears for the first time that day.

As if by mutual agreement, they stopped talking about the murder, and instead talked about the upcoming Labor Day sales. They still had to do some planning if they were going to make the most of the back-to-school bargains.

It wasn't until they were on the "coffee and pound cake" portion of the evening, that Maggie brought the conversation back to the matter at hand.

"Claire, I know you probably don't want to talk about this, but if we're going to help you, we need to know about you and John Templeton," she said.

"There's nothing to tell," Claire said quickly, too quickly. She shrugged and tucked the right side of her blonde bob behind her ear. Without meeting anyone's gaze, she took a sip of her coffee.

If Sam Collins was correct about the signs of lying, looking away and shrugging, then Claire was definitely being less than truthful. Maggie sighed. She didn't want to push her friend too hard, but she didn't know how to help her if Claire withheld information from them.

"So you haven't had any contact with him at all since you left Baltimore?" Maggie asked.

Claire shook her head, but didn't speak.

"Claire, you know I love you," Ginger said. "But that *beep-beep-beep* we're all hearing is the manure truck backing up and unloading a whole pile of sh—"

"What Ginger is trying to say," Joanne interrupted, giving Ginger an exasperated look, "is that we were wondering about the missing slice of Ralph's cake."

"Huh?" Claire looked bewildered.

Maggie nodded. "Oh yeah, I forgot about that. That's a good place to start. Yes, tell us about the cake."

"What about the cake?" Claire asked exasperated.

"When you showed up at Maggie's, it was missing a piece," Ginger said. "Did you happen to give a piece to this Mr. Templeton before you joined us at Maggie's house?"

"I . . . well, that's just . . ."

Someone knocked on the door, cutting off whatever she had been about to say.

"I'd better get that," she said.

The three women watched her go.

"She's hiding something," Ginger said. "She had the same look on her face that I've seen on each one of my boys when they've tried to keep something from me."

"What do you think it is?" Joanne asked. "I mean, you don't think . . . it couldn't be . . ."

The three of them exchanged glances.

"Nah," they all said together.

"Claire didn't stab him," Maggie said definitively. "But I do think she saw him, which for some reason she doesn't want to talk about."

They heard voices at the door. The low voice of a man and Claire's rather shrill reply.

Maggie hopped off her stool and moved to stand in the arched doorway that separated the kitchen and the living room. She supposed it was terrible of her to eavesdrop, but she wondered who would be stopping by Claire's house so late in the evening and why.

It only took her a moment to recognize the greasy black hair and red Converse sneakers. Max, the attorney, was here.

"Hi, Max," she called out. "I thought you'd be here earlier. Come on in and grab some food."

Max shifted to the side to peer around Claire. He gave Maggie a smile that didn't meet his eyes but instead wobbled, as if trying to be brave.

"Hi, Maggie," he said. "I'm afraid there's no time to eat. Sheriff Collins is on his way over here with an arrest warrant for Claire."

Chapter 13

The sound of two chairs scraping back on the tile floor broke through Maggie's stunned silence.

"What?" she asked. "But why?"

"Claire's fingerprints are on the cake knife," he said.

"Well, yeah. It's her knife," Maggie said. "Of course her prints are on it."

"But there are no others," Max said. "It seems Claire is the only one to have touched that knife."

"But that's completely circumstantial," Ginger protested. "Any fool knows that."

"Either way, it warrants questioning," Max said. Looking older than his years, he turned to Claire. "They will be here any minute. If there's anything you need to do, get it done. I have no idea how long they plan to keep you."

Max stepped all the way into the house and closed the door behind him. They migrated into the kitchen. Joanne nibbled another piece of cheese while Ginger downed the last of her wine.

Claire looked stricken. Then she turned and looked at Maggie. "Will you take care of Mr. Tumnus?"

"Of course," she said.

"His food is in the pantry. I give him a can in the morning and at night, and he likes to go out in the yard in the morning and watch the birds. I don't let him out alone, however, because I'm afraid . . ."

As if sensing his person's distress, Mr. Tumnus hopped down from the window and trotted into the kitchen and began to rub himself against Claire's ankles. She scooped him up and snuggled him close.

"I'll take him home with me. Josh will love him, and I'll sit on the sun porch with him every morning," Maggie said.

Claire gave her a watery smile, "He'll like that."

"Not that it's going to come to that, because I'm sure you'll be released before the night is through."

Claire looked over Mr. Tumnus's head with doubtful eyes, and again Maggie knew for sure that Claire hadn't told them everything.

"You could run, you know," Joanne said.

"What?" Max looked shocked. "I did not hear that. That's completely and utterly . . ."

"Peru would be good," Maggie interrupted Max's tirade. "Laura has a pen pal in Peru. Do you have a passport?"

"Yes, but I can't—" Claire began but Ginger cut her off.

"I can drive her to the airport," Ginger volunteered. "The rest of you can stall the police until her flight has taken off."

"No! You're not acting rationally. You can't just take off! How would it look?" Max asked, but they all ignored him.

"Go now!" Joanne ordered. "Don't even pack, just go."

"But . . ." Claire protested, but Maggie, Joanne and Ginger began to hustle her toward the door.

"Stop!" Max shouted. "If she runs, she'll be a fugitive, and the police will hunt her down. If they focus on her, then they won't be searching for the real killer. Is that what you want, Claire? To be on the run for the rest of your life?"

Claire blew out a breath and shook her head. "No."

Maggie, Ginger and Joanne pulled her into a group hug. Given Claire's resistance to hugs, it showed her frazzled state that she not only joined in the group hug, but clung to her friends as if trying to pull their collective strength into herself.

A car pulled up in the drive, and they all tensed. While the others went to the large front window to see who was there, Maggie clutched Claire by the shoulders and forced her to look her in the eye.

"You saw him that morning, before our Good Buy Girls meeting, didn't you?" Maggie whispered.

"Yes," Claire admitted. "But I didn't kill him. I swear to you, Maggie, the last time I saw him, John Templeton was as mean as ever; in fact, I would have sworn he was too mean to die."

"It's Sheriff Collins," Ginger called from the living room. "And he's got a couple of deputies with him."

"I believe you," Maggie said. "And I'm going to do everything I can to get you out of this."

Claire kissed her cat's head and handed him over to Maggie. She took off her glasses and pulled off the oversized T-shirt that was her painting smock. She wore a black T-shirt under it, which she smoothed out with her hands. She finger-combed her hair and put her glasses back on.

When she looked back at Maggie, she looked resigned. "Maybe this is just what I deserve."

Before Maggie could ask any questions, Claire turned and left the kitchen.

A knock sounded on the door, and Claire reached it first.

She pulled it open and there stood Sheriff Collins with a sheaf of papers in his hands. "Claire Freemont, I have a search warrant for your home."

Max held out a hand to examine the papers, and Sam shook his head as if he still couldn't believe Max was an attorney, but he handed them over.

With so many people in the front room, the small house seemed even smaller. When Max gave a nod of approval and handed the papers back to Sam, the sheriff motioned for his deputies to come in making the house feel tiny.

"Do you want us to wait outside?" Claire asked.

"That won't be necessary, since everyone will be leaving, including you, Ms. Freemont," he said. His voice was stern. "The warrants aren't just to search your home. I have one for your arrest as well."

The Good Buy Girls gasped as one.

"Ms. Freemont, you are under arrest for the murder of John Templeton."

Maggie had thought she could be cool. She'd known what was coming—after all, Max had prepared them—but she found herself swamped by a rage so fierce and so ferocious that she was storming across the room, handing Mr. Tumnus to Joanne en route and confronting Sam Collins before her good sense had a chance to kick in.

"Is this how you do your job?" she asked. "You go after the easiest target? I mean, heaven forbid you actually do some leg work and investigate."

Sam crossed his arms over his chest as if he were trying to contain his own temper by literally holding it back. His voice when he spoke was placating, which to Maggie's ears was the same as patronizing, which did not soothe her ire in the least.

"I'm sure this is very difficult for you, Maggie, given that Ms. Freemont is your friend . . ."

"Huh!" Maggie broke in with a huff of outrage.

"But let me assure you," he continued through gritted teeth, "that from what we have learned so far, Ms. Freemont is a very likely suspect, and we are following the proper protocol by taking her in."

"Taking her in?" Maggie snapped. "What a nice way to say you're putting her in prison. You big oaf, don't try to candy-coat it for me."

A hand wrapped around Maggie's elbow and forcibly yanked her back. She swung around and saw Ginger looking at her as if she were afraid Maggie was about to have a grand mal seizure.

"What?" Maggie snapped.

"You need to calm down," Ginger hissed. "This isn't helping Claire at all."

Ginger motioned to the door with her head as Claire was stepping through it, escorted by one of the deputies and Sam Collins to a waiting squad car.

"I'm going to follow them," Max said.

"I'll come with you," Maggie offered.

"No, you won't," he said. For a twenty-year-old, he

suddenly sounded very assertive, making Maggie feel as if she were the equivalent of a tantrum-throwing toddler.

"I'll go with Max," Ginger offered. "You stay here with Joanne and lock up the house when they're done and, for pity's sake, don't antagonize Sam anymore."

Maggie blew out a breath. Ginger was right. She was letting her personal dislike of Sam get in the way of her good judgment. She needed to be here for Claire, not shooting off her mouth because she found Sam Collins to be an arrogant, insufferable . . .

He walked back into the house. Maggie was pleased to see that his blue eyes looked troubled, almost as if he regretted the current turn of events. She shook her head. She had to get a grip, truly. Sam was doing his job as sheriff, and Maggie was playing her role as the chief suspect's best friend. It was not surprising, given their history, that they had ended up on opposite sides. In fact, it seemed to be their way.

Sam walked past Maggie without saying a word. The other deputy, the one who had stayed behind to help Sam, stepped up to her and Joanne, and said, "If you ladies wouldn't mind waiting outside."

Maggie was about to protest, but Joanne plopped Mr. Tumnus in her arms and gave her a shove.

"Certainly," she said. "We'll be on the front porch."

"Thanks, ma'am," the deputy said. He looked relieved when Maggie was led out the door, and she figured he had been dreading a tongue lashing from her. She could have reassured him that her beef was only with his boss, but she didn't.

Once outside, Joanne retrieved the cat carrier from the stand-alone one-car garage that Claire used primarily as a storage shed. When she returned, Maggie gently put Mr. Tumnus in through the hatch on the top. He yowled, but seeing that they weren't letting him out, he turned his back on them and began to lick his front paw.

A shadow passed across the front window. Maggie turned and glared at what she assumed was Sam Collins going through all of Claire's belongings.

"What do you suppose they're looking for?" Joanne asked. She had pulled her long ponytail over her shoulder and was twining the ends around her finger. Maggie had noticed that Joanne always did this when she was nervous.

"At a guess, I would say something that links her to the murder," Maggie said. "Probably proof that she's been in contact with him."

"Do you think she has?" Joanne asked.

Maggie didn't answer, not wanting to voice out loud what she knew. When Joanne glanced at her, she gave a small nod. Joanne pursed her lips as if that confirmed what she thought, too.

Maggie sank into one of the two lounge chairs on Claire's front porch. She wished she had her glass of wine or, even better, a fat slice of Ginger's pound cake.

"What do we do now?" Joanne asked.

"Now we wait," Maggie said.

Chapter 14

For two hours they sat outside Claire's small bungalow. After the first half hour, Maggie took the cat carrier back into the house and let Mr. Tumnus out.

When Sam gave her an inquiring look, she said, "I really don't think he'll bother your investigation."

She shut the door before Sam could respond.

When they were finally allowed back in, it took all of Maggie's self-control not to ask if they'd found anything. She knew Sam wouldn't tell her, and it would just invite another uncomfortable scene between them.

She had to admit that, for all their searching, both Sam and his deputy had left the house looking surprisingly untouched. While she appreciated that, she was still so irritated by the entire situation that she couldn't trust herself to do more than nod at them when they left. She left it to Joanne to finesse the situation, which she did admirably. Together they packed up the remaining cake and cold cuts, storing them in the fridge for when Claire returned home. Then Maggie packed up Mr. Tumnus's favorite toys and food and put him back in his carrier and headed for home.

"Auntie Maggie!" a small voice chirped at the side of Maggie's bed the next morning. "Look what I found."

She glanced over the side to see Josh in his train pajamas, holding a very put-upon gray tabby around the middle. She smiled at the cuteness of the new friends, even though the sight of the cat reminded her of Claire's predicament. She pushed aside the bedclothes and slid her feet to the floor.

"You've met Mr. Tumnus," she said. "We'd better get him some breakfast."

She led the way out of her room to the kitchen. Josh helped her feed the cat, who cleaned his bowl and then stretched and headed toward the sun room at the back of the house.

"Is that coffee I smell?" Sandy asked as she joined Maggie in the kitchen.

"Sorry, did we wake you?" Maggie asked.

"No, Mr. Tumnus managed that with a well-placed pounce on my bed."

Maggie smiled, taking in Sandy's sleep-tossed hair and puffy eyes. "Were you up late studying again?"

"Let's just say microbiology and I are not friends," Sandy said, and poured herself a cup of coffee. "But that's hardly news. Please, tell me what's happening with Claire. The entire town is abuzz with her . . . situation."

"She's been arrested for the murder of John Templeton," Maggie said.

"But that's ridiculous," Sandy protested. "Claire's not a killer. She's the nicest person I know. If it weren't for her using her library contacts to track down used medical textbooks for me, I never would have been able to afford the books for nursing school."

"She's great like that," Maggie agreed. "My TBR—to be read—pile is perilously high because she keeps giving me books that I—"

"Just have to read," Sandy said with her, and they both smiled.

"Do you think they'll keep her in jail long?" Sandy asked.

"I don't know," Maggie said. "I don't know much about the process, which is why I brought Max in to help."

"He's brilliant. He'll help figure it out," Sandy said. "Which reminds me, when all of this is over, I should see what he knows about microbiology."

Maggie smiled and took a restorative sip of her coffee.

"So, what are you going to do now?" Sandy asked.

Maggie sighed. "There's only one thing I can do, find the real killer."

Chapter 15

Maggie spent the morning watching Josh so that Sandy could do some studying. Jake, Sandy's husband, would be calling from Afghanistan, and Maggie knew that Sandy was having a hard time concentrating with Josh flitting around and her own excitement over hearing from her man.

She and Josh went out to the garden to pick several bowls of blackberries before the birds got them all, and then they played trains on the porch so that she could keep her promise to Claire and spend time with Mr. Tumnus, too.

Sitting on the floor and running her favorite trains, Donald and Douglas, across the wooden tracks, she mulled over the events of the day before while Josh ordered her trains about, doing a fair imitation of Sir Topham Hatt, the boss of all trains.

"Josh, your dad is on the computer! Come see him!" Sandy poked her head around the doorway.

"Daddy!" Josh clutched his train and toddled with his mother into the small bedroom, converted into an office, in the back of the house.

Maggie followed behind them—she always liked to see for herself that Jake was okay, and then give the couple their alone time.

The computer was on, and there beaming out of the screen was Jake. A handsome man, his hair was cut military short, and he was wearing his fatigues, which made him seem even more manly. It had to be that "man in a uniform" thing, Maggie thought. She had known Jake since he was in high school, and sometimes she still saw the knock-kneed, sweaty-palmed boy who had arrived on her sister's doorstep with a wilting lily corsage to give to Sandy on their prom night.

Despite his grown-up good looks, Maggie couldn't help but notice that he looked tired—not "I haven't slept lately" tired, but more of a bone-weary tired, like if he ever got the chance to rest, he would sleep for a month.

He and Sandy talked using Skype, a free computer program that allowed them to see each other while they spoke, which was at least once a week. Sandy hefted Josh onto her lap, and he waved at his dad, who beamed even brighter at the sight of his big baby boy.

"How ya doin', Josh-by-gosh?" Jake asked.

"Daddy, make the train whistle," Josh demanded.

"Okay," Jake agreed with a smile. Then he did a spot-on impression of a train whistle. Josh clapped in delight.

"Daddy, I smashed Auntie Maggie's train!" Josh said. Then he made a loud crashing sound.

Jake laughed delightedly.

Maggie popped her head into the group and said, "Hi, Jake!"

"Hi, Aunt Maggie," he said. "These two rascals aren't giving you too much trouble, are they?"

"Define *trouble*," Maggie said with a grin.

"Hey!" Sandy said. "I resemble that remark."

"Daddy home soon?" Josh asked.

"Yeah, I'll be home soon, son," Jake said.

He looked a little sad, but then Josh said, "We play trains when you come home, Daddy."

"Yes, we will."

"Make the whistle, Daddy," Josh ordered, and Jake smiled and did another perfect imitation of a train whistle.

Josh pumped his fist and then leaned forward and kissed the computer monitor.

"Love you, Daddy," he said. Then he wiggled off of his mother's lap and headed back to his train table.

Maggie leaned forward and blew a kiss to Jake. "Take care of yourself, Jake."

"You, too, Maggie," he said, and he winked.

Maggie knew that Sandy and Jake had only minutes to talk, so she went to keep Josh occupied so they could spend their precious time alone.

"How are you, baby?" Sandy asked.

Maggie turned away, but she heard the sadness in Jake's voice when he answered, "It's been a rough week, hon. Two of my squad were killed by IEDs."

The devastation in his voice made Maggie want to turn around and offer some comfort, but she heard Sandy say, "Oh, Jake, I'm so sorry."

Quietly, Maggie shut the door behind her. She closed her

eyes, her thoughts with the families who had lost their men. But another part of her was so desperately grateful that it wasn't Jake who had been killed, she felt guilty for even thinking it.

She found Josh back at the train table. She sat down with him and let him boss her trains around some more. Sandy joined them about fifteen minutes later. Her face was pale and her eyes watery. Maggie opened her arms, and Sandy sank onto the floor and leaned into her.

"He's okay," Maggie said, knowing it was a cold comfort at best. But Sandy nodded and pulled back.

"Be present. Live today," she said. "I got to see him today."

Maggie nodded in approval. Her own throat was too tight to speak.

"Mommy, look!" Josh launched his train down the steep part of the track, and Sandy watched him with amused eyes.

"Sandy, I didn't mean to eavesdrop, but I heard Jake talk about the two men in his squad."

"He'll be all right, but it was bad," Sandy confirmed.

"I can't even imagine what he's going through," Maggie said. "Jake's tour will be done soon, though, yes?"

"Six more months," Sandy said, and closed her eyes, as if trying to imagine it.

Maggie squeezed Sandy's shoulder. Josh had five of his trains lined up now, and he was sending them into the round-house one by one. Sandy sat down to play with him, and Maggie stepped away, letting them have some mother-and-son time.

She couldn't help but think of the cake knife sticking out of John Templeton's chest. Not exactly an IED, but then again, who used a cake knife—an everyday, ordinary object—to kill?

"How long is Claire going to be held?" Maggie asked Max through the window of the Frosty Freeze. She and Ginger had decided to have ice cream while they pestered Max about Claire's case.

"At her arraignment this morning, the judge denied bail," Max said.

"But she has ties to the community," Ginger protested.

"And she's a good person," Maggie added.

Max blew out a breath. "Yes, but her fingerprints are on the knife, and she has a history with the victim. I couldn't get them to budge."

He looked defeated as he passed Maggie her hot fudge brownie sundae through the window and handed her a spoon.

"I'm sure you did your best, Max," Maggie said. "How did Claire take it?"

An odd look crossed his face, and Max said, "She didn't seem surprised."

"What happens next?" Maggie asked.

"Preliminary hearing," he said. "The prosecution will do their best to prove that they have enough evidence to hold Claire for a trial, and I will do my best to prove that they don't."

He looked stressed, and Maggie wondered if it was time to call in an attorney with some years behind him. She didn't want Max to carry this burden alone.

As if reading her thoughts, he said, "I've been in contact with my mentor. He's agreed to oversee Claire's case."

Maggie smiled at him. She should never have doubted the boy genius.

"Can we see her?" Ginger asked. She was already working on her hot caramel sundae with extra pralines.

"That's probably going to be up to Sheriff Collins," Max said. "Given that Maggie is not on his list of friendlies, I don't see him letting her in to see Claire, but you might stand a chance."

"Well, that's rude," Maggie said.

"Maybe if you played nice for once, he'd let you talk to her," Max said. "I don't know what is between you two, but you're really not helping my client with your hostile attitude."

"There's nothing between me and Sam Collins!" Maggie protested. "I simply loathe the man."

"You're not normally such a grudge-holder," Ginger said. She waved her spoon at Maggie. "Was it really so awful that he teased you as a kid? Shouldn't you let it go? For Claire?"

Maggie wanted to protest. She wanted to come clean and tell Ginger everything, but then how would she explain that she'd never told her before? Ginger was her bff, and what had happened between her and Sam Collins was definitely the stuff of midnight chats over cheesecake and wine with your best friend forever.

"I can try," she said. "But I just find him so infuriating."

"The feeling appears to be mutual," Max said. "Now, if you two will excuse me?" He nodded his head, and Maggie turned around to see that a small line had formed behind them. She and Ginger shuffled to the side and then strolled over to the picnic table nearby to sit and eat their ice cream.

"So, can you be on your best behavior so we can go and talk to Claire?" Ginger asked.

"I can try," Maggie said. "Maybe we'll get lucky and he'll be out ticketing someone for a broken headlight, and I won't have to see him."

"That's the spirit," Ginger said with a shake of her head.

"Well, if it isn't the little shoe thief," a voice said from behind Maggie.

Since that particular voice always managed to make the hair on the back of Maggie's neck stand up, and not in a good way, she knew it was Summer Phillips before she even turned around.

"Hello, Summer," she said. "I hate to argue, but if anyone is a shoe thief, it's you."

She let her eyes run up and down Summer's latest eye-popping ensemble, from the platform sandals to the Daisy Duke shorts and halter top that barely kept her girls restrained. Ruby red lipstick, fake eyelashes and a head of platinum hair that had been teased to add another three inches to her overall height capped off her "look at me" outfit. Maggie found it hard to pull her gaze away, as if from a train wreck.

"Why, hello, Ginger." Summer ignored Maggie and turned her attention across the table. "I saw your son the other day, the oldest one. My, he has turned out just as handsome as his daddy."

Maggie saw Ginger's nostrils flare. The mother lion in her was obviously gearing up to take down the long-legged, underdressed gazelle in front of her.

Summer, not being entirely stupid, must have sensed that she was in mortal peril, as the next words out of her confirmed.

"But obviously, he is too . . . immature for me," she said.

"If by that you mean you're *way* too old for him, then you'd be right," Maggie said. She scooped some of her sundae into her mouth with a smile.

Summer looked like she wanted to use her red talons to claw the smile right off Maggie's face. Thankfully, they were in public, and Ginger was a witness.

With a toss of her big blonde head, Summer seemed to get a grip on her rage, and she gave Maggie a smug glance. "What's the matter, Maggie? Are you jealous?"

Summer had caught her on an inhale, and a chunk of brownie stuck in her throat. She coughed and then gagged. Ginger looked ready to jump up and pound her on the back, but Maggie held up her hand to indicate that she was okay.

"Jealous of what?" she managed to ask in her most scathing tone.

"Why, me and Sam Collins, of course," Summer said. "Everyone knows you've had the hots for him since high school."

Later, she couldn't say that what happened next had ever been a fully formed thought. Premeditated, so to speak. She supposed it was really just an instinctive reaction, like ducking when a ball is lobbed at your head. Either way, Maggie's hot fudge brownie sundae landed splat on Summer Phillips's big blonde head.

Chapter 16

Summer stared at Maggie with a look of horror that would have been comical had she not immediately begun to hunt for a weapon. She lunged toward Ginger, who stepped back with her sundae just in time.

"My hair!" Summer cried. "You've ruined my hair! I'm calling the sheriff! I'm going to have you arrested for assault!"

A chuckle sounded from the Frosty Freeze, and when Summer whirled in that direction, Max quickly yanked his head in and slammed the window shut as if afraid she would launch herself into his ice cream palace.

Maggie and Ginger used her momentary distraction to race to Maggie's car. They had barely slammed their doors shut when Summer hurried after them as fast as her platform sandals would allow, which was thankfully not fast at all.

"Punch it!" Ginger ordered, and Maggie threw the car

into reverse and backed out of the lot, put it into drive and raced down the road. Her last sight of Summer was of her shaking her fist as ice cream and hot fudge flattened her hair and dripped down her face like snow off the mountaintops in summer.

"What were you thinking?" Ginger demanded. "She is going to have you arrested."

"Really? A dead guy was found with a cake knife in his chest, and she's going to have me arrested for dumping my ice cream on her head?" Maggie asked. "Sam may be a horse's behind, but even he wouldn't do that."

"If she hollers loud enough, he'll do it just to shut her up. If there is a will, there is a way and, believe me, Summer has the will," Ginger said. "What do you have to say to that?"

"Oops?" Maggie asked with a shrug.

"Why do you let her get under your skin so easily?" Ginger said. "Obviously, she's just trying to yank your chain by saying you had the hots for Sam Collins back in high school. I mean, everyone knows you can't stand him. Why do you let her wind you up?"

Maggie blew out a breath. Again, here was another opportunity to tell Ginger the truth, and yet, she couldn't do it.

Why had she reacted so strongly to Summer's words? Well, duh, it was because for a terrified second she had thought that Summer knew about her and Sam. It was ridiculous. No one knew about them. It was one crazy summer so long ago that it hardly mattered, and yet, it did matter. To her.

"I don't know," she lied. "Summer just pushes all of my buttons."

"Pushes your buttons?" Ginger repeated. "Honey, that was a direct hit, and you fell for it."

"I know, I know," Maggie said. "I suppose I owe her an apology."

"I don't know that I'd go that far," Ginger said. "This is Summer Phillips we're talking about. After what she said about my boy, I was ready to douse her with a sundae myself. But yes, you should try not to react so strongly to her, per-haps."

As they cruised down Main Street, the sheriff's car passed them going the other way. Maggie and Ginger exchanged a wide-eyed look. Sam Collins had been driving the car, and while the lights hadn't been flashing, he was still driving in the direction of the Frosty Freeze like he meant business.

"Hmm," Maggie hummed. "Since we're already in trou-ble, should we go for broke and see if we can get in to see Claire?"

"We? What we?" Ginger asked. "You mean *me* not *we*, because you are in trouble and I am not. However, I promise to come visit you when Sam locks you up for assault with a deadly maraschino cherry."

"Aw, that's my bosom buddy," Maggie said. "So how 'bout it? Are you feeling charming?"

"Why not?" Ginger sighed. "The worst they can do is say no."

"Or lock us up," Maggie said. At Ginger's alarmed look, she added, "But that would be highly unlikely."

Being the county seat, St. Stanley had one courthouse adjacent to the sheriff's department, which had a small jail. Usually, it was just a drunk tank for anyone picked up with a DUI after the Friday night high school football game, but presently the lone resident was Claire.

Maggie parked outside the sheriff's department, and Ginger loaded the parking meter with change. The only metered parking in St. Stanley was in front of the courthouse, the sheriff's department and the jail, and Maggie wondered if it was to discourage anyone from lingering.

The buildings were all made from red brick with wide stone steps, and each had an imposing glass front door. They went to the building on the right, as the courthouse was on the left. Maggie was really hoping they weren't going to have to go there anytime soon.

Ginger and Maggie hit the steps, and Maggie noticed that her palms were sweaty. She was nervous about seeing Claire. Max had seen her briefly earlier in the day, and he said she'd been holding up okay but, really, how good could she be doing? She was in jail!

They entered the building to find it fairly quiet. At the front desk sat a deputy who was talking on the phone. Ginger and Maggie waited for him to hang up, perfecting their smiles of ingratiating sincerity.

When he did, he glanced up and recognized Ginger right away. "Hello, Mrs. Lancaster. What can I do for you?"

"Stephen Rourke, well, look at you," Ginger said. She gave him a big smile. "The boys told me you had gone into law enforcement, but I didn't know you were working here as a detective."

"Oh, I'm just a deputy, ma'am," Stephen said.

He looked to be about the same age as Ginger's oldest. Maggie pressed her lips together to keep from smiling at how thick Ginger was spreading the flattery.

"Well, a smart fellow like you, I'll bet you're running this place in no time," Ginger said.

Maggie looked at her out of the corner of her eye. She was afraid Ginger was going overboard, but as she glanced back at the deputy's flushed face, she realized her friend was spot-on in her approach.

"Now, Stephen, I'm wondering if you can do us a little favor," Ginger said. "My friend Claire has been arrested for murder, and Ms. Gerber, here, and I were hoping we could get in to see her."

Stephen started to shake his head, but Ginger just pushed forward as if he were nodding.

"Aren't you a dear?" she asked. "Isn't he, Maggie?"

"Oh yes," Maggie said. She decided to play it to the hilt and put on her most relieved voice. "You are a lifesaver—literally. You see, I'm taking care of her cat, and he's been getting sick—hairballs and whatnot all over the place. I need to ask her what to do."

"Oh, I don't know about this. The sheriff was very clear that while he was out no one was to go back there."

"But you know me," Ginger said. "I've fed you custard pie since you were knee-high to a tadpole."

"You do make a fine custard pie, ma'am," he said.

Maggie almost felt bad, strong-arming him like they were. But this was ideal, getting to see Claire without Sam around. And there was no telling how long Summer would keep him occupied with her complaint against Maggie.

"Aw, come on, Stephen. You wouldn't want a poor little cat to suffer, would you?" Ginger asked.

"Well, no, ma'am, but . . .'"

"Great, then it's all settled," Maggie said.

"Of course, we wouldn't want you to get in trouble," Ginger said. "So, I'll just stay here and keep you company while Maggie goes to ask Claire about the cat. It won't take more than a minute."

Stephen frowned at them. "Well, since it's for a cat, I suppose it would be all right. You'll need to leave your things here, though."

"Sure." Maggie handed her purse and keys to Ginger.

He hit a button on his desk, and the half door beside him popped open.

Maggie glanced at Ginger, who nodded toward the window, letting Maggie know that she would act as a lookout in case Sam got back before Maggie was done.

"Follow me, ma'am," Stephen said. He led the way through another set of doors toward the back. They passed through a metal detector and came to a small lobby. Two hallways ran off of it. One led to the men's jail and the other to the women's.

Stephen led her though another door. A female deputy was sitting at another desk, and she looked up when they entered.

"What's this, Deputy Rourke?" She looked suspiciously at Maggie and at Stephen.

"A visitor for Ms. Freemont," Stephen said.

"I thought she wasn't supposed to have any visitors unless Sheriff Collins is present," the woman said. She was short and sturdy with dark brown skin, and her hair was combed back and held in a tight bun at the nape of her neck. Her uniform was the same as Stephen's, a dark brown shirt over tan pants, with a star on the left side and her name on a badge on the right.

"Deputy Wilson," Maggie said, reading her badge. "I'm Maggie Gerber. I'm taking care of Ms. Freemont's cat, and he's been very sick. I just need to ask her a quick question, and then I'll be out of your hair."

"What kind of cat?"

"A gray tabby," Maggie said. "And he's very old."

"Oh, I have a gray tabby named Puddin'," Deputy Wilson said, looking sympathetic. "Five minutes. That's it."

She stood and unlocked the door behind her. With a nod to Stephen, she led Maggie into a room full of small cells. They approached one at the end, and Deputy Wilson tapped on the bars with a pen from her pocket.

"Ms. Freemont, there is someone here to see you. I have to get back to my desk. Five minutes, and I'll be watching." She stared hard at Maggie, who nodded.

The young deputy left them, and Maggie turned to see Claire rise from the thin cot in the corner. She was in an orange jumpsuit that made Maggie's breath catch. The orange, zip-up onesie was an affront to the senses, no question, but the worst part was that it made it all too real: Claire could go to jail for a crime she didn't commit, and there was nothing Maggie could do to stop it.

Claire adjusted her glasses and sighed. "It's not my best color, I know."

"Oh, sweetie." Maggie put her hands on the bars, and Claire put her hands on top of Maggie's. "That color makes you look like a pile of pumpkin vomit."

Claire busted out with a surprised laugh, which had been Maggie's intent.

"What, fluorescent orange isn't the new black?" Claire teased. "How's Mr. Tumnus?"

"He's good. In fact, if the guards seem to think he's not good, just go with it," Maggie said. "Excessive hairballs were my excuse to get in here."

Claire nodded.

"Now listen, I get that you don't want to talk about John Templeton," Maggie said. "But you've got to help me so I can help you."

"I don't know what I could say that would help," Claire said. "As you know, I dated John back in Baltimore—not for long, we weren't even together for a year, but then I got the job here, and I moved and that was that."

"Claire, no single girl in her early thirties leaves a sweet, full-time position in her chosen profession and a boyfriend to move to a tiny town in another state to take a job as the second fiddle in a puny library," Maggie said.

"Ouch, that's harsh," Claire said. She took her hands off Maggie's and stepped back.

"You were the head of one of the Baltimore branch libraries, weren't you?"

"Yes, but—"

"No, don't give me the buts," Maggie said. "No one is going to believe you came here because you wanted to live in a Podunk town as an assistant director. Now, why did you leave Baltimore, Claire. What were you running from?"

Claire stared at her from behind her narrow glasses. She moved her fingers over her lips as if trying to keep in the words that desperately wanted out. Maggie waited. Claire lowered her hand.

"I was running from him—John Templeton," she said.

Chapter 17

Maggie blew out a breath. She had figured there was something there, but hearing it confirmed only gave her more questions and no answers.

"What happened?" she asked. "Why did you have to run from him? Did he hurt you? You know if he abused you, you could say it was self-defense."

Claire barked out a bitter laugh. "He didn't hurt me, and I didn't kill him, Maggie."

"Then why—"

"Why did I run from Baltimore?" Claire asked. "That's easy. I ran because I saw him kill someone."

"Oh, wow," Maggie said. She didn't know what to say. This was beyond anything she had imagined. She had expected a tale of love gone wrong, not one of murder. "Who was it?"

"I don't know," Claire said. Her voice cracked, and she looked down at her feet.

"Tell me what happened, Claire."

"I can't," she said. "It's bad."

"Worse than being in jail for a crime you didn't commit?" Maggie asked. "I can help you, Claire, but you have to tell me what happened in Baltimore."

Claire glanced over her shoulder, taking in the thin cot with one blanket and a flat pillow on it, the astringent smell and the steel toilet in the corner.

"John and I had been dating a few months. He seemed like a decent, hardworking guy. I knew he was well connected within the community, and I knew he was a venture capitalist, you know, someone who invested in small companies to help them get their businesses started or to help them grow.

"One night we had tickets to the symphony at the Meyerhoff, and John didn't show up to get me, so I took a cab to his office."

Claire sucked in a breath, and Maggie nodded for her to continue. She glanced at the door to see if anyone was coming. She didn't want to rush Claire, but she knew they were running out of time.

"It's okay," Maggie said. "You can tell me."

"I walked into his office and I found him, with another man, carrying a body toward the stairwell."

The door at the end of the hallway opened, and Maggie feared Sheriff Collins had arrived. But no, it was just Deputy Wilson. Obviously, their five minutes were up.

"Then what happened?"

"I demanded to know what was going on, and he said it was none of my business and that if I told anyone what I'd seen, he would tell everyone about me and my past," Claire said. "So, I panicked and I ran. St. Stanley seemed far enough away and small enough. I thought I'd be out of his reach. I was wrong."

"Time's up, ladies," Deputy Wilson said.

"It's going to be all right," Maggie said. She reached through the bars and squeezed Claire's hands one more time. "I promise."

Claire looked at her with sad eyes, and Maggie could tell she didn't believe her.

The door at the end of the hall opened, and Ginger poked her head through.

"Maggie, time to fly!"

Ginger's eyes were huge, and Maggie knew that meant that Sam was back. *Uh-oh!*

"Hang tough," Maggie said to Claire. "We'll figure this out. You'll see."

Claire nodded, trying to look brave.

"Thanks, Deputy Wilson," Maggie said. "You've been a huge help."

"Just take care of that cat," the deputy said.

Maggie nodded and ran. Ginger popped the door open wider, and Maggie dashed though it.

"He just pulled into the lot," Ginger said. "If he comes in the back, we're clear. Go, go, go!"

"Thanks, Stephen," Maggie said. She snatched her purse off of his desk.

She didn't wait for him to open the half gate that would let them out. Instead, she hopped over it and turned around and held her hand out to Ginger, who grumbled while she swung her legs over it and grabbed Maggie's hand to give her some forward momentum. Together they broke into a sprint for the front doors.

Maggie pushed open the glass front door just as the side door to the station opened. She shoved Ginger out ahead of her so she wouldn't be seen. Maggie saw Sam Collins stride through the side door. Their eyes met for a nanosecond, and then Maggie was running down the stairs behind Ginger. As they bolted down the walkway, Maggie hit the button on her key fob to unlock the doors to her Volvo. Without breaking their stride, both ladies jumped into the car. Maggie was just pulling away from the station when Sam Collins appeared on the front steps, glaring at her disappearing taillights.

"So, that went well," Ginger said. "Is it too early in the day to have a drink?"

"It's five o'clock somewhere."

"Thank God."

They were sitting on the padded, wrought-iron furniture set that had been Maggie's grandmother's, each with a glass of wine, when Joanne arrived. Maggie had called her immediately and invited her over so they could discuss what Maggie had found out.

"I can't believe you went to the jail and talked to Claire," Joanne said. She strode onto the sun porch with a small bag from the Perk Up coffee shop in one hand.

"Oooh, what did you bring us?"

"Red velvet cupcakes," Joanne said, and she put the box

down on the wrought-iron table. "Gwen had just marked these down to half off when I was going by, so I got a half dozen."

"Those will compliment the wine perfectly," Maggie said. She handed Joanne a glass and went to get plates and forks for the cupcakes.

"Two-buck Chuck from Trader Joe's," Joanne said as she poured. "My favorite."

"You can't beat the price," Ginger agreed. "I wish Claire were here to enjoy this, too."

"Speaking of Claire, spill it," Joanne said.

Maggie put the plates on the matching iron coffee table, and they each helped themselves to a cupcake. She recounted what Claire had told her while Joanne and Ginger listened as they chewed.

Maggie took a big bite of red velvet cupcake—she had a weakness for cream cheese frosting—as soon as she finished talking.

"Is it just me," Ginger said, "or do you two feel like there is more to the story?"

"There has to be," Joanne said. "I mean, she saw him dragging a body out of his office, and she didn't go to the police?"

Maggie swallowed the bite of cupcake and washed it down with a sip of wine. That was exactly what had been bothering her. Why hadn't Claire gone to the police?

"I can't help but wonder what she meant when she said that he threatened to tell everyone about her and her past," Maggie said. "We have to find out what is in Claire's past."

"Doesn't that seem intrusive?" Joanne asked. "I mean, if she wanted us to know, she would have told us, right?"

"She might have told me today, but she ran out of time," Maggie said.

"If we're going to help her, what we really need to do is find out more about John Templeton," Ginger said. "If he was a venture capitalist, I may have some sources in the accounting world that can help."

"Excellent," Maggie said. "And I'm going to see what I can find out about Claire."

"You're going to investigate her?" Joanne looked appalled.

"No, but I am going to stake out the jail, and when I get a chance, I'm going to question her again, and hopefully she'll have enough time to tell me why she was so afraid of Templeton exposing her past."

"Girlfriend, you are flirting with disaster," Ginger said. "If Sam catches you . . ."

"He won't," Maggie said. She was pleased that her voice sounded more confident than she felt.

"And I'll ask Michael what he knows," Joanne said. "He's in a young entrepreneurs group, and he said Templeton came to a few of their meetings. Maybe he knows someone who invested with him who can tell us what he was like."

"That works." Maggie lifted her glass in a toast. "To setting our fellow GBG free."

Ginger and Joanne clinked glasses with her, and Maggie felt optimistic for the first time since she'd seen Claire in her hideous cantaloupe-colored coveralls.

After Joanne and Ginger left, Maggie had dinner with Sandy and Josh. She volunteered to give Josh his bath and read him a story, as Sandy was prepping for an exam the next day and needed to get in her study time.

Maggie and Josh snuggled in the rocking chair in his room while they read his favorite Thomas the Tank Engine book for what Maggie was sure was the five hundredth time. The nice thing about reading a book so many times was that her mind could drift to other things while she said the words aloud without paying attention.

Naturally, her mind drifted to Claire. What was in her past? She was a librarian. What could she possibly have done? Maybe she'd been a hooker? Maggie tried to picture it with the blonde bob and the glasses . . . er . . . *no*.

Maybe she'd been a member of a gang. Yeah, that didn't fit either.

Josh closed the cover of the book, alerting Maggie to the fact that she'd read the last page. She hefted him up into her arms and sang a lullaby. His head drooped onto her shoulder as she swayed back and forth, rubbing his back with one hand while she cradled him close with her other arm.

His hair was still damp from his bath, and the scent of it brought back memories of holding her own daughter like this seventeen years ago. Rationally, she knew Laura was away at school fulfilling her dreams, but sometimes Maggie missed her so much it was just a black hole of ache in her chest, a void that would never be filled.

When Josh's breathing evened out, Maggie laid him down in his crib. At two, he had almost outgrown it, but he never tried to climb out and loved it so much that Sandy wasn't ready to move him to a big-boy bed just yet.

Maggie was just closing the bedroom door when she

heard a knock on the front door. She passed the office where Sandy was studying, and said, "I'll get it."

Sandy grunted acknowledgment, not even looking up from the piles of notes that surrounded her.

It was only seven thirty. The summer sun hadn't set yet, and the air was still thick with humidity. Maggie hoped they'd get a storm soon to break up the unrelenting haze of heat.

She peeped through the eyehole in the door and felt her heart slam down into her feet. Why hadn't she been expecting him? After the incident at the sheriff's department, she should have anticipated this visit.

Standing on her front steps in his starched white shirt and badge and with a gun on his hip was Sam Collins. And he did not look happy.

Chapter 18

Maggie thought about not answering. She thought about pretending that no one was home, but given that her car was parked in front of her garage, it seemed unlikely that he would fall for it.

Of course, she could tiptoe down into the basement and pretend to be doing a load of laundry, but what if he pounded on the door and woke Josh? That wouldn't be good. There was no telling how long it would take the little guy to get back to sleep. With a sigh of resignation, Maggie opened the door.

A blast of sticky air hit her in the face like a slap. She kept the air conditioner set at a thrifty eighty degrees but even so, it was much more comfortable inside than out. She debated leaving Sam out on the stoop while they talked, but her mother had raised her better than that.

"Evening, Sam," she said.

"Hi, Maggie," he said.

"Do you want to come in?" she asked. Her voice betrayed her feelings, and the invitation sounded as if it had been forced out of her at gunpoint. She glanced at the gun on his hip. Probably a bad analogy.

He gave her a small smile, as if he knew how much it pained her to be polite to him.

"I don't mind if I do," he said.

She stepped aside, and he entered her house. A small house to begin with, it shrunk to the size of a mushroom once he entered.

He scanned the room, which was full of pictures of her daughter and a few of her husband. He took in the comfy furniture with a few antiques scattered here and there, giving the room some character.

"You have a nice home," he said.

"Thanks." She watched him watching her. If things got any tenser between the two of them, Maggie was pretty sure she was going to spontaneously combust. She drew on the generations of Southern hospitality she had grown up on with her grits and okra.

"Can I get you some iced tea or lemonade?" she asked.

"Lemonade would be real nice," he said. "Thanks."

Maggie grunted and led the way to the kitchen.

"I suppose there is a reason you're here?" she asked.

She poured them each a glass from the pitcher in the fridge and handed his to him with just a hint of put-upon, manners be damned. Again, he smiled as if he knew exactly how she was feeling and he was amused by it.

"I have some questions about your visit with Ms. Freemont today," he said.

"Oh, that." Maggie had figured as much and had mentally prepared to sound casual. "Yeah, I'm watching her cat and he's been horribly sick, so I needed to know what to do for him."

"So my deputies told me," Sam said.

He walked through the small kitchen and out onto the sun porch. Maggie followed closely behind him. She got the feeling he was looking for something, and she had a pretty good idea what. Mr. Tumnus chose that moment to run past them as if his tail were on fire.

"That's the cat, isn't it?" Sam asked.

Maggie pursed her lips and wondered how much trouble she'd get into if she didn't answer.

Mr. Tumnus ran past again. This time she could see he was chasing a cricket.

"Mr. Tumnus, right?" Sam asked again.

"And would you look at him go?" Maggie said with wide eyes. "Praise the lord, it's a miracle. He's going to live."

"Uh-huh," Sam said.

He didn't look impressed with the miracle before him, more like annoyed. He sat on the wrought-iron furniture, making the couch look smaller than it was, and said, "Maggie, I think it's time you and I had a little chat."

"Really?" she asked. "What about?"

Her grandmother had always said you catch more flies with honey than with vinegar. Of course, Maggie had always wondered why you'd want to, but since she'd been throwing nothing but vinegar at Sam since he'd gotten back and he still hadn't left her alone, maybe she needed to toss a little sugar his way. He might just run for the hills, which did seem to be his modus operandi.

He narrowed his eyes as she sat in the seat adjacent to his. He didn't trust the nice her. Smart man.

"What were you really doing at the jail today?" he asked. When she opened her mouth to speak, he added, "And please do not give me any baloney about a sick cat. We both know he's fine and always was."

"Claire is my friend," she said. "I wanted to see that she was all right."

She took a sip of her own lemonade, trying to look the part of a worried friend who had no ulterior motives. One of Sam's eyebrows lifted, and he watched her like a hawk tracking a field mouse. She stared at the rim of her glass, the picture of innocence.

"Did she tell you about Baltimore?" he asked.

Maggie's gaze flew up to meet his blue one. Did he know about John Templeton? Had Claire told him about what she'd seen? Or was he trying to trick her?

"Mostly, we talked about how she was feeling," Maggie said.

She didn't like lying to a law enforcement officer, but since he hadn't said he was here in an official capacity, and since she *had* been talking to Claire about her feelings, she felt pretty good about her answer.

"And how is she feeling?" he asked.

"About what you'd expect," Maggie said. "Miserable."

"Listen," he said. He leaned forward and set his glass on the table. He rested his elbows on his knees and gave Maggie a very direct, no-nonsense stare. "I don't think your friend killed Templeton."

Maggie sucked in a breath of surprised relief. This was great. Hopefully, he'd let her out of jail and turn his attention toward finding the real killer.

"But," he said, and raised his hand as if to halt the happy bubble that was beginning to float up inside of her, "your friend knows things about John Templeton that would help me to find his real killer, and she's not talking."

"What makes you think that?" Maggie asked.

"A woman does not abandon a promising career in a large municipality to take a job as second banana in a midsize town with no growth potential," he said. "Unless she's trying to get away from someone or something."

Maggie felt her heart pound hard in her chest. How could she have forgotten that Sam was as smart as he was good-looking? She should have expected him to connect the dots and come up with the same question mark she had.

Of course, she now knew why Claire had abandoned her life in Baltimore, but Maggie had no idea what impact it would have on Claire if she told Sam. Besides, she really didn't think it was her place to say.

"She told you, didn't she?" he asked.

"I don't know what you're talking about," she said.

Sam blew out a breath. "I'm not playing games, Maggie. This is your friend's life at stake. If she doesn't cooperate, she's going to go down for the murder of John Templeton."

"So, she hasn't told you anything. This is just a fishing expedition for you," Maggie said. She was feeling annoyed at being caught between her friend and the law, and at not knowing what she should do. "So, what does that make me—the big-mouthed bass?"

Sam opened his mouth and closed it—remarkably like a big-mouthed bass, in fact.

"You really thought that you could intimidate me into telling you anything my friend told me in confidence," she said. She rose to a standing position. This conversation was over.

Sam rose to his feet as well. "Then you admit that she told you something."

"I admit nothing," Maggie protested.

A knock on the door frame sounded, breaking them out of their staring contest, and they turned as one to the door.

"Sorry to interrupt, but the wee man is sleeping," Sandy said. "Do you think you two could keep it down?"

She glanced between them, and Maggie knew she was taking in their tense posture, rapid breathing and the palpable hostility polluting the air between them.

"I'm very sorry," Sam said. "I didn't mean to disturb you, any of you."

"He didn't wake up," Sandy said. "So, no harm, no foul."

"I'm sorry, too, honey," Maggie said. "Fortunately, Sam was just leaving."

He looked back at her in surprise. Obviously, that had not been his plan, but it was certainly hers. Unless he had a warrant for her arrest, she saw no earthly reason why she should even be talking to him.

A knock on the front door sounded, and Maggie turned to Sandy. "Are you expecting someone?"

"No," Sandy said. "Study group is tomorrow night."

"Speaking of which, you should get back to it," Maggie said. She shooed her niece away with her hands. "I'll get the door, you hit the books."

Sandy gave them one last considering look before disappearing back down the hallway.

"I'll show you out," she said to Sam, and led the way from the sun porch.

Sam didn't put up a fuss, but followed her to the front door. Maggie undid the latch and pulled the door open. Joanne stood there, looking puffy-eyed and trembling.

"Joanne, are you all right?"

"I talked to Michael." Her words were fast, like a stream when it tumbles over the rocks in its path. "He said he knew John Templeton, that he had actually loaned us money for some of our investments. Michael met him through the young entrepreneurs group, but he didn't tell me because he didn't want me to worry about the money."

"Oh," Maggie said. "Well, that's interesting. Thanks for stopping by, Joanne. I'll see you tomorrow."

She tried to shut the door on Joanne before she said anything else within Sam's earshot. Maggie could feel Sam beside her, just behind the door, looming like a dark shadow at midnight. She didn't know how much he had heard, but given that Joanne wasn't being quiet in her blubbering, she was betting he'd heard all of it.

"But, Maggie, don't you want to—" Joanne began, but Maggie interrupted.

"Meet for coffee in the morning? Yeah, that sounds great."

She didn't know how to get Joanne to stop talking without letting Sam know that that's what she was trying to do. Damn it.

"I can't wait to talk in the morning. Maggie, don't you realize what this means?" Joanne wailed. Maggie shook her head, frantically trying to get Joanne to shut up.

"It means," Sam said, stepping out from behind the door, "that you and your husband have just landed on my list of suspects."

Chapter 19

Joanne gasped as she took in the sight of the sheriff in Maggie's house. She looked at Maggie in horror.

"Oh, it does not!" Maggie snapped at Sam. "Stop being a bully."

"I am not—" he protested, but Maggie hushed him by holding her hand up.

Joanne burst into big hiccupping sobs and moaned. "Oh, I can't go to jail, I just can't. It would mess up everything, my shots and taking my temperature. They probably don't let you have thermometers in jail."

"Joanne, are you on hormone shots right now?" Maggie asked.

Joanne nodded and then let out another sob. Maggie pulled her into her arms and let Joanne cry on her shoulder.

"She and her husband are going through in vitro fertilization right now," Maggie whispered to Sam.

"Maggie!" Joanne pulled back and gave her a furious look. "Why don't you take out an ad in the daily paper?"

"Joanne, we have to tell him," Maggie said. "Look at you, you're a mess. He needs to know that it's your hormones and not that you're nuts."

"I'm not hormonal," Joanne argued. "I'm in here. I'd know if I was hormonal, wouldn't I?"

Maggie stared at her until Joanne burst into tears.

"Oh, God, I am hormonal, aren't I?"

"Little bit," Maggie said. "Come on in and sit down. I'll get you some lemonade."

"Okay." Joanne sniffed and followed Maggie to the sun porch.

As if afraid to be alone with the crazy, hormonal woman, Sam followed Maggie into the kitchen while she got a glass for Joanne.

"Is she always like that?" he asked.

"Only when she's on shots," Maggie said. "She gets very weepy."

"Reason number five hundred and one that I'm glad I'm a dude," he said.

Maggie shook her head at him. "How very sensitive of you."

"What?" he asked.

"Weren't you leaving?" she asked.

"Not now," he said.

"What do you mean?"

"I'm staying," he said. "I want to hear what Mrs. Claramotta has to say."

"You can't! That's illegal," Maggie said.

"No, it isn't," he argued.

"Well, it's unethical," she said. "Not that I ever thought you suffered from an overabundance of ethics anyway, but still."

Sam glared at her as if he were considering strangling her. Maggie tipped her chin up in defiance. She wasn't scared of Sam Collins.

A breath hissed out between his teeth. "Listen, I can either talk to her here or haul her down to the station and get a formal statement. Up to you," he said.

Maggie watched as he nosed around her counter, obviously giving her a few seconds to weigh her options, until he found her large ceramic cookie jar. He lifted the lid and peered inside.

"Yes, there are oatmeal raisin cookies in there," she said, taking the lid away from him. "No, you can't have any. I am plum out of hospitality for you."

"That's too bad," he sighed. "Those are my favorite, and I'm a much nicer person with a few cookies in me."

"Fine. Three cookies and not one raisin more," she said. "And you had better not make Joanne cry again, or it's the last time you'll ever see the inside of my cookie jar."

A grin spread across his face as Maggie felt a hot flush of mortification spread across her own.

"I did not mean that the way it sounded," she said. "I mean, I did mean that the way it sounded—oh, why are you here?"

"I'm beginning to wonder myself," he said. He fished three cookies out of the jar. "But it's nice to see you're thinking about giving me access . . . to your cookies."

Maggie was clutching the ceramic lid in her hand so

tightly she was afraid it might shatter. That would be better than throwing it at him, she supposed.

Sam started to walk back toward the sun porch but turned around and said, "You should bring her some cookies. I bet that'll make her feel better."

Maggie glared at him. She didn't need him telling her what would make her friend feel better. She did, however, put some cookies on a plate and brought them as well as a glass of lemonade into the sun room, where Joanne sat, looking like a weepy, miserable mess.

"Mrs. Claramotta," Sam said. "I'm Sheriff Collins, but please call me Sam."

Joanne looked up at him as if he were a snake and she was trying to figure out if he was poisonous or just creepy. Maggie would have told her just creepy, but she doubted it would endear her to Sam. Not that she cared what he thought, but she didn't want this to be any more traumatic for Joanne than it already had been.

"Sam," Joanne said as if trying it out. "My name is Joanne."

"Nice name," Sam said.

Maggie rolled her eyes. Joanne didn't see her, but Sam must have because he stepped on her toes, and when she jerked her leg back and frowned at him, he gave her a bland "I have no idea why you're mad at me" look.

"Joanne, neither you nor your husband are in any trouble with the law," he said.

"We're not?" The shoulders that had been clenched around her ears slowly lowered.

"No, but I do have some questions about John Templeton,

and anything you can tell me may help me catch his killer, which would be great for your friend Claire."

Joanne looked at Maggie, who gave her a small nod.

She'd have to trust that whatever Joanne told Sam wouldn't incriminate Claire any more than she already was.

"What do you know about John Templeton?" he asked.

Joanne took a sip of her lemonade. She looked at both Maggie and Sam, and said, "Not very much. My husband Michael might be a better person to talk to, but I can tell you what he told me."

"Thank you," Sam said. He finished off his cookies and fished a small pad and pen out of his shirt pocket. Then he nodded at Joanne to continue.

"My husband belongs to a young entrepreneurs group," she said. "Several local businessmen in St. Stanley belong, like Jay Morgan from the Perk Up and Mr. Santana, the grocer, and Jerry Paulson, who owns the hardware store. There are others, but I can't think of their names right now."

Sam wrote down the names she had said and nodded for her to continue.

"Anyway, about a year ago, Mr. Templeton came and spoke at a group meeting," she said. "He told them he was a venture capitalist and looking to invest in St. Stanley because he really believed it could become the next hot suburban community for Richmond."

"Huh," Maggie grunted. She didn't like that at all.

Sam gave her a quelling look, which she ignored.

"Anyway, Mr. Templeton offered to find capital for anyone looking to buy up some small businesses to increase their net worth. Michael, my husband, took him up on it, and we bought two apartment complexes on the edge of town."

"Which ones?" Sam asked.

"Arbor Cove and the Windscape apartments," she said.

Sam made a note and glanced up at her. "Go on."

"There isn't much more to tell," she said. "Michael had an attorney check the deal out, so we knew it was legit. Now we're paying on those apartment buildings, and trying to keep our tenants happy. We didn't kill John Templeton. We had no reason to."

It was silent in the sun room as Joanne broke down sobbing and Maggie glared at Sam.

"What?" he asked. "I didn't accuse her of anything."

"Can't you see that she's not at her best right now?" Maggie snapped.

Sam looked from Maggie to Joanne and sighed. "You're right. I should be talking to her husband anyway. This young entrepreneurs group sounds like a promising lead."

"Oh no," Joanne wailed. "Now they're all going to be mad at me, and they'll probably kick Michael out, and he loves that group."

As Joanne spiraled into yet another meltdown, Maggie looked at Sam and jerked her head in Joanne's direction. Sam gave her a confused look, and Maggie bugged her eyes at him in a clear signal for him to say something to calm her friend down.

"Oh!" Sam cleared his throat. "I don't think there will be any need to tell the other members of the entrepreneurs group where I got their names from."

"Really?" Joanne sniffed.

"Really, it's all public record, and I'm sure we would have gotten to them eventually on our own," he said.

Maggie dialed back her glare just a little. At least the big oaf was showing some humanity. She rose from her seat, and said, "Can I show you out now, Sheriff Collins?"

He raised his eyebrows at her abrupt tone, but slowly rose to his feet.

"Good night, Joanne," he said. "Thanks for the information. You've been a big help."

"Good night, Sam," Joanne said. She reached for a cookie as Maggie and Sam left the room.

"Here's your hat, what's your hurry?" Sam said as he followed her through the living room to the front door.

Maggie stopped by the door and turned to face him. "I think you officially owe me."

"Owe you?" he asked.

"Joanne said a lot more to you than she would have if I hadn't been here. In fact, if she had come at any other time, you wouldn't know any of this."

Sam rocked back on his heels and considered her. "Maybe."

"There's no maybe about it." Maggie could feel her temper getting wound up. How did this man manage to do that to her with one word? *Argh.* It was maddening.

"So, if I owe you one, and I'm not saying that I do," he said. "How do you plan to collect?" His voice was full of innuendo, and so was his steadfast blue gaze for that matter.

Maggie shook her head. "You really think pretty highly of yourself, don't you?"

He shrugged. It was a practiced move that showed off more muscle than it should have. Maggie turned her head in disgust.

"Please, save it for Summer Phillips and your other female fans," she chided him.

They were standing by the door. Maggie had her back to it, and Sam reached out and braced himself against the wall with one arm, effectively trapping her between him and the door. Yet another practiced move, she was sure.

"Are you saying you're not a fan?" he asked.

His face was just inches from hers and, as she met his gaze, she was transported back to those summer nights all those years ago, when they snuck out of St. Stanley in his old beat-up pick-up truck and went swimming in the abandoned quarry on the edge of town.

She was also made infuriatingly aware of how handsome Sam Collins, the football star and valedictorian of his graduating class, still was. Before she heard Karen Carpenter's voice start singing about birds suddenly appearing, Maggie closed her eyes and shook her head as if she were trying to shake off a bad case of fleas. When she opened her eyes, she felt her good sense return.

Sam watched her, tilting his head as if he was trying to figure her out and it would be easier from a sideways angle. Then his gaze moved down to her lips, as if looking for her answer and daring her to deny that she had been a fan of his. Maggie slipped under his arm and sidestepped away. She turned the knob on the door and yanked it open, leaving him no choice but to move his arm.

"Sorry, not so much," she said.

She saw his jaw clench as if he knew she was lying, but didn't know how to prove it.

"So, if I owe you," he said, ignoring the open door. "What do you want?"

"I want to see Claire tomorrow," she said.

Sam crossed his arms and considered her. Gone was any

remnant of the past between them. He was looking at her now with his sheriff face on, considering how he could grant her request and make it work for him.

"I want you to tell me everything she says," he said.

"Why would I do that?"

"Because if you don't, she's going to go to jail for murder," he said.

He stepped out the door and the dark night absorbed him like a raindrop vanished into the ocean.

Chapter 20

Maggie spent more time than usual on her appearance the next morning. She told herself it was because she had to go into the office to work on billing for Dr. Franklin after she stopped by the jail to see Claire. But given that she was known to work at Dr. Franklin's in a jean skirt and sandals, this was a blatant lie and even she knew it, although she refused to acknowledge it.

In her own defense, she felt that looking professional would make Sam respect her more, but that wasn't it either. Having been hit by the blinding realization that Sam was still hot, Maggie was determined that he should feel the same way about her. Level the playing field as it were, not that she had any interest in playing on any field of his, however. Right.

When she entered the kitchen, Sandy stared at her over the rim of her coffee cup. Then she let out a low wolf whistle.

"What's the occasion?" she asked. "Is someone getting married?"

"I don't know what you mean," Maggie said. She poured a cup of coffee and perused the bananas.

"Oh, please. That's your Sunday best to the tenth power," Sandy said. "The only time I have ever seen you pull out your Steve Madden peep-toe pumps and your Nanette Lepore sheath dress is when you were going on a date. And look at your hair. It's all loose and wavy. You never take time with your hair. So, who is he?"

"Who's who?" Maggie asked. She could feel her heart thump in her chest. Was it possible that Sandy knew what she was up to?

"Who do you have a date with?"

"I don't have a date," Maggie said. "It's just been a while since I've worn this outfit, and you know my rule."

Sandy shook her head in exasperation. She knew the rule well: *If you don't wear something at least once a year, you need to get rid of it.*

"Exactly," Maggie said. She could feel her pulse decelerate.

"Has it really been a year since your last date?" Sandy asked.

"Something like that," Maggie said.

"Well, that's ridiculous," Sandy said. "We need to get you hooked up. I mean, look at you: You're beautiful, too beautiful to be sitting at home every Saturday night."

"And that is why I love you, niece of mine," Maggie said. She gave Sandy a kiss on the head. "Don't worry about me. I like my Saturdays just the way they are."

Maggie grabbed a banana and glanced out on the porch.

Josh had finished breakfast and was already hard at work on the railroad. She gave him a kiss on the head, too, and he beamed at her. Reaching up with a chubby hand, he pulled her face down to his and kissed her cheek.

"Aunt Maggie pretty," he said.

"Thank you, Josh," she said. Somehow when a child paid a compliment, it seemed so much more valid than when it came from another grown-up. Probably because kids were unfailingly honest, even when you'd rather they weren't.

"I'm off," Maggie called as she headed through the living room toward the front door.

"It's pizza night," Sandy said. "Josh and I'll do the pickup. He likes to watch them twirl the dough."

"Take a twenty out of my stash," Maggie said. Sandy waved her off, and Maggie gave her a firm look. "That's not negotiable."

"Have a nice day," Sandy said. "Hey, maybe you'll meet someone, since you're all dolled up."

Maggie gave her a small smile and shut the door behind her.

The drive to the sheriff's department was short. When she parked, she noticed her palms were damp. Not wanting to ruin her dress, she grabbed a hand wipe out of the case she kept in the car for post-playground cleanup with Josh.

She wished the little thing was big enough to run over her whole body, because what had seemed like a good idea in her bedroom this morning, now just seemed obvious and ridiculous. She almost put the car in reverse and left without going to see Claire, but she couldn't do that to her friend.

With a muttered curse, Maggie got out of the car and

strode up the stone steps and into the red brick building, trying to look like a woman on a mission.

Deputy Wilson was manning the front desk today, and she glanced up at Maggie with a polite smile.

"Good morning, ma'am," she said. "How can I help you?"

"I'm here to see Claire Freemont," Maggie said.

Deputy Wilson narrowed her eyes at her. She was wearing her standard-issue uniform of dark brown shirt and light brown pants. Her hair was scraped back in its usual bun. She pursed her lips as she looked Maggie over. Then she blinked as if the light of recognition had hit her like a camera's flash.

"I remember you," she said. "How's the cat?"

"The who?"

"The cat," Deputy Wilson repeated. Her eyes still narrowed in suspicion.

"Oh, yeah," Maggie said. "He's good, great, really good."

Oh, crud. Maggie knew she sounded like a big, fat liar, which she was.

"Uh-huh." Deputy Wilson crossed her arms over her formidable chest. The she leaned close to Maggie and sniffed the air.

"Something wrong?" Maggie asked.

"Are you wearing perfume?"

"Yes, why? Am I not allowed to wear perfume in here?"

"Women only wear perfume when they are looking for a man."

"Oh." Maggie wasn't sure how to respond.

"Your perfume is the good stuff." Deputy Wilson smiled. "And you are definitely on the hunt."

"I am not," Maggie argued.

"Oh, please, a woman only wears the good perfume if she's trying to impress that special someone," Deputy Wilson said.

"Or if she knows how to get the good stuff on the cheap," Maggie said.

"Do tell." The deputy leaned her chin on her hand and studied Maggie.

"Samples," Maggie said. "When you go to the department store, always be sure to see if they have samples of the good stuff at the makeup counter."

Maggie opened her purse and unzipped the small side pocket on the inside. She kept part of her stash in her purse. She took out three small vials of perfume.

"Here," she said. "You can have these."

"We're not supposed to accept gifts." The deputy shook her head with a sigh.

"These aren't gifts, they're freebies," Maggie said. "Look, I have Joy, Beautiful and Lovely."

"So, how do you get them to hook you up?"

"Well, over the years, I've become friends with one of the ladies at the makeup counter. I used to go in with my mother when I was a girl, so she's seen me grow up. Now I have to buy my mother's anti-wrinkle cream for her. She's in Florida with my sister, but they don't have the stuff she likes, so when I pick up her cream, my pal always hooks me up with whatever perfume samples she has. I haven't bought perfume in years."

"That's very . . . thrifty," the deputy said.

Maggie shrugged. "I try."

"Thanks for these," the deputy said. She sniffed each one appreciatively. "But I still say you're looking for a man, because you're wearing the most expensive of the three."

"Good nose," Maggie said. "But really, I was just in the mood for that one today. I really am on my way to work, and I'm just stopping here to check on my friend first."

"Uh-huh," Deputy Wilson said. "Sheriff Collins is out."

"I don't care!" Maggie said. The deputy's eyebrows lifted, and Maggie knew she'd been too fast. She glanced at her watch. "Really, I just have to get to work."

Deputy Wilson hit the buzzer on her desk and the half-gate latch popped. Maggie hurried through it before the woman changed her mind. She left her purse behind the counter, and Deputy Wilson led her through the door at the back.

She looked at Maggie over her shoulder, and said, "If it's any consolation, the sheriff had to leave on a call. Before that he was pacing the lobby like a caged cougar."

"I really couldn't care—"

"And he was wearing aftershave," the deputy added. "He's never worn aftershave before today."

Maggie met Deputy Wilson's knowing brown eyes, and she felt the corner of her mouth quirk up. "Aftershave, huh?"

"The expensive kind."

"So, when you see him—"

"Tell him that Mrs.—"

"You can go with Ms."

"That Ms. Gerber has legs up to her neck," Deputy Wilson said. "Too bad he missed it."

"That works for me," Maggie said with a delighted grin. "What's your name, your first name?"

"Everyone calls me Dot, short for Dorothy."

"Dot, I think we're going to be great friends."

"Hook me up with a pair of those shoes on top of the perfume, and you've got yourself a lifer in the gal pal department," Dot said.

"I'll see what I can do." Maggie smiled and slipped through the open door into the lobby area.

Another deputy was sitting there. He was older, with a spindly build and thinning gray hair, and he seemed rather cranky at having to put down his newspaper to let Maggie into the back room. The name on his uniform read Deputy Crosthwaite. He walked her down the hall to Claire's cell.

"Freemont, you have a visitor!" he snapped. Then he looked at Maggie and pointed to his eyes with his index and middle finger and then pointed the fingers back at her and said, "I've got my eye on you."

"Okey-dokey," she said. She wondered how the heel of her peep-toe pump would feel on his geriatric instep, but she refrained from letting him find out—just barely.

"Maggie," Claire said as she rushed up from the cot. "How is Mr. Tumnus? How are you? I'm so bored, I think I might go out of my mind."

"I'll bet," Maggie said. She glanced at the cell behind Claire and desperately wished she could let her out. This whole thing was just crazy.

"Listen, I have news. Joanne came over to my house last night," Maggie said.

"Oh, how is Joanne?" Claire asked. She sounded as if she hadn't seen her in months, instead of just days.

"She's fine. Well, no, actually, she was in tears, but that's not the point. The point is that she told Sheriff Collins and me—"

"Whoa, back up," Claire said. "What was Sheriff Collins doing at your house?"

"Pestering me about why I had really been here to see you," Maggie said. "He didn't believe the sick-cat story."

"So, he's good-looking *and* smart," Claire said. "How unfortunate."

"Indeed," Maggie said. "Now here's where it gets interesting—"

"Wait, one more question," Claire interrupted again. "Why are you all gussied up today? Don't you have to be at Dr. Franklin's in an hour?"

Maggie blew out a breath. This was the downside to close friends: They knew you too well.

"I am just wearing this outfit so that I don't have to weed it from my closet," she said.

"The one-year rule?" Claire asked.

"Yes, exactly."

"But you wore that two months ago when we all went into Richmond because we had that Groupon to eat one hundred dollars' worth of food for only fifty at Chez Nous, that snazzy French restaurant," Claire said.

"Oh, I forgot," Maggie said. She felt her face grow warm, and she was annoyed that Claire was going to figure her out if she didn't get her distracted and quickly. "Now, do you want to hear what Joanne had to say or not?"

"Yes, I do," Claire said. "Sorry. I think being stuck in here is making my brain go sideways."

"Okay, Joanne was in tears, because of the hormone shots," Maggie said, and Claire nodded. "But she told us that John Templeton had approached Michael's young entrepreneur's group about investment opportunities and, in fact, Michael used Templeton's company to buy those two apartment buildings that he and Joanne own."

"No!" Claire said. "But this means there could be other investors who have much more reason to kill John than I did."

"Exactly," Maggie said. "I talked to Max last night and, in light of the new information, he thinks he can get the judge to set your bail at a more reasonable sum. You may be out in time for the two-for-one breakfast at the House of Bacon on Saturday."

Claire sagged against the bars. Silent tears coursed down her cheeks. Maggie patted her hands where they rested on the bars.

"Hey, this is good news," she said. "Come on, chin up."

Claire reached under her glasses and wiped her eyes. She snuffled a bit and then turned to blow her nose on a piece of toilet paper, a roll of which sat on the shelf by the severe metal bowl in the corner.

"There is one thing that will help you to get out faster," Maggie said.

"What's that?"

"You have to tell Sam what you told me, about what you saw that night that you fled Baltimore."

"I can't." Claire shook her head.

"I don't think you're going to have much choice," Maggie said. "They're going to keep investigating, and if they link the body you saw being hauled out by Templeton with your flight from the city, it's going to look very bad. Claire, you have to tell them. You have to tell them what you saw, and you have to tell them what John Templeton was holding over you."

"John knew about my past. He knew, and he was going to tell. I would have been ruined," Claire cried.

"What happened in your past?" Maggie asked. "I can't help you unless you tell me."

Claire turned away as if she couldn't face Maggie. Her voice was so low, Maggie had to strain to hear her.

"I was involved in a robbery, and someone got shot."

Chapter 21

A sucking sound echoed around the sterile chamber, and it was a moment before Maggie realized it was her, gasping in shock. Of all the things she had expected Claire to say, this was not it.

Claire turned back to Maggie. "When I was sixteen, I got involved with a gang of bad girls. It was pure reckless stupidity, but they decided to rob a convenience store, and I went along with it to fit in. I was the only one with access to a car, and I knew how to drive, so I was the driver."

As Claire paused to catch her breath, Maggie could see her reliving the horror of that long-ago day. The painful memory weighed heavily upon her, and Maggie could swear that Claire shrank as she uttered each word.

"No one was supposed to get hurt, but the girls I was with, well, one of them was wild. When the clerk refused to empty his drawer, she went crazy. I could see her screaming at him and yelling, so I knew something had gone wrong. I left the car and went in to get the others. I figured our bluff had been called, and we needed to get out of there."

Claire was silent so long, Maggie asked, "And then what happened?"

"The wild girl, Rita, she leaned over the counter and shot the clerk in the leg. I couldn't believe it. I didn't even know she had a gun. Turned out it was her brother's, and it was loaded. The rest of them ran, but I stayed and called nine-one-one."

Silent tears slipped down Claire's face, and Maggie reached through the bars to grab her hands. They were cold to the touch, and she wished she could get into the cell to hug her friend.

"You stayed," Maggie said, not at all surprised that her friend had done the right thing.

"Well, if I hadn't rushed in there, demanding that they all leave, she probably wouldn't have shot him. I felt like it was my fault."

"It wasn't," Maggie said. "Yes, the robbery was a stupid thing to do, no question. I mean really, what were you thinking?"

Claire cleared her throat. "I just wanted them to like me. I was sixteen, remember."

"Oh, yeah, sorry." Maggie shook her head. "I got off track there. What happened next?"

"The ambulance came, and it turned out that it was just a flesh wound. The clerk testified that I tried to get the others to leave and that I stayed with him after he was shot. But still, the other girls' lawyer pointed out that I was a part of the robbery; I was the driver, so I had to do some time. I was sent to juvie for three months, and because I cooperated, my records were sealed."

"And John knew this?" Maggie asked.

"Apparently he had me investigated when we first started dating," she said.

"But your records were sealed," Maggie said.

"Not tightly enough," Claire said.

"He threatened to go public with it, didn't he?"

"Can you imagine, a librarian with a record? It would have ruined me," Claire said. "I knew I couldn't trust him not to keep using my past against me, so I called in a silent witness report about what I saw that night and I ran."

"Oh, Claire," Maggie said. "You must have been terrified when he showed up here."

"Pretty much," Claire said. "I tried so hard to cover my tracks. I even took my stepfather's name."

"Your name isn't Freemont?" Maggie asked.

"It is now," Claire said. "But it wasn't then."

They were silent for a moment. Maggie was trying to process all that she had learned, and Claire seemed to be lost somewhere in the past.

When the door opened at the end of the hall, Maggie glanced up, expecting to see Sam Collins. When she recognized the crotchety deputy making his way toward them, she was surprised to find she felt disappointment instead of relief.

"Time's up," he said. "We're having a shift change."

Maggie glanced at her watch. She had to get to Dr. Franklin's anyway.

"Listen, Claire, I know telling me all of this was hard for you, but I'm glad you trusted me," she said. "It's going to help you get out of here. I promise."

"Thanks, Maggie," Claire said. "And not just for the pep talk."

Maggie tilted her head. She wasn't sure she understood.

"What I mean is, thanks for not treating me any differently now that you know everything," Claire said. "You're a good friend."

"So are you," Maggie said. "No matter what happened when you were a teenager, you are a good person, and you did the right thing. Is it all right if I tell Ginger and Joanne?"

Claire nodded. "Yes, I trust you—all of you."

"Yeah, blah blah," the old deputy said. "You're cutting into my break time. Let's go."

Maggie reached through the bars to give Claire a half hug. "I'll be back later today or early tomorrow," she said. "And I know Max is coming by later. I'll see if we can get you something to read in there."

Claire looked like she might weep with relief, "Oh, please! All this time on my hands with no books is killing me."

Maggie grinned. Claire was such a librarian.

With a wave, she followed the deputy out to the front desk, where she retrieved her purse.

"Bye, Dot," she said.

"Bye, Maggie. Remember my shoe size is seven and a half."

"On it," Maggie said. She swept out the front door, feeling optimistic for the first time in days. They were going to get Claire out of jail, and they were going to prove she was innocent by catching the real killer.

Of course, she had no idea how they were going to do

that; it just seemed more in the realm of possibility than it had yesterday. She hurried down the sidewalk. She had parked farther away, around the corner at the unmetered parking. As she strode toward her car, she heard a set of heels clicking purposefully behind her.

She glanced over her shoulder to see Summer Phillips bearing down on her like a warship with its canons primed. Perhaps it was because she was leading with her bust like the carved wooden figurehead on the bow of a ship. In any event, Maggie wanted to get out of firing range.

She supposed Summer was out for revenge for the ice cream incident, which would not be out of order, but Maggie really didn't have time for a tussle before work. She was pushing being late as it was.

"Do not try to outrun me, Gerber," Summer barked.

Which told Maggie, of course, that that was exactly what she should do. She picked up her pace, and she heard Summer pick up hers as well. Darn it. This is when peep-toe pumps were not helpful, not at all. She didn't want to go faster for fear of a taking a header, but Summer had at least four inches in leg length on her, and the odds were good that she would be able to make up the ground between them pretty quickly. Maggie poured on a burst of speed.

Two men dressed in fluorescent orange vests were surveying the street, trying to determine if they needed to add a streetlight on the corner of Chestnut and Main. They did this every year, as old man Wilcox, who lived in the big house on the corner, attended every town council meeting and complained loudly that he could never cross the street on account of there not being a light.

So every year it was surveyed, and every year they

discovered that Mr. Wilcox was just moving slower and slower and, no, they would not be putting in a light.

This, of course, made old man Wilcox mad, and he would soon be dragging his lawn chair out to the sidewalk to count the number of cars that turned the corner onto Chestnut. He would then make a fancy colored graph showing the peak traffic times and how they correlated with his day's schedule of trying to cross the street. Then he would attend all of the council meetings until they agreed to have the corner surveyed again. Maggie thought they should just give the old man his light. Really, was it asking so much?

Both of the surveyors stopped what they were doing and took in the sight of Maggie trying to outrun Summer. Maggie could hear Summer wheezing up behind her and suspected she was about to have all of her hair pulled out by the roots.

Abruptly, a blue sedan screeched to a stop right in the middle of Chestnut Street, and the passenger door popped open.

"Jump in, she's gaining on you!" Ginger ordered.

Chapter 22

Maggie jumped into the car, and Ginger zipped away before she had even shut her door. Maggie scrambled around in her seat, slamming the door. She glanced back to see Summer stomping her size twelve high heel on the sidewalk. The two surveyors stared openmouthed as Summer let loose a string of curses that could have bubbled the tarmac.

"How did you know I needed back-up?"

"One of my boys was at the Perk Up getting an iced coffee and saw you leave the jail with Summer hot on your tail, so he called me," Ginger said. She glanced at Maggie out of the corner of her eye. "He said he wasn't sure it was you, given that you were all decked out like you were going on a date or something."

"It's the one-year rule," Maggie said.

"But you wore that when we—"

"I know," she said. "Claire already reminded me. So I

forgot? Sheesh. Why is everyone making such a big deal about it? Do I normally look so terrible?"

"Is that a rhetorical question?" Ginger asked. She smiled as she drove around the corner and parked under a large, shady maple tree. The morning was already heating up, and both ladies rolled down their windows to allow for a cross breeze.

"As scintillating as discussing my wardrobe is, I have bigger news," Maggie said. She then told Ginger all about her conversation with Claire.

"Oh, wow," Ginger said. "This certainly fits in with what I've found out about Templeton so far."

"What do you know?"

"His venture capital company is really just a giant shark swallowing up any guppies stupid enough to invest with him."

"What do you mean?"

"Okay, you know how the country is in an economic bust, partly because people used their houses for ATMs and took out home equity loans at high interest rates, and then found when their home values tanked that they now owed more than their homes were worth?"

"Yeah," Maggie said. She felt her tightwad insides pinch at the thought.

"Well, Templeton's venture capital company pretty much did that with all of the small businesses they financed. If I'm reading the financials right, he loaned money, waited for the company to fail, and swooped in and bought them out."

"So, he was like the black death of financing," Maggie said.

"He was definitely a parasite," Ginger agreed. "And of

course his real profit came when he unloaded the dead business onto a new buyer."

"Well, that would certainly give someone a motive to kill him," Maggie said.

"Agreed. So, what next?" Ginger asked.

"I have to go in to work," Maggie said. "But then I want to meet with Max and see how this new information will affect getting Claire out of jail."

"It might not help her," Ginger said, chewing her lip.

"Why, because she committed a crime as a youth?"

"No, because she fled a crime scene before," Ginger sighed. "She may be perceived as a flight risk."

"I didn't think of that."

"What can I do to help?" Ginger asked.

"For starters, would you mind dropping me off at work?" Maggie asked. "I can hoof it back to get my car later. I'm afraid Summer is going to camp out next to it."

"Not a problem," Ginger said. "I'm going to go back to the office and see what I can find out about the young entrepreneur's group, as in who invested with Templeton and how much."

"You can do that?" Maggie asked.

"I have some sources." Ginger put the car in drive and pulled out onto the main road.

Maggie gave Ginger an impressed look.

"I had no idea accountants were so well connected."

"We know where the bodies are buried—financially speaking." Ginger took two right turns and pulled into the long driveway in front of Spring Gardens.

"Thanks, Ginger," Maggie said as she opened her door. "You're a lifesaver, and I do mean that literally."

"That's what I'm here for." Ginger said. "But repayment with some blackberry cobbler would not be refused."

Maggie laughed. "How did you know Josh and I spent yesterday picking blackberries off my bushes?"

"I saw him with Sandy at the park, and his fingers were still purple."

"Excellent. Recon at my house at seven?" Maggie said. "And I'll let you bring the vanilla ice cream."

With a wave, Ginger headed back out of the lot, and Maggie hurried into the entrance she used for Dr. Franklin's office.

"Well, look what the wind blew in," Cheryl Kincaid said. Cheryl was Dr. Franklin's longtime nurse practitioner and had become a good friend of Maggie's over the years. "So, do you have a hot lunch date or what?"

"No, I'm just behind on laundry," Maggie said. Man, she wished she'd never worn this dress today. It all seemed so stupid, since she'd never even seen Sam.

"Well, you'd better stay in your office or you're going to give my older male patients heart attacks," Dr. Franklin said as he stepped out of the exam room with a chart in his hand.

"Oh, aren't you sweet," Maggie said.

Dr. Franklin was tall and thin, with a thick thatch of white hair on his head. Maggie had learned years ago that she could mark the time of day by his hair. In the morning he always started with a head of properly pomaded and sculpted hair but, by the time lunch rolled around, his hair would escape its chemical bonds and would have less of an Elvis and more of an Einstein thing going. By the end of the day, it was full-on mad scientist.

His wife, Alice, had tried every beauty product available

on his hair, but nothing could tame Dr. Franklin's crazy mane for long. Maggie knew she had managed to arrive on time today, as not a hair was yet out of place.

"Unless, of course, we need Maggie to restart a heart," Cheryl teased. "In that dress, she might be able to pull it off."

Cheryl was short and stocky, played in the town softball league and was known for her love of beer, brats and brawn. She and Tim Kelly, who owned the local tavern, had been a couple for years, but they had never married and didn't live together. Cheryl said it was because they liked their space, and this relationship worked out fine for both of them. Maggie couldn't fault it. They seemed happy.

"Thank you both," Maggie said. She was feeling embarrassed and longed to duck into her office. "Would you look at the time? I'll just get to work then. I want to see if we've heard back from Mr. Stevenson's insurance company. They're being awfully evasive about covering his heart medication."

"Coffee is hot if you need it," Cheryl called after her.

Maggie's office was in the back of Dr. Franklin's suite of rooms. Nestled between the bathroom and the exterior wall, she was happy to have a window that overlooked the grounds, even if the occasional flushing noise made her bladder spasm.

She turned on her computer and waited for it to boot up while she went through her voice mail. She had several messages from insurance companies that she had to return, as well as some from patients. She didn't love doing the billing for Dr. Franklin; in fact, sometimes she was sure her brain was turning into tapioca dealing with all of the insurance companies and their ridiculous parameters for care.

But still, she knew she was making a difference for Dr. Franklin's patients and for Dr. Franklin and Cheryl, because no one got paid until Maggie got the money in.

On particularly bad days, she envisioned herself storming the offices of the insurance companies, swinging a baseball bat and threatening to smash some skulls until she left with what they owed Dr. Franklin. But that was only on particularly bad days.

She turned her radio on low to NPR and listened to the news while she worked her way through the files in front of her. She had been billing for Dr. Franklin for so long, she knew which companies she had to call, who she had to send letters to and who she needed to turn over to collections. She didn't enjoy doing that, but sometimes even she needed to call in the heavies.

"Knock knock."

Maggie turned to her door to find Dr. Franklin standing there. His hair was mussed, indicating that they were about halfway through the workday.

"What's up, Doc?" she asked with a smile. He shook his head. How many years had she been teasing him with that one? Too many to count, and yet he always smiled.

"Do you have a minute, Maggie?"

"For the boss? Always."

"I wanted to talk to you about Claire Freemont," he said.

Maggie waved him into her little office, and he sat in the only other available chair. She reached over and switched off the radio right in the middle of the local weather forecast. They were predicting thunderstorms. Not a big surprise in southern Virginia in August.

"I take it you've heard," Maggie said.

Dr. Franklin was well into his sixties, and his face was lined with wrinkles. Most were laugh lines, but Maggie knew the deeper creases came from worry, worry about patients he couldn't cure or patients who wouldn't follow the treatments he prescribed.

Claire was one of his patients—as were all the GBGs, since they were referred by Maggie—and Maggie knew Dr. Franklin well enough to realize that Claire's situation would concern him greatly.

"I went to see her this morning," Maggie said. "She's bored, but otherwise, I think she's holding up very well."

Dr. Franklin nodded. "Good, that's good. She's had a— very difficult life."

Maggie tilted her head and studied him. Had Claire told him about Baltimore?

Dr. Franklin's eyes were a pale blue, and he watched Maggie as if he was waiting for her to put it together without him having to break any patient confidentiality.

Yep, she had told him.

"Things were difficult for her," Maggie said. "But she made several good choices, and I'm hoping that will weigh in her favor when Max tries to get her bail set."

"Ah, the young Mr. Button," Dr. Franklin said. "How is he holding up under the strain of his first big case?"

"Well enough to boss me around," Maggie said. "And his mentor, a defense attorney in Richmond, is helping him with the case."

Dr. Franklin nodded. "Excellent. I heard Judge Pearson is presiding. He's very fair-minded. Max should do well with him."

"I'll be there to help, too," Maggie said.

Dr. Franklin looked alarmed.

"What?" Maggie asked.

"Won't Sheriff Collins be there?"

"Probably," she said. "I suppose he may be called upon to testify. Why?"

"Do you think it's wise for you to be in the same room with him?"

Maggie shrugged and avoided his kind gaze. Dr. Franklin always had the ability to make her feel as if she were still a teenager. She had begun working for him when she was seventeen, part-time and after school; it had worked well with her schedule.

When things had ended between her and Sam, she had tried to pretend nothing was wrong. She worked through her tears, learned her new job and never said a word to anyone. Then one night when they were closing the office, Dr. Franklin invited Maggie to take a walk with him.

They had strolled around the town green, not talking until he finally said, "Maggie, I'm a doctor, but I don't need my stethoscope to diagnose a broken heart. Are you all right?"

Maggie had been fine . . . well, she'd been doing a fine job of faking it until Dr. Franklin gazed at her with those worry lines creasing his forehead. Then she had fallen apart.

They had ended up sitting in the gazebo in the middle of the town green while Maggie cried her eyes out into his handkerchief. He had *tsk*ed in all the right places as she recounted the story, but he had never offered her any advice or told her she'd been a fool. He'd let her cry it all out, and then he invited her to dinner with him and his wife, Alice.

Maggie had always liked Dr. Franklin before, but from

that day forward she loved him like the father she'd never had, the uncle she wished she'd had and the grandpa who had died too young for her to know him.

"So much time has passed since that teenage heartbreak," Maggie said. "I married Charlie, a wonderful man, gave birth to our beautiful daughter and had to bury my dear Charlie entirely too soon. That was *real* heartbreak. I'm a different person now. I really think I'm over Sam, and I can handle being in a courtroom with him."

"So, the outfit is for . . . ?"

"I may be over him, but that doesn't mean I don't want him to notice that the years have been good to me," she said.

Dr. Franklin gave her a dubious look. Then he gave her a slow smile that took in her outfit. "So, did you see him at the station today?"

"No, he was out on a call," she said. She gave a frustrated sigh.

"Shall I call in a crime and get him over here?" he asked. "It'd be a shame for him to miss out on your . . . er . . . need to do laundry."

Maggie smiled. "I think calling in a false report *is* a crime, and I already have my hands full visiting Claire, but thanks for offering."

"I know it's cold comfort," Dr. Franklin said. "But I'd bet my last tongue depressor that he regrets what happened all those years ago."

"Eh." Maggie waved a hand as if she didn't care. But there was a treacherous part of her that really hoped Dr. Franklin was right.

"Well, as long as you're all right." Dr. Franklin rose from his seat, and the sound of flushing could be heard from the bathroom next door. He checked his watch. "Marshall Pinter, right on schedule. Excuse me, Maggie."

"Of course." She nodded.

"And if you find that you're not as 'eh' as you think, I hope you know you can talk to me," he said.

"Thank you, Dr. Franklin, I really appreciate that," she said.

The door closed softly behind him, and Maggie sagged back in her chair. What was she doing? She glanced down at her dress. She was flirting with disaster, that's what she was doing. Really, trying to make Sam notice her, and for what? He had left her once and never looked back; surely, twenty-four years and one outfit were not going to make him change his mind. She shook her head.

"I'm an idiot," she muttered. Then she turned up her radio and got back to work.

Chapter 23

At mid-afternoon, Maggie walked back to her car. It wasn't a long walk, but the afternoon had a pre-storm stickiness to it that seemed to rise up from the cement sidewalk in waves. Cicadas hummed as if in a dither over the possible change in the weather, and Maggie wondered if they were warning one another to take cover or if they were looking forward to a good soaking.

She kept a wary eye on the few people out in this heat. She was half expecting Summer Phillips to leap out from behind a mailbox to get her. Not for nothing, but she quickened her pace.

She glanced at the sheriff's department as she went by. She wondered if Sam had made it back to his office. She wondered what had called him away. She wondered if Dot had really told him that Maggie had legs up to her neck. And she wondered why she cared.

Sam had left her busted up and broken when he took off without so much as a backward glance. Maggie had stayed in St. Stanley. She'd worked for Dr. Franklin and gone to the community college part-time and gotten her two-year degree. She had planned to go on and attend the university, but just when she'd been about to leave, she'd met Charlie Gerber, the new deputy in the St. Stanley sheriff's department.

He was kind and funny and he made no secret of the fact that he thought Maggie was the most perfect woman he'd ever met. He was a balm to her wounded soul, and she fell head over heels in love with him. Somehow, college got pushed aside for a wedding, and then she was pregnant with Laura.

Maggie had figured she'd get back to college once Laura started school, but it hadn't turned out that way. Charlie was killed in the line of duty, and suddenly all the dreams Maggie'd had of growing old with her husband evaporated like fog under a warm sun, and she found herself alone with a child to raise.

She was lucky. She had a job and plenty of friends to help her along the way, but still, she'd be a liar if she didn't admit that when times were tough and she wasn't feeling strong, she wondered how her life would have turned out if she and Sam Collins had stayed together.

Maggie fished her keys out of her bag, relieved to be at her car and looking forward to cranking on the AC. She could feel a rivulet of sweat run down her neck and imagined her hair had gone quite limp during her walk. Ah, well, dressing up had seemed like such a good idea this morning.

Feeling sluggish, she decided a caffeine pick-me-up was in order. She still had her punch card from the Perk Up, and today she could cash it in for a freebie. Feeling much more motivated, Maggie fired up her Volvo and circled the town green until she found a parking spot just down the street from the coffee shop.

The bells on the door jangled when she pushed her way inside. The scent of roasted coffee beans filled her nose and the cool air of the shop washed over her skin. The place was empty of customers.

"Hi, Maggie," Gwen greeted her from behind the front counter. "What can I get for you?"

"Something frozen and heavily caffeinated, please."

"How about an Almond Cappuccino Frost?"

"Perfect," Maggie said. She handed Gwen her punch card. "Can I have it to go?"

"Sure." Gwen put the card in the register. "Do you want to start a new card?"

"Yes, please," Maggie said. Gwen handed her a blank card, and Maggie put it in her wallet.

The front counter wrapped around the side of the shop and had several stools for patrons to sit there as well. Maggie slid onto one of the tall stools.

She watched as Gwen hustled behind the counter, fixing her drink. Gwen was tall and thin, with sharp features. She didn't smile often, which Maggie thought was unfortunate, because her whole face lit up when she did.

Gwen and Jay Morgan had come to St. Stanley several years ago and opened the Perk Up. It had become the place to hang out in town, but lately, Maggie had noticed that business seemed to be a bit slower for them. She wondered if the coffee shop franchise that opened on the edge of town last year had driven down their sales. Of course, there was no polite way to ask this, so she didn't.

Gwen wasn't generally one for chatter, but since no one was in here today, Maggie thought she'd ask her what she thought about the murder. Given that the Perk Up was still busy in the mornings, maybe Gwen had a good idea of what people in town were saying.

"So, what do you think about that murder in the library?" she asked.

"I try not to think about it," Gwen said. "A small town like this—that sort of thing shouldn't happen here."

"Well, when times are tough, crime goes up," Maggie said. "People get desperate."

"Claire Freemont has a cushy job at the library," Gwen said. "What did she have to be desperate about?"

"Claire didn't do it."

Gwen stopped fussing with Maggie's drink and stared at her. "That's not what I heard. It was her knife in his chest, wasn't it?"

Maggie opened her mouth to give a well-thought-out rebuttal, but of course she didn't have one. And in a moment of blind clarity, she realized that this was what Max was facing. Why was it Claire's knife sticking through the victim's chest? And with her fingerprints, no less.

Gwen pushed the beverage in its plastic cup across the counter toward her, and Maggie handed her a tip for service.

Maybe it was the panic of knowing how badly it looked for Claire, but Maggie didn't leave right away. Instead she took a sip of her frozen drink. It was delicious.

She watched as Gwen wiped down the counter, and even though she found the other woman intimidating, she screwed up the courage to say, "Gwen, can I ask you something?"

"Shoot," Gwen said without stopping her work.

"What was your impression of John Templeton?"

Gwen looked at her with a frown. "I never met him, so I don't have one."

"But I thought he spoke to the young entrepreneurs group," Maggie said.

"Maybe he did," Gwen said. "I don't go to those meetings. They're too boy's club for me."

"Is Jay here?" Maggie asked. "I'd like to know what he thought of him."

"No, he's out buying supplies," she said. "If you'll excuse me, I really have work to do."

"Oh, sure," Maggie said.

Since the hint to go away was given with all the finesse of a kick to the temple, Maggie hopped off her bar stool with her drink and headed for the door. She glanced around the empty café one more time before she pushed through the doors and stepped back out into the muggy heat.

To the west she could see a thunderhead perched, as if gathering its strength before it moved in and struck like a sledgehammer. She glanced at the row of dogwood trees planted along the perimeter of the town green. She couldn't help but notice as the hot breeze picked up that the leaves closest to the ground seemed to be turning over, as if beckoning the coming storm to bring them some rain.

Maggie checked her watch. It was getting late, and it was pizza night. She didn't want to miss that, especially since she'd skipped lunch and she was starving. She hopped in her car and headed home, mulling over the events of the day and feeling a little ridiculous that she'd dressed up for nothing.

Dwelling on her own foolishness did nothing for her self-esteem, so she turned her thoughts over to the question of who had killed John Templeton. It was very apparent that he'd been a bad man, but still, someone had committed murder. The question was, why?

She knew it looked bad for Claire. If Maggie was honest, Claire's motive to kill Templeton was extraordinary. People certainly killed for less, but Maggie knew her friend wasn't capable of taking a life.

Claire said she hadn't told anyone about why she had fled Baltimore, but that didn't mean that John Templeton hadn't told someone about Claire. If he had and that person wanted him dead, well, wouldn't Claire be the perfect fall guy?

As she pulled into her driveway, Maggie hoped that Ginger had some luck pulling up information about Templeton's other investors. There had to be someone out there with a bigger motive than Claire's, and it was up to the GBGs to find them.

Chapter 24

"Okay, the topping deal was a bust, so I had to go with double cheese," Sandy said. "They wanted entirely too much money for the puny amount of pepperoni they were going to scatter on this pizza."

"Double cheese works for me," Maggie said.

She had changed out of her dress and heels and into a comfy tank top and shorts. As the storm flirted with the outskirts of town, the mugginess had become oppressive. Even though she didn't love the rattle and boom of thunderstorms as much as she had when she was a kid, Maggie was ready for the relentless sticky misery to be over.

They took their pizza out onto the sun porch. Sandy had cut Josh's up into bite-size pieces, and he sat in his plastic chair while Maggie and Sandy each took one of the padded wrought-iron chairs.

"Do you have study group tonight?" Maggie asked.

"It was canceled," Sandy said. "Some of the others were worried about being caught in the storm."

Maggie glanced through the glass windows that enclosed the room. The wind was beginning to whip the trees into a frenzy.

"I think that was a wise choice," she said.

"What about you, any plans tonight?" Sandy asked. "Did you get asked out on a hot date today?"

"No." Maggie shook her head. "In fact, it'll be a while before I wear heels all day again. I am so out of practice."

She stretched her bare feet, feeling the kinks in them protest. Did it always hurt like this after she wore heels, or was she just getting old?

They spent the rest of the meal recapping the day's events, and then Maggie baked a fresh blackberry cobbler and did cleanup while Sandy got Josh ready for bed.

When the storm hit, the first boom shook the house. A flash of lightning lit up the sky soon after. The storm was here.

Maggie hurried down the hall to Josh's room. He didn't like storms, but she met Sandy backing slowly out of the boy's room.

"He's asleep," she said. "I put the air filter on, so hopefully the hum will keep him from being disturbed by the storm."

"Good idea," Maggie said. "Are you going to study now?"

Sandy nodded.

"Call me if you need me," Maggie said. "Ginger is supposed to be coming by with the others."

"Another strategy session?" Sandy asked.

"I really want Claire out of jail," Maggie said. "It's so depressing."

Another boomer rumbled through the night. They both jumped, and then a faint knock sounded on the door. Maggie went to get it while Sandy disappeared into the little office to hit the books.

The wind whipped around the front door when Maggie opened it, propelling both Ginger and Joanne inside. The smell of rain, although there wasn't any falling yet, gave the air a pungent, earthy smell.

"Is Max with you?" Maggie asked.

"He went to the jail," Ginger said. "He talked to Sam today and was told he could bring Claire some books and things."

"Oh, good," Maggie said. "Josh is asleep and Sandy is studying, so let's go out to the porch where our talking won't disturb them. We can watch the storm out there, too."

Joanne's cell phone chimed, and she pulled it out of her pocket. "It's Michael. He's out with the guys. I have to text him that I've arrived."

She rolled her eyes at her husband's overprotectiveness, but it was obvious that she was pleased by his concern. Joanne and Michael Claramotta were such a nice couple, Maggie really hoped the baby thing worked out for them, and soon. It would be one lucky baby to have such loving parents.

While Joanne hammered on the keypad of her cell phone with her thumbs, Maggie and Ginger went into the kitchen. Ginger had brought the vanilla ice cream, as promised.

The blackberry cobbler was cooling on the stovetop. Maggie hauled a pitcher of iced tea out of the fridge while Ginger gathered plates.

"Do you want to do the honors?"

She handed Ginger the pie cutter and, while Ginger dished the cobbler, Maggie scooped the ice cream. Then she loaded up a tray to bring out to the porch. Ginger followed her.

"Again, it just feels wrong without Claire here," Ginger said.

"I know," Maggie agreed. "We have to get her out of jail, and soon."

They took their seats and Maggie set the tray down on the table. The thunder rumbled outside and the lightning flashed, but Maggie felt safe on her cozy porch. She hoped Claire was doing all right at the jail.

"Well, to that end, I have information," Ginger said.

"Do tell." Joanne slipped her phone into her pocket and took the plate Maggie held out to her.

Ginger dug into her large purse for a small notebook and her reading glasses. She perched the glasses on her nose and flipped until she found the page she wanted.

"Okay, here's what I got from my background check on John Templeton," she said. "He was fifty-four, lived in Baltimore, but had investments all down the east coast."

"All the way to Florida?" Joanne asked.

"Yes, and he was very interested in scooping up post–Hurricane Katrina properties in New Orleans."

"Married?" Maggie asked.

"No, and no children either," Ginger said. "He started his venture capital company in the early nineties, and it has slowly grown into a multibillion-dollar company."

"He's been audited by the IRS several times, but has always gotten away without any fines being levied against him," Ginger said.

"Good accountants?" Maggie asked.

"Or government workers who take bribes," Ginger said. "Hard to say."

Maggie blew out a breath. "Okay, what else?"

Ginger scanned her notes. "I have lots of money stuff, but what I deemed most important were the businesses here in St. Stanley that had a 'working' relationship with John Templeton."

"Other than Michael and me, who have you got?" Joanne said.

Maggie was pleased that Joanne wasn't in a puddle of tears tonight. This was the no-nonsense Joanne Claramotta, the "there is a scuff on these shoes, so I want twenty-five percent off" Joanne Claramotta that they knew and loved.

"Well, it's a pretty long list," Ginger said. "With the recession, almost everyone is squeezed to the max, so people are borrowing from whoever is lending, and at disgusting interest rates, too."

"Can we narrow it down by who is in trouble?" Joanne asked.

"Already on it," Ginger said. "We have Jay and Gwen Morgan of the Perk Up."

"I was just in there today, and Gwen said she'd never met him," Maggie said. "I wonder if Jay did a deal and didn't tell her. You know, the place looked dead."

"That franchise on the outskirts of town is killing them," Joanne said. "It has a drive-thru."

"We also have Hugh Simpson of the Frosty Freeze," Ginger said.

"No!" Maggie and Joanne said together.

"And then there are a few ties for third place," Ginger

said. "The Clip and Snip hair salon and the thrift store My Sister's Closet over on Main Street."

"Okay, this makes no sense," Maggie said. "Why would anyone invest in virtually every business in a town this small and in businesses that are so diverse?"

"I am delighted that you asked me that," Ginger said. She smiled at Maggie as if she were her prize pupil. "I thought the same thing, too. Usually venture capitalists have a specific interest. This guy is all over the place."

"A thrift store, a deli, an ice cream place and a hair salon . . . you think?" Joanne asked.

"But there is one thing they all have in common," Ginger said.

"They're all in St. Stanley?" Maggie asked.

"You're getting warmer," Ginger said.

"They're all on the town green," Joanne said.

"Exactly," Ginger said. She flipped through her notebook. "I looked at other towns Templeton has invested in over the past two decades. They are virtually unrecognizable."

"What do you mean?" Maggie said.

"The mom-and-pop shops are gone," Ginger said. "Wiped out. And who has a vested interest in the franchises that take over?"

"John Templeton," Maggie said.

"He did it to midsize towns all up and down the coast," Ginger said. "It's like he was on a mission to homogenize the entire eastern seaboard."

"That's awful," Maggie said. "And not just from a financial standpoint."

"Agreed," Joanne said. "I mean, as a small business owner you hope to franchise one day, but to have all the small businesses be swallowed up by franchises, well, how will anyone ever break into business ownership if everything starts with an established franchise?"

"What did you find out from Michael?" Maggie asked Joanne.

"Not as much as that," she said. "He did say, though, that Templeton seemed almost disappointed when Michael made his payments on time, and he always found that a bit odd."

"Well, now we know why," Ginger said.

"What did you find out from Claire?"

Another boom of thunder followed rapidly by lightning caused them all to jump and glance out the windows. In a burst, the rain started to fall, not the pitter-patter of happy rain, but rather the incessant sound of a chorus of hammers pounding on the roof and against the glass.

"Let's finish our cobbler, and I'll tell you what I know," Maggie said.

They each tucked into the decadent dessert, with Joanne having two pieces. While they ate, Maggie told them what Claire had told her. Ginger accepted the story without flinching, as she'd already heard it, but Joanne was upset.

"Why didn't she tell us?" she asked. "We could have helped her."

"I think she was hoping her past would stay there," Maggie said.

"The minute he showed up back in town, she should have told us."

"She probably found it difficult to work 'By the way, I saw my former boyfriend dragging a body out of a building once' into the conversation," Ginger said.

"Kind of a show-stopper, that one," Maggie agreed.

Joanne opened her mouth to protest, but then huffed out a breath instead. "You're right. Poor thing. That must have weighed as heavily upon her shoulders as Summer Phillips's last boob job does on hers."

Maggie busted out with a laugh as the storm roared overhead. When both her laughter and the storm quieted, they could just make out a faint knocking on the front door.

"That must be Max," she said. "We need to tell him about Hugh. Maybe he can help."

Maggie yanked open the door and there stood Max Button, esquire. He had a hot fudge splat on his LEGO T-shirt, which he wore over cargo shorts and flip-flops. His hair was plastered to his head, and his acne looked a bit worse than usual.

"Max, come in, come in," she said. She stepped back and swung the door wide. Max stepped into the entryway and began to drip all over the small, tiled area. "Here, let me grab you a towel."

Maggie dashed down the hall to the master bathroom. She found a big, fluffy towel and then opened the small closet to grab her peach-colored, satin-trimmed terry cloth robe. It wasn't terribly masculine, but at least it would keep Max from freezing to death.

She raced back down the hall and handed him the fluffy towel. He used it to wrap his hair, and Maggie held the robe out for him.

"I really don't think that's my color," he said.

"Aw, it's just us girls," Maggie said. "Come and have some cobbler. We'll do your nails while we chat."

Max gave her an alarmed look as he shrugged on the robe. Maggie busted up.

"I'm joking," she said. "Come on."

Max squished behind her in his flops. Ginger and Joanne exchanged a look when he entered the porch.

"Trying on outfits for court?" Ginger asked.

Max grinned and turned this way and that, modeling the robe. "I think it really brings out the sallow in my skin, don't you?"

"The towel totally makes the outfit," Joanne said. "All we need is one shot of you in the towel and it will go viral. We could start selling them as the latest haute couture accessories."

Max struck a pose, and they all laughed. Maggie remembered when he'd first come to her house to tutor Laura. He'd been so shy, he'd almost been paralyzed. He'd stammered and stuttered through the social niceties until they'd finally ended his suffering by opening a math book, at which time he became quite the loquacious speaker. Maggie had realized that Max was fine when he was in boy-genius mode. It was every other waking moment of his life that was torture.

Maggie had watched him mature over the past four years and develop into the kind, confident young man that he now was. She was pleased to have been a part of his life then and now. She had no idea where his overly large brain was going to take him, but with degrees in every subject under the sun, she hoped he'd be leaving the Frosty Freeze sooner rather than later—especially if Hugh, the owner, had some shady business deals happening.

Ginger cut Max a man-size slice of cobbler topped with a healthy scoop of vanilla ice cream, and he settled onto the couch to eat. While he ate, they told him what they'd learned, and he chewed thoughtfully when they mentioned that his boss, Hugh Simpson, was one of the biggest investors with the venture capital company.

"So, that's why he looked so weird when I told him who Claire was accused of murdering," Max said. "He knew John Templeton."

"Did he say that?" Maggie asked.

"No, he didn't say a word."

"Don't you think that's odd?" Joanne asked. "I know if I knew somebody who'd been murdered, I'd say so."

"Unless you had something to hide," Ginger said.

Max's fork stalled halfway to his mouth. "You don't . . . . but that . . . that's crazy talk."

"Is it?" Maggie asked. "You know how much Hugh loves the ice cream stand. Maybe he killed to keep it."

"Whoa, whoa, whoa," Max said. "Hold the phone. For all his seventies macho-man chic, Hugh is just a big marshmallow. He has a hard time calling in the exterminator. He certainly isn't one to snuff out a life."

"Desperation makes people do crazy things," Maggie said.

As if to emphasize her words, a boom of thunder rattled the windows. They were all still until the sound died away.

"Maggie, I just don't see Hugh shoving a cake knife into anyone's chest, no matter how desperate he was," Max said.

"Would you be willing to search his office?" Joanne asked.

"For what? Remnants of birthday cake frosting?"

"For anything that links him with the John Templeton," Maggie said. "Max, I wouldn't ask, but this is for Claire."

"All right," he groaned. "But you have to follow up on the other names."

"We will," Maggie said. "Ginger, why don't you take My Sister's Closet, since they gave you such a good deal on the shoes and handbag that you obviously have an in there. I'll take the Perk Up and see if I can talk to Jay this time. Joanne, can you handle the Clip and Snip hair salon?"

"Oh, an excuse for a mani pedi," Joanne said. "And I have a coupon for twenty percent off."

"Nice." Ginger gave her a high five.

Maggie looked at her own fingers. Her nails looked like she'd been dragging them up and down the sidewalk for giggles. Darn it. She should have picked the Clip and Snip.

Thunder rolled but it now sounded distant, as if the storm was done punishing St. Stanley and was slowly moving away.

A knock sounded at the front door, and Maggie glanced at the others. With Max here, they were all accounted for except for Claire, but Maggie sincerely doubted that she'd been released. Then again, maybe St. Stanley's crackerjack new sheriff had solved the murder and arrested the perpetrator.

"I'll be right back," she said.

"I'll come with you," Max said. He rose from his seat. "After all, there is a murderer on the loose. You can't be too careful."

Chapter 25

He looked concerned and Maggie was touched that he felt the need to protect her. She didn't have the heart to tell him that, in his head towel and robe, the only people he was likely to scare off were the fashion police.

With Max at her back, Maggie pulled open the door, and there stood Sam Collins, with rain pouring off the brim of his sheriff's hat.

She leaned into the doorway, barring his entrance.

"Can I help you?" she asked.

Sam looked over her shoulder at Max and narrowed his eyes. "He's a little young for you, don't you think?"

Maggie shrugged. "He's of age."

Sam's mouth dropped open and Maggie rolled her eyes.

"Don't be ridiculous," she said. "He was soaked from the rain, so I let him borrow a robe and towel. I can get you a matching one if you'd like."

"Hi, Sheriff Collins," Max said. He slouched back into his relaxed stance since it wasn't a crazed murderer on the other side of the door.

"Button," Sam returned. He looked unhappy, which naturally made Maggie feel quite pleased.

"Uh, Maggie, I'm going to go dry off," Max said.

She glanced over her shoulder at him and nodded. Poor guy, he seemed to have just realized that he'd greeted the sheriff in a peach-colored, satin-trimmed robe.

"What can I do for you, Sam?" Maggie asked.

"The deal was that if I let you see Claire, then you tell me what she said."

"You weren't there today, so I couldn't, now could I?" she asked.

"Which is why I'm here now," he said.

"You could have called first," she said. "I might have had a date."

"From what I heard, you must have had a hot date today," he said. He took in her tank top and shorts. "Too bad I missed the outfit, but this is nice, too. It brings back a lot of memories."

"Really, of what?" she asked.

She met his gaze, and that's when she understood the term *smoldering look*. She was pretty sure Sam Collins could ignite kindling at fifty yards with that look.

Instinctively, she stepped back, which of course Sam took as an invitation for him to enter the house. He removed his hat and let the excess water run off onto her front steps before he came in, but still, here he was again. Maggie wasn't sure she liked this pattern.

"Sam," Ginger said as she came strolling into the room.

"Hi, Ginger," he said. They gave each other a half hug and a kiss on the cheek.

Maggie felt a hot lick of jealousy spurt up inside of her. Not because of the hug or the kiss but because they had the easy familiarity of old school chums, and that was something she and Sam would never have.

"Hello, Sheriff Collins . . . er . . . Sam," Joanne said.

Sam gave her a kindly smile, and they shook hands.

"Good to see you again, Joanne," he said.

Max walked into the living room. His clothes were still damp, but his hair was mostly dry.

"Listen, Maggie, I have to go prepare for Claire's preliminary hearing," he said.

Maggie could see he was back in lawyer mode.

"All right," she said. She glanced at the group. "So, we're all clear on what we need to do?"

They all nodded, and Sam glanced around the room at each of them. Before he could detain them, however, they dashed out into the rain and Maggie shut the door behind them.

"Why do I have a really bad feeling about that?" he asked.

"I can't imagine," she said.

"You're not taking this further than you should be, are you?" he asked.

"Meaning?" Maggie turned away and went back to the sun porch to start cleaning up. Perhaps if she stayed busy, he'd leave sooner.

Sam followed, placing his hat on a chair arm before helping her carry into the kitchen the dishes left behind by the mass exodus.

"You are not, I repeat not, supposed to go poking any further into the murder," he said.

"Now why would you think I'd do that?" she asked. She opened the dishwasher and began to rinse and stack the dessert plates inside.

Sam looked at the lone piece of cobbler in the pie dish on the counter beside her.

"Go ahead," she said. She handed him a clean plate and a fork but he only took the fork.

"No need to make more dishes for you," he said as he tucked in.

"Gee, thanks," Maggie said.

She shook her head as she continued with the dishes. She had forgotten what it was like to have a man in her kitchen. They took up too much room, she decided, and they ate too much. Honestly, she had no idea how Ginger put up with five of them under foot. The woman should be sainted.

"So, what did Claire say?" he asked.

"You know," Maggie said, "technically you left before I agreed to tell you everything that she said."

Sam paused while chewing and stared at her hard.

"I didn't agree, we didn't shake on it—in fact, we didn't even pinky swear—so I think that makes your demand for full disclosure null and void," Maggie said.

Sam very carefully put the pie plate on the counter. Maggie glanced into it to find it empty. She took it and the fork out of his hand, rinsed them and loaded them into the dishwasher, too.

"Maggie, if you don't tell me what she said, I can't help her," he said. "Whatever bad feelings you have about me, you shouldn't let them get in the way of helping your friend."

"I don't have any feelings about you, good or bad," Maggie argued. "And I certainly wouldn't let them get in the way of helping my friend."

His gaze met hers. He looked like he didn't believe her. He looked like he wanted to call her out on it, but he didn't.

"Fine," he said. "Then tell me what she said."

"I can't," Maggie said. "I don't know how it will affect things for her at the preliminary hearing, and until I do, I can't just blab out what she told me."

"You know, I could arrest you," he said. "Obstruction of justice, impeding an investigation, etc. and so forth."

Maggie felt her heart hammer in her chest. The thought of being arrested terrified her. Then she saw a tiny sparkle in his blue eyes, and she lost her temper and snapped her dish towel at him.

"But I gave you cobbler and cookies!"

He backed away from her, and a grin broke across his face. His voice was low, and he said, "You always take me by surprise Maggie O'Brien."

They stared at each other for a moment until Maggie looked away.

"It's Gerber now," she said. Her voice was softer than she would have liked, but it was weird hearing her maiden name after all these years.

"That's right," he said. She glanced back at him and saw his smile fade like afternoon sunshine. "You married Charlie Gerber. I heard he was a good man."

"He was," she said.

They fell silent. Only the rain dripping off the roof in time with the kitchen clock broke the silence.

"Listen, Maggie," he said. "I'm going to be honest.

I didn't expect a murder my first week on the job. I've been away from St. Stanley for a long time, and I don't know it like I used to."

Maggie watched him. He looked as if the words were caught in his throat and he was forced to choke them out or suffocate.

"What are you trying to say?" she asked.

"Maggie, I need your help."

Chapter 26

Maggie raised her eyebrows. She lifted a hand to her ear and cupped it as if she were hard of hearing. "What was that? I couldn't quite make it out."

"You heard me." He wasn't smiling now, but his lips twitched.

"You'll have to forgive me, it sounded like you need . . ."

"Help!" He reached out and grabbed the dish towel in her hand and pulled her close. He took the towel and dropped it on the counter and then laced his fingers between hers in a gesture as familiar as if he did it every day. "There. I need your help. Are you satisfied?"

Maggie glanced down at their hands. Her breathing felt oddly constricted, and she pulled her hand out of his, patted her upper chest and coughed.

"Okay, then, I'll help you," she said. She turned away from him and led the way back into the sun room.

"Are you all right?" he asked.

"Me? I'm fine," she lied.

A pot of honey and an army of fire ants would not get her to admit that she'd about keeled over when he grabbed her hand. After twenty-something years, he shouldn't have that sort of impact on her. Obviously, she needed to start dating again, and soon.

"It's getting late, so let me tell you what I can," she said. She gestured for him to sit and he did. She felt his blue gaze on her face, but she kept her eyes on the windows as if she was watching the storm as it meandered its way out of the valley.

She took a deep breath and told him what Ginger had discovered about Templeton's business scheme to destroy and sell the local mom-and-pop shops. Sam took notes, asked intelligent questions and seemed pleased with the additional information.

"Is there anything else?" he asked.

"No, I think that's it," Maggie said. "If you want me to tell you what Claire told me, you're going to have to subpoena it out of me. It is her life, and it just isn't my place to say."

She turned away from the window and met his eyes. He gave her a slow nod.

"I'll let it go, for now," he said. "Nice work on Templeton. Did you ever consider a career in law enforcement?"

"No," she said. "When Charlie was killed, that pretty much curbed any enthusiasm I might have had for a career with the sheriff's department."

Sam nodded. He gave her an empathetic look. "I'm sorry for your loss."

"Thank you," she said.

"My partner was killed," he said. "We were deep undercover, trying to bust up a drug ring. One of the suspects got twitchy and the next thing I knew we were in a full-on shootout. My partner was hit and died before they could get him airlifted to the hospital."

"So, you know."

"Yeah, I know."

Maggie didn't talk about how Charlie had died. She didn't need to. It was enough to know that Sam understood what she had gone through.

She wasn't sure how, and she wasn't sure that she liked it, but as she showed Sam to the door, she felt as if a truce had settled between them, at least for now.

Maggie took Josh to story time the next morning. The library had reopened, but it seemed odd without Claire there. They got to see Linda, who looked ready to drop that baby any second, and Freddy. And, of course, Josh very proudly showed his hand stamp to everyone he met.

The rest of the morning was spent on chores, baking a strawberry rhubarb pie and playing trains. The summer air after the storm was surprisingly cooler and drier, as if the storm had pulled the mugginess away with it. Maggie and Josh worked up quite a thirst weeding the garden—well, she weeded and Josh played with the worms—but still, it was a nice morning all the same.

When Sandy returned from her class, Maggie had lunch waiting and, afterward, she put Josh down for his nap so Sandy could hit the books. Once the house was quiet, Maggie decided to walk into town and treat herself to a coffee at the Perk Up. She didn't have a coupon, but she could get her first hole punch on her new card.

She changed from her muddy gardening outfit to a cotton sleeveless blouse and denim shorts. She glanced at her fair, freckled skin in the mirror and sighed. There was no hope for it; with the sun at its brightest, she was going to have to wear her ginormous sun hat and slather on the sunscreen.

She stopped by the office on her way out. Standing next to Sandy, she propped her hip on the desk.

Sandy had her own red hair twisted up onto the top of her head and held in place by several pencils. She was tapping an eraser on the page of her textbook, as if trying to commit it to memory with a Latin beat.

"I'm going to take a quick walk into town," Maggie said. "Need anything?"

"Someone to tell me what the O antigen of Enterobacteriaceae is."

Maggie looked around at the walls and then slowly backed out of the room.

"I think I hear Josh calling me," she said. She covered her mouth and said in a high-pitched voice, "Aunt Maggie!" She lowered her hand and said, "Yep, that's definitely him. Gotta go."

Sandy started laughing. "It's okay. I don't expect you to know my homework questions."

"You know, you could always ask Dr. Franklin," Maggie said. "He lives for that stuff."

"I may have to put him on speed dial," Sandy said.

Maggie walked back in and kissed the top of her niece's head. "I'll be back shortly."

"Aunt Maggie, can I ask you something?"

Something in her tone alerted Maggie that it wasn't about microbiology.

"You can ask me anything, you know that," she said.

"Is there something between you and Sheriff Collins?"

Maggie sucked in a breath.

Sandy shook her head. "I'm sorry. It's none of my business. It's just that he looks at you . . ."

"Like he wants to bite me?" Maggie asked.

"Yeah," Sandy said and then grinned. "But not in a bad way."

Maggie felt her face grow warm, but she shook her head. "Sam Collins and I have been at war since we were Josh's age. I don't see that ending anytime soon."

"I don't know," Sandy said. "I think there's more there, at least on his part."

Maggie thought about the uneasy truce that had seemed to form between them and the way he had held her hand last night. Could he feel more for her than annoyance?

Nah. The man seemed to goad her every chance he got. If they were getting along right now, she was sure it was temporary.

"That man goes out of his way to aggravate me. I sincerely doubt he feels anything but irritation at my presence."

"If you're sure," Sandy said.

"Oh, I'm sure," she said. She scooped up her hat as she headed out of the room.

Maggie locked the front door behind her and plopped her hat firmly on her head. Today was one of those days when it just felt wonderful to be alive. The sun was warm, and the breeze was cool. The birds chirped in the trees as if they, too, were just happy to be.

She hopped down the steps onto the walkway that led to the sidewalk. She turned in the direction toward town and thought about how she was going to broach the subject of John Templeton with Gwen if she was at the shop instead of Jay. The woman had already made it clear that she hadn't met him and was convinced that Claire had done the deed. If this thing went to trial, Maggie sure hoped Gwen wasn't called up for jury duty.

She was lost in thought, and it took her a moment to register someone calling her name.

"Maggie! Maggie Gerber!"

She glanced around until she saw old Mrs. Shoemaker, two houses down, standing on her front porch waving at her.

Mrs. Shoemaker was ninety-one going on sixty. She was short and stout and favored floral-print house dresses and sensible black shoes that she wore laced up tight. Her gray hair was worn in a tight bun at the back of her head, and her pale blue eyes twinkled behind her silver-rimmed glasses. She moved quickly for a woman of her years, and she was off the porch and hurrying down the walk before Maggie had reached the gate in her white picket fence.

"Afternoon, Mrs. Shoemaker," she said.

"Well, look at you, Maggie Gerber, aren't you a pretty picture today," Mrs. Shoemaker said.

"Why, thank you," Maggie said. "You look lovely as always."

Mrs. Shoemaker patted the bun on the back of her head.

"Mr. Shoemaker, God rest his soul, always liked my hair this way. He said it reminded him of Kate Hepburn."

"He certainly had fine taste when it came to the ladies," Maggie said.

"Oh, go on." Mrs. Shoemaker waved a hand at her. When Maggie was silent, she said, "No, really, go on."

Maggie laughed. She had always had a warm spot for Mildred Shoemaker.

"Morning, Mrs. Shoemaker, Maggie," a voice called from behind them.

Maggie spun around to find Rich Hardaway approaching them from his mail truck.

"I have a package for you, Mrs. Shoemaker," he said.

Mrs. Shoemaker clapped her hands together and took the small box from his hands.

"Mrs. Shoemaker," Maggie said. "Did you buy more cookie cutters?"

"Just two," Mrs. Shoemaker said. She clutched the package closer to her chest as if Maggie might take them away. "They're vintage and very rare. I got them on eBay for two dollars."

Maggie looked at the happy light in Mrs. Shoemaker's eyes and didn't have the heart to diminish her joy.

"Congratulations," she said.

Mrs. Shoemaker gave her a pleased smile and then waved at Rich as he went on to the next house.

Maggie glanced over Mrs. Shoemaker's head at the house behind her. Built in the 1920s, it was small and compact like Maggie's. But where Maggie's contained manageable clutter, Mrs. Shoemaker's was out of control.

When her husband died ten years ago, she had begun

collecting things. Silly things, like the cookie cutters, but as her children had hooked her up with a computer to keep in touch when they moved out of state, Mrs. Shoemaker had discovered the joy of online shopping and bargain sites. Maggie had frequently debated having an intervention for her, but the little things brought Mrs. Shoemaker such joy that Maggie was loath to stop her.

"So, are you going to be making cookies today, Mrs. Shoemaker?" Maggie asked.

"No, these are too precious to use," she said. "But if you go to see Claire today, tell her I have a cake knife she can have. I used to collect those, too, but really how many cake knives can a girl use?"

Maggie felt her breath stall in her lungs. "Mrs. Shoemaker, do you think Claire killed John Templeton?"

"Oh, goodness no," Mrs. Shoemaker said. "Not Claire. She's such a lovely woman. She's always loaning me her personal books, because with my eyes not being what they used to be, I am such a slow reader. I can never finish a book before it's due back at the library, so she gives me hers."

"Yeah, that's our Claire."

"But someone did take her knife and use it," Mrs. Shoemaker said. "So you tell her I have one for her when she's back from her trip."

Maggie smiled. *Her trip* was, of course, Mrs. Shoemaker's euphemism for Claire's time spent in jail.

"I'll let her know," Maggie said. "Bye, Mrs. Shoemaker."

"Bye, dear." Mrs. Shoemaker headed to her house with a renewed spring in her step that Maggie knew was because she now had more stuff to add to her collection.

Whatever gets you through the day, Maggie thought.

She remembered that after Charlie died, getting out of bed had been so difficult. Even with her daughter, Laura, there to prod her up, Maggie had struggled. She found that if she could just get Laura into the stroller and get her shoes on, then Maggie could get herself outside and start moving.

She'd jog around the neighborhood as if she could outrun her grief, and then, when she was out of breath and too weak to cry, she would treat herself to a sticky bun from the old bakery. It took about six months of this routine, but it got her through the worst of it.

Maggie continued her walk, thinking about how much the loss of a loved one impacted those left behind. She wondered whom John Templeton had left behind. There had to be someone, some family, and yet she hadn't heard anything about mourners. His body had been shipped to the medical examiner's office, and that was that.

She wondered if Sam would tell her anything if she asked, and she wondered how she could ask him so that he would tell her without thinking she was overstepping her boundaries. Nothing brilliant leaped to mind.

She turned onto Main Street and noted that last night's howling wind had done some damage to the usually picturesque square. The dogwoods had lost some limbs, and leaves were scattered. A few of the town's maintenance trucks were parked along the curb as the workers cleaned up the mess.

Maggie headed straight for the Perk Up. She hoped it was having the same afternoon lull as yesterday. She pulled the door wide and entered to find there was a group of customers at a table and a lone man sitting at the counter. Jay was manning the coffee bar. Maggie glanced about for Gwen, but there was no sign of her.

"Hey there, Maggie," Jay said. He was on the tall side of medium in height, with an inner tube of forty-something paunch around his middle. The only hair he had left was a fringe to remind him of what used to be. But his smile was wide and welcoming, and it occurred to Maggie that the Perk Up might do better if Jay worked the front counter more often than the somber Gwen.

"What can I get for you today?" Jay asked.

"A big cup of go juice straight up," she said.

"That's what I like to see, a woman who does not sissify her beverage. For here or to go?"

"Here," she said. She slid onto a bar stool and watched while Jay fussed with her coffee.

"So, how was the storm out at your place?" Jay asked. "Any limbs down?"

"No, I got lucky," Maggie said. "No damage at all. How about you?"

"We're good," Jay said. "We lost one shutter off of the house, but I can live with that."

"It's sure been a crazy week," Maggie said.

"I'll say," Jay agreed. "First that guy gets murdered, then Claire is arrested and then we have a bad storm. Kind of makes you wonder what's next?"

"Well, I think next they find the real killer," Maggie said.

"You don't think Claire did it?" he asked.

"Claire? Heck no," Maggie said. Then she realized how perfect it was to have the owner of the coffee shop spread the word that Claire was innocent. He probably ran into people all day long.

"Wow. Gwen seems pretty sure it was her. Who do you think did it then?" he asked.

"I don't know," she said. "I heard he spoke at your entrepreneur's meeting. Did he strike you as someone who had a lot of enemies?"

"That was about a year ago," Jay said. He rubbed his chin with the back of his hand while he thought about it. "He was full of himself. You know the type. He had a Rolex on his wrist, drove a Mercedes and had one of those walks, you know, like this."

Jay stepped back from the counter and began to walk in a rolling swagger that looked like he was caught by a strong wind that was knocking him side to side like a badminton birdie.

Maggie couldn't help but laugh. "Was he really that bad?"

"Ugh. And his cologne!" Jay said. "You could smell that guy coming when he was twenty feet away. It was like a bad diaper smell filling up the room. There was no ducking it."

"Ooh," Maggie said. "That's bad."

Jay put a full ceramic mug down in front of her with cream and sugar on the side.

"Honestly, I didn't like the guy," Jay said. "I got a bad vibe off of him."

"Did his investment in the Perk Up work out for you?"

"Oh, we didn't take the investment," Jay said. "I saw those interest rates and I said no way, and now we're doing all right. I told Gwen it would turn around."

"Good for you," Maggie said. She frowned. She wondered if Ginger's information had been in error. Jay certainly seemed very clear that they hadn't taken any of Templeton's money, or maybe he just didn't want to admit it.

Maggie studied his face. She thought again of Sam's five tells for lying. Jay showed none of those. So, either he was very good or he was telling her what he believed to be true, which meant that Gwen had lied to her when she told her that she had never met Templeton. One of the Morgans seemed to have done a deal with Templeton, and if it wasn't Jay, then it had to have been Gwen.

Maggie glanced at her watch. It was just about time to reconvene with the others and see what they had learned. Her cell phone chimed, and she looked down to see the number for the Frosty Freeze. That would be Max.

"Hi, Max," she said.

"Maggie, you need to come over here right now," he said. His voice was higher than normal, almost girly high in fact. Maggie knew him well enough to know that this meant he was having a stress meltdown.

"Did you find something?" she asked.

"Get. Here. Now." *Click.*

Seriously? Maggie looked at the phone as if it were a live snake. What was happening to her pliable Max?

She paid for her coffee and left her tip on the counter. She waved to Jay, who had headed down the bar to talk to the lone guy who had finished his espresso and was holding up his tiny cup for a refill.

Okay, they had planned to meet up, but Max was on the other side of the town square from where she was, so she figured she would stop by the Clip and Snip and see how Joanne was doing. She had better be done with her mani pedi and then together they could head to the Frosty Freeze and ask Ginger to meet them there.

Maggie hurried down the sidewalk toward the salon. The brim of her hat flapped in the breeze, and she was forced to hold it down on her head. The Clip and Snip was the only hair place in St. Stanley, so it did a steady business with everyone from the blue hairs, for their rinse and sets, all the way to the two-year-olds getting their first haircuts.

Eva Martinez owned the salon. She had bought it seven years ago from old man Zucker, who had been the town barber for fifty years before that. Being a smart (not to mention sultry) woman, Eva had the brains to hire an older man who gave the best straight-edge razor shave in the state, and she had redesigned the shop so that it was gender separated. So she had effectively opened up business to the entire town and, as far as Maggie could tell, was doing fabulously. Why she would have had anything to do with John Templeton was a mystery to Maggie.

Maggie hurried into the Clip and Snip and found Joanne sitting with her nails under the little hand dryer. She had chosen to go with the French manicure and, luckily, Eva was the one sitting with her.

"Hello, Maggie," Eva said. "Here to make an appointment?"

"No, just here to get Joanne," she said.

"Pity," Eva said. She looked at Maggie as if she were an ancient painting that could be magnificently restored if Eva could just get her sharp shears on her.

Maggie was afraid of Eva. She could admit it. Not to Eva, of course, but to herself. When she booked her very rare appointments at the salon for a trim, she always made sure she got a different hairdresser.

She wasn't sure why, but Eva exuded sex appeal like a sun-ripened peach evoked summer. Maybe it was her long, thick, curly black hair, or the way she looked at customers from under heavily lidded brown eyes, or perhaps it was the perfect ten she had for a body, which she dressed in tight-fitting tops, miniskirts and hoochie-mama shoes. The reality was that she made Maggie feel as dull as dishwater, and she was afraid that after spending an hour with her, she'd come out with horrid self-esteem. It was a gamble she was not yet prepared to take. That being said, she found Eva fascinating and could have spent hours just watching her walk around her salon, interacting with her customers.

"Eva, help!" A new hairdresser in a pink smock was standing by the dryers over the head of Mary Ellen Whitfield. She was biting her lip and looking stressed and Maggie had the feeling Mary Ellen was about to have a bad hair day.

While Eva bent down to examine the girl's work, Joanne turned to face Maggie and hissed, "I got nothing."

"What?"

"Bupkes, nada, zilch, zip, zero," Joanne said. "I tried. I really tried, but every time I went to ask a question, I just panicked."

"So, you didn't ask her about Templeton?" Maggie asked.

"I'm telling you I panicked," Joanne said. "She's got some kind of witchy-woman voodoo power thing going."

"But you're the one who comes here the most," Maggie said. "You have a rapport with her, or at least your wallet does."

"So sorry, but it just doesn't include asking your beautician if she's a murderess!"

"Is something wrong?" Eva asked. She had resumed her seat behind the nail desk and was checking Joanne's manicure. Afraid or not, Maggie figured she was just going to have to bluff her way out of this one.

"Joanne and I were just talking about John Templeton's murder," she said.

Eva's perfectly sculpted eyebrows rose, and she pressed her ruby red lips together in an uncompromising line.

"What about it?" Eva asked. Although she had lived in the United States for years, her voice still had the faint flavor of Puerto Rico in it, adding to her exotic appeal.

"We were just wondering who did it." Maggie said.

"The librarian did it," Eva said. "And if I ever get my hands on her . . ." She switched over into a tirade in Spanish that Maggie could only get every other word of, but it was enough to know that Claire would not be getting her hair done at the Clip and Snip anytime soon.

"Whoa, the way she's going on, you'd think Templeton was her husband," Joanne whispered to Maggie.

Maggie studied Eva for a moment and had to concur that, yes, she looked like a jealous lover in the throes of a passionate tantrum.

"Eva, was there something going on between you and John Templeton?"

Chapter 27

"What do you call this?" Eva asked, and held out a hand that had a diamond as big as a Fourth of July sparkler on it. "He gave that to me for our one-month anniversary."

"Wow," Joanne said. "I could get pregnant with triplets, and I don't think I'd get a ring that big."

"So, you two are . . . were a couple?" Maggie asked. "I'm sorry, I didn't know."

Eva raised her hands in the air. "We broke up. That man, he broke my heart for her, the bookish one."

"Claire?" Joanne and Maggie said together.

Eva turned and gazed into the mirror. "Look, my beauty is fading. I don't have 'it' anymore."

Maggie looked at the gorgeous woman before her. How could she possibly think that?

"Eva, you're stunning," she said. "You'll always be

stunning. You're the kind of woman who stops traffic, literally."

"Oh, Maggie, you're very kind," Eva said. "But the mirror doesn't lie."

"I think she's having some confidence issues," Joanne whispered, as if Eva couldn't hear her.

Maggie glanced at her watch. Max had called her ten minutes ago. She really didn't have time for this. Tough love was in order.

"You're right, the mirror doesn't lie," Maggie said. She put on her no-nonsense voice, which she had used on Laura during the ugly adolescent years. "You are beautiful, and everyone knows it. Now, from all that I have heard, I can tell that John Templeton was a big, stupid jerk. If he dumped you, well, how can I put this?"

Maggie paused, and Eva stared at her with her eyes wide, willing her to continue. There was just no way to candy coat it.

"Did you ever stop to consider the fact that you were more woman than John Templeton could handle?"

Maggie knew she had played right into Eva's vanity, and it was working. The other woman looked back at the mirror and preened.

"He was older," she said. "He got tired very easily."

Joanne and Maggie nodded at her in silent agreement with what she was saying.

Eva tossed her hair and beamed at her reflection. "You are right. He could not handle a woman like me."

Maggie silently thought that there weren't many who could, but she was glad to see Eva looking confident again.

"How long ago did you two break up?" she asked.

"Oh, it was spring," she said. "I remember because he brought me tulips, and then he dumped me. And after I had agreed to his crazy investment scheme, too."

"Investment scheme?" Maggie asked. She and Joanne didn't look at each other in an unspoken effort to appear nonchalant.

"As if I want to expand this place," she said. "I agreed because he talked such a good game, but I didn't spend the money, and then, when he dumped me, I paid it all back. I wanted nothing to do with him."

"Then what happened?" Joanne asked as she handed over her coupon.

Eva rang up the sale, and Joanne paid in cash, giving Eva a nice tip. Maggie figured she was giving her more for the wealth of information they were getting, and she had to agree it was a good move.

"He was so angry with me," Eva said. "It was a little exciting, you know?"

Maggie thought about Claire's story about John Templeton carrying a body and shivered. *Exciting* wasn't the word, and she wondered if Eva would ever know how lucky she had been to get away from him.

"What makes you think he had a thing with Claire?" she asked.

"Well, because she killed him," she said with a shrug. "He must have met her on one of his trips here, and I'm sure he used the same charm on her that he used on me. He was a dog, that man. I knew that, but for certain compensation, I was willing to look the other way."

Eva admired her ring as it sparkled from the glow of the overhead fluorescent lights.

"Boys will be pigs, you know," she said.

"I thought he was a dog. I'm getting confused," Joanne said. Maggie hushed her.

"So, you knew he was seeing Claire?" Maggie asked. Her heart was pounding in her chest. Claire hadn't told them that she had seen Templeton other than the day before his murder. Had she been seeing him again for weeks before-hand, even after she'd fled her old job and home to get away from him? If so, why hadn't she told them? What had he wanted from her? This could not be good.

"Oh yes," Eva said. "I found the evidence after one of their trysts in his car. He denied it, but I knew there was another woman, and when she stabbed him, I knew who it was."

"Evidence?" Maggie asked.

"A bra," Eva said. "Not in my size. I have to order custom-made support."

Okay, Maggie had to look. She knew Eva was built, but she had never really checked her out before.

She glanced at Eva's figure. Yep, there was no question. Eva and Claire were not in the same league; in fact, they weren't even in the same sport.

"You have a lovely figure," Maggie said. "So, did you confront him about it, the bra?"

Eva tossed her head. "No. After all, I have my admir-ers, too."

Maggie wasn't sure what she meant but didn't want to seem like a complete dunce, so she just nodded.

"So, what do you think happened to Templeton?"

"Maybe she found out he was a dog, or maybe he changed his mind and didn't want to be with her anymore. Either way, she was angry enough to stab him through his cheating heart."

Maggie did not point out that this gave Eva an excellent reason to have committed the murder herself. She tried to picture Eva sneaking into the library, luring Templeton down to the basement and stabbing him. Nah, it didn't work.

She supposed it was possible—anything was possible, after all—but Eva really struck her as the sort of flamboyant woman who would drive over a man if she was that angry at him. In fact, she'd probably run him down and then back up over him a few times to make sure she'd gotten the job done and, most likely, she'd do it with his own car.

"Next time you come in, Maggie, I will fix your hair," Eva said. "And I'll give you a discount."

"Can't argue with that," Joanne said.

Maggie forced a smile. For a discount, she might have to reassess her fear of Eva. The woman certainly knew her way around a pair of shears. Maybe it wouldn't be so bad.

Her cell phone sounded, and she fished it out of her bag.

"Where are you?" Max asked as soon as she opened it.

"I stopped to get Joanne," she said. "We're on our way."

"Well, get here already," he said. *Click.*

Huh! Maggie was not sure she was as fond of the uptight lawyerly attorney Max as she was ice cream cone Max.

"What's up?" Joanne asked.

"Max is having some sort of drama," she said. "We'd better hurry."

Maggie dialed Ginger's number as they hustled out of the Clip and Snip with a wave at Eva. The dark beauty watched them leave, and Maggie had a moment of doubt.

Was Eva capable of murder? As if reading her mind, the hairdresser gave her a small smile and turned away.

"Hello? Maggie?" Ginger's voice came out of her phone, and Maggie was forced to bring her attention back to the situation at hand.

"Ginger, what's the good word?" she asked.

"Don't have one. My Sister's Closet is a dead end," Ginger said. "They already sold out to Templeton. The deal was that they'd stay operational until the end of the summer, but now, with Templeton dead, I don't know if they'll stay open or have to close or what. I'll tell you more about it when we meet up, but I'd say they're in the clear, since their deal with him was hammered out months ago. Where are you?"

"Joanne and I just left the Clip and Snip—very interesting—and I had an enlightening chat with Jay at the Perk Up. We're walking to the Frosty Freeze to see Max. He keeps calling, and it sounds urgent."

"I'll meet you there," she said.

Maggie ended the call, and she and Joanne quickened their pace. The Frosty Freeze actually had a line outside the little window. About five people stood looking at the posted menu. A woman stood at the front with two children, a boy and a girl, looking irritated as the boy and girl took turns shoving each other and running away.

Maggie peeked in the little window and saw that no one was there.

The woman rapped on the window with her knuckles and hollered, "Hello?"

Maggie and Joanne exchanged a glance and hurried around the side of the building to the back entrance.

Maggie tried the doorknob. It was unlocked. She opened it and walked in.

"Max?" she called as she pulled the hat off of her head. "Max, are you here?"

There was a mumbled response.

The back of the Frosty Freeze was not nearly as appetizing as the glossy photos that decorated the front of the building.

Maggie and Joanne passed a small closet that was full of cleaning supplies and smelled faintly of ammonia. Next came the pantry, which was full of industrial-size boxes of napkins and sprinkles and all of the other yummies that go on top of ice cream. After that was the vintage walk-in freezer that kept the ice cream cold.

Finally they came to the closet that had been converted into an office. Max was sitting there, staring at the monitor of an ancient computer.

"Max, you have customers," Maggie said. She tossed her hat onto a nearby shelf and raked her hair with her fingers. "Get out there before Hugh finds out you're shirking."

Max turned a concerned gaze toward her. "That's going to be the least of his worries."

"What did you find?" Joanne asked.

"Check this out," Max said.

They crowded closer to his chair, and Max scooted out of his seat to let them have a better view.

"Hello?" an irate voice, the mother, called from the front.

"Go! We'll read while you help the customers," Maggie said.

Joanne sat in the seat. It was an e-mail correspondence

between Hugh Simpson and John Templeton. She scrolled down to the bottom of it to start at the beginning.

What started as a business proposition and then turned into a business transaction, with Hugh borrowing a large sum of money from Templeton, rapidly deteriorated into demands for payment from Templeton, which, judging by the responses from Hugh, were met with several profanity-laced threats. The last e-mail from Hugh, dated before Templeton was killed, gave a vivid although misspelled description of how exactly Hugh was going to eviscerate Templeton with an ice cream scoop.

Chapter 28

"Oh my," Joanne said.

"Oh my what?" Ginger appeared in the doorway, making both of them jump.

Maggie put her hand over her chest.

"What did I miss? You both look completely freaked out," Ginger said.

"Read this," Maggie said. She pointed to the computer, and Joanne rose so that Ginger could have her seat.

They stood silently as Ginger read. Max popped into the doorway just as Ginger turned away from the computer.

"Does the man really not have the brains to have deleted these messages?" Ginger asked. "I mean, if I threatened to do what he said he would do with an ice cream scoop and the guy turned up dead, well, I'd delete the message."

"He did," Max said.

"Then how did you find it?" Maggie asked.

"He uses a work station, client-based e-mail program, so even though he deleted it, it's retrievable from his hard disk."

"Oh," Maggie said. She had no idea what he was talking about, but the point was that he'd gotten the e-mail.

"So, do you think Hugh killed Templeton?" she asked.

"It sure sounds like it," Joanne said.

"I have to agree," Ginger said. "Can we print this?"

"I already did, but I feel terrible about it," Max said. "I mean, he's my boss. This is a total violation of his trust."

"But if he killed someone, then you have to do what's right, which means you have to turn that e-mail over to the police," Maggie said.

"Max!" a voice bellowed form outside. "Max!"

Max's eyes went round. "That's him!"

He frantically started punching keys on the computer, trying to erase the evidence.

"Why aren't you out front, Max?"

"I have to use the bathroom," Max yelled back. "He's going to come in. He can't find you three here. Hide."

Maggie looked around the tiny office.

"Where?" Ginger asked.

Max yanked the computer's plug out of the wall, shoved the sheaf of printed e-mails into Maggie's hands and started pushing them toward the door.

"The storeroom," he said.

Joanne hurried across the hall with Ginger and Maggie right behind her. The storeroom was barely big enough for one person to turn around in, so the three of them had to mash up against the wall while Max pushed the door shut.

As soon as he closed the door, they heard the back door open, and Hugh Simpson lumbered in.

"I don't pay you to go to the bathroom," he barked at Max. "And you'd better have washed your hands."

"Yes, sir," Max said.

Maggie held her breath as she heard one set of feet head to the front of the ice cream shop and another go into the office across the hall. When the door to the office shut, she slowly let out her breath.

She was wedged between Ginger and the door, and she didn't think she could move without tipping an entire stack of waffle cones.

"Now what do we do?" Joanne asked. Her voice was muffled, so Maggie assumed Joanne was as cramped as she was.

"I don't know, but I have to piddle," Ginger said. Then she giggled.

"Oh no, don't you start," Maggie hissed. Ginger had been like this since they were kids. She could never play hide-and-seek because she always had to go tinkle and she got the giggles.

It was the silent laughter that did it.

Ginger was trying to cork her giggle fit, but her shoulders were shaking, bumping against Joanne and Maggie and causing the Tupperware tubs of sprinkles to shake on their steel shelf.

"Stop it, Ginger," Maggie whispered.

But she felt her own laugh hiss out her nose right after she said it. The harder she tried to contain it, the more it wanted to erupt out of her, and she was forced to make noises like a cat coughing up a hairball as she tried to hold the laughter back.

Ginger's shoulders started shaking harder, and Joanne was making panting noises that Maggie knew were her attempts at silent laughter, which only made her own cat-gagging noises worse.

"I'm going to pee my pants," Ginger said between shoulder shakes, which only set Maggie and Joanne off again.

A door banged open in the hall and they all went still.

"Max!" Hugh bellowed.

"Yes, sir?" Max called from the front of the shop.

"There's something wrong with my computer. Would you look at it?"

"Yes, sir," he said. His voice was getting louder as he was walking toward them. "Could you, uh, watch the front while I do that?"

Hugh let out a sigh. "Sure. It's just dishing ice cream. It's not like I'm paying you to do brain surgery out there."

Hugh's footsteps got quiet. Maggie waited for Max to open the door, but he didn't.

"What do we do now?" Ginger hissed.

Maggie could hear Joanne shifting in the back. She bumped Ginger, who knocked into Maggie, who banged into the door with a thud. They all held their breaths, but no one came.

"What are you doing?" Maggie whispered.

"Weg crum," Joanne said.

"What?" Maggie and Ginger asked together.

They heard Joanne swallow, and then she said, "Leg cramp."

"Are you eating?" Ginger asked. She was trapped with

her arms pinned to her sides, and she could just turn her head to get a glance at Joanne behind her.

"There's a bag of marshmallows back here," Joanne said. "I couldn't resist."

The doorknob turned with the sound of metal clicking into metal. Someone was opening the door.

Chapter 29

Collectively, they all gasped and froze, as if the person opening the door would find it perfectly normal to see three grown women hiding in the supply cupboard if they weren't moving.

Maggie was wondering how good of an impersonation of a can of hot fudge sauce she could do when the door opened and Max's head appeared.

"What are you still doing here? Go!" he cried.

"Max!" Hugh called from in front.

Maggie sidled by Max with Ginger and Joanne hot on her heels. They were almost at the back door. She reached for the knob, quietly opened it and had just slipped through with Joanne and Ginger behind her when she glanced up and saw Summer Phillips standing right in front of her.

Summer was holding an enormous banana split. Maggie just had a chance to register her evil grin before the split slammed into her face with an icy punch to the nose and a sticky splat to her temple. In the ice cream sundae wars, Maggie had just been TKO'd.

Max, however, felt no sympathy for her plight. He gave Ginger and Joanne a shove, which pushed Maggie face-first into the gloating Summer's front bumper.

Summer leapt back with a shriek, but it was too late. Her turquoise, formfitting halter top was covered in whipped cream and fudge sauce. While Maggie used her fingers to scrape the banana and pineapple from her eyes, Ginger started bellowing at Summer and Joanne ran around the front of the building to grab a handful of napkins for Maggie.

As if Maggie's humiliation was not complete, at that moment one of the sheriff department's squad cars lurched into the parking lot and out stepped Sam Collins. She wondered if she were to lay down in the parking lot if she could be mistaken for a speed bump.

"Good afternoon, ladies." Sam strode forward. Although, she had to blink the whipped cream off her lashes, Maggie could still see the smile that tugged at the corner of his lips.

"It was a sneak attack," Ginger said. "Summer snuck up on Maggie and nailed her with the banana split. It was premeditated. It was assault . . ."

"With a deadly banana?" Sam asked.

Maggie wanted to kick him in the shins or maybe a little higher.

Joanne thrust a handful of napkins at her, and Maggie tried to wipe the sticky mess off her face, but little bits of paper napkin just got stuck to the goo, making a bad situation worse.

"That was payback," Summer said. "You cost me six hundred dollars in hair ex . . . accessories . . ."

"You mean extensions," Ginger cut in. Her brown skin was flushed with anger, and she was clenching her fist as if she was about to take a swing at Summer.

"Ginger and Joanne, why don't you go see if Max has a towel Maggie can use?" Sam asked.

They both looked at Maggie and dashed around the building in a sprint, confirming to Maggie that she looked even worse than she had supposed.

"Maggie, are you planning to press charges?" he asked her.

Much as Maggie loved the idea of having Summer locked up—oh, howdy, how she loved it!—she was honest enough to admit that she deserved the sundae smack-down at least a little.

"No, no charges," she said.

Summer looked triumphant and Maggie almost took it back, but Sam cut in and said, "Perhaps, it is best if you go now, Summer."

"If you say so, Sam," she said. "You're such a brave man to put yourself between me and someone who wants to cause me harm."

She shook out her fake blonde hair and batted her false eyelashes at him. Maggie felt her gag reflex kick in, but luckily she didn't actually puke. Summer sashayed away, making sure Sam got the best view of her posterior. Maggie was pleased to see that he didn't notice her seductive stroll, and instead turned his gaze on Maggie. Apparently, he was not as taken in by Summer's charms as she thought he was. *Hmm*.

Sam squinted at her face and then reached forward with

a finger. Maggie was proud of herself for not flinching when he dabbed his finger against her temple. When he pulled his finger back, it had something red on it. Maggie's eyes widened in alarm. Had Summer managed to cut her?

Sam popped his finger into his mouth and smiled.

"Raspberry sauce," he said. "My favorite."

"I hate you," she said.

"Aw, what's the matter?" he said. "Did Summer put you in a bad a la mode?"

Maggie closed her eyes, as if by sheer force of will she could make him disappear. When she opened her eyes, he was still there and he was laughing.

"I really, really hate you," she said.

"Now, there's no need to get all frosty," he said. He doubled over, and Maggie had to fight the urge to dump a sundae on him.

Mercifully, Joanne and Ginger arrived with a wet towel, and Maggie was able to look away from Sam and start to scour off the ick that covered her.

"So, what brings you three to the Freeze?" he asked.

It was an innocuous question, and they could have bluffed their way out of it by saying they'd come for ice cream, but Joanne, a terrible liar by nature, turned bright red and began to stammer.

"Uh . . . we . . . uh," she said.

"Had to get something from Max," Ginger said. "You know, just a thing."

Sam's face grew serious, and he looked at Maggie as if he considered her the ringleader.

"So, a thing, huh?" he asked.

Maggie glared over her towel at the other two. Clearly,

Josie Belle

these ladies were lacking in the fine art of keeping their lips zipped.

"Yeah," she said. "Just, you know, a bill for services rendered."

"Oh." He nodded.

Just then the door opened, and Max popped his head out.

"Maggie, are you okay?" he asked.

"I'm fine, Max," she said. "Don't worry about me. Don't you have customers to take care of?"

"Nah, having Hugh behind the counter scared everyone away."

"So, Max," Sam said, "I hear you're charging for your legal services now."

Max looked puzzled and Maggie took the opportunity to ball up her towel and fire it at his pie hole before he could utter a word.

Sam looked at her, and she said, "Thanks for the towel, Max. I'll bring that bill over to Claire asap."

Max lowered the towel and saw that Maggie was staring at him like a pointer dog at a fallen pheasant.

"Oh, yeah," he said. "Right. Thanks."

"Okay, well, this has been fun," she said. "Gotta go shower now."

Sam opened his mouth to say something, but she cut him off by raising up a hand. "Stop. Whatever you're about to say, just stop."

He pressed his lips together and looked down.

Maggie turned and walked away from the Frosty Freeze with Ginger and Joanne flanking her, as good wingmen should.

"So, that's it? You're just going to make like a banana

and split?" Sam called after her. Obviously he just couldn't contain himself. He sounded as if he were actually choking on his laughter.

Out of the corner of her eye, Maggie saw Ginger start to look back.

"No, don't look!" she said. "Let's try to maintain what little dignity we have left."

"What about the e-mails?" Joanne whispered.

"Not here," Maggie said. She clutched her purse a little closer to her side.

She knew Sam was too far away to hear them, but she couldn't help being a little paranoid.

"But shouldn't we give them to him?" Ginger asked.

"With Hugh right there?" Maggie turned and waved as they passed the front of the ice cream shop.

Hugh was standing in the Frosty Freeze frowning at them. He did not wave back. Probably, he thought they should buy an ice cream from him, but Maggie figured she had a built-in excuse, since Summer had ambushed her.

"Joanne, you go back to the deli. Don't say anything to Michael until I give you the all clear. We don't want Sam to find out what we did until I tell him. Okay?"

"What should I do?" Ginger asked.

"Go home and lay low," Maggie said. "And the same thing goes for you. Don't tell Roger anything. I know he and Sam are friends from their football days, and we can't risk him blabbing."

"What are you going to do?" Joanne asked.

"I'm going home to clean up," Maggie said. "Then I'm going to make copies of these e-mails and turn them over to Sam."

Both Ginger and Joanne looked at her as if they doubted her.

"What?" she asked.

"You hate Sam," Ginger said. They had made their way down the sidewalk to the corner and paused before More than Meats, Joanne and Michael's deli. "I have a hard time believing that you are willingly going to tell him anything."

Maggie opened her mouth to argue, but she knew Ginger was right. She really didn't see herself calling Sam willingly—ever, even with their current truce. That having been said, this was bigger than their past or her dislike. This was about Claire's life and the possibility that she could get out of jail sooner rather than later. Like it or not, Maggie had no choice. She was going to have to tell Sam what they'd found.

"I don't like it," Maggie conceded. "But I'll do the right thing."

"Good," Joanne said. "Because I am really bad at all of this. I'm going to have to avoid Michael all evening just to make sure I don't blab."

Maggie smiled at her. "I'll text you both as soon as I give Sam the papers."

Maggie gave Joanne an air hug, so that she didn't get her sticky with sundae residue. Ginger gave Joanne a big squeeze, and they walked in the direction of Ginger's house. Ginger turned down the side street that led to her historic house, and again Maggie offered up an air hug.

"Good luck," Ginger said.

"Thanks," Maggie blew out a breath and continued on around the square and down the side street that would lead to her neighborhood.

She was only a short way from her house when she noticed a car was slowly coming up behind her on the left. She didn't want to turn, because she felt it would be betraying the fact that she knew she was being followed. No, she was going to try to play it cool.

With her heart pounding in her chest like a bass drum, she wondered if it was Hugh. Had he figured out what they'd done? Had Max blabbed? Was he coming to kill her, too?

She glanced up the street and wondered if she could outrun him, or if that would force his hand and he'd run her down with his car. Decisions, decisions.

Chapter 30

"Maggie! Hey, Maggie!"

That was not Hugh Simpson's voice. Maggie whipped her head around and saw Sam peering at her through the open passenger's window from his spot in the driver's seat of his squad car.

She stopped short and let out a relieved breath. Sam stopped the car to watch her.

"Are you all right?" he asked. "You look a little freaked out."

"I'm fine," she said. "What happened? Did you think of another pun that you just had to use?"

He grinned, but when he saw her scowl, he quickly forced it back into a somber expression.

"Actually, I just came to offer you a ride," he said. "I figured walking all sticky like that had to be gross, so I thought it would be nice of me to offer you a lift."

"It would be nice," Maggie said. "Making it completely out of character for you."

"Aw, come on," he said. "I'm not that bad."

She refrained from comment. He pushed open the passenger door and it swung wide to the curb. The thought of arriving that much sooner to her shower was more temptation than Maggie could resist. She climbed into the car and shut the door.

"Excellent," he said. He pulled away from the curb. "Also, I wanted to ask you about the papers you took from Hugh Simpson's office."

Maggie's hearing went fuzzy. She could not have heard that. No, how could he possibly know about that, unless . . . Max! Damn it. He wasn't supposed to say anything until she'd made a copy of the papers.

"I don't know what you're talking about," she said.

Sam sighed. "Really? You really want to play it that way?"

"What way?" Maggie said. Back in the good old days, her mother had taught her a very valuable life lesson: When all else fails, play dumb.

When times were tough, Maggie's mother would occasionally float a check at the grocery store, just to keep the family fed, and the bank would invariably call to chastise her. Maggie's mother always played stupid with a bucketful of charm, and Mr. Costas, the bank manager, always forgave her.

The money was always repaid to the bank as soon as Maggie's mother got paid for her work as a secretary at the car dealership in Dumontville, and she kept food on the table. She wasn't proud of what she had to do, but she had drilled it into Maggie that sometimes playing dumb could help you get out of a tough situation.

"I'm not buying it, Maggie," Sam said as he pulled up to her house. "You and I both know that you were not at the Frosty Freeze getting ice cream—well, at least not to eat."

Maggie scowled.

"What exactly did Max say to you?" she asked.

"That he found incriminating e-mails on Hugh's computer and that he thought I should read them. Oh, and that you had them in your purse."

"I really need to talk to him about knowing when to keep his yap shut," Maggie said. She pushed open her door.

"Oh, don't be too hard on him," Sam said. He reached over the backseat and handed Maggie her hat, which she had left in the Frosty Freeze. "He was a little freaked out, given that I went into Hugh's office to talk to him about his account of your ice cream—uh—incident and found your hat."

"Hmm." Maggie took the hat and strode up the walkway to her house.

"Um, Maggie, the papers?" Sam said.

She turned to look at him. She didn't think he'd wrestle her purse out of her arms to get them, but then again, she wasn't so sure.

"Would you like some strawberry rhubarb pie?" she asked. "I made it fresh this morning."

Sam narrowed his eyes at her. "There you go, being nice to me again. Summer's ice cream assault must have given you a brain freeze."

"Personal differences aside, I know we're on the same team," Maggie said. "Come on in. I'll clean up and give you the papers."

"And pie?" he clarified.

"Yes, pie, too," she said.

She led the way into the house with Sam behind her. The house was quiet, so she assumed that Sandy and Josh had gone to the park. Josh did love to feed the ducks.

Maggie led the way into the kitchen. She handed Sam a plate and a fork and lifted the cover off the pie plate.

"Help yourself," she said.

"Where are you going?" he asked.

"I have to clean up before I go mental," she said. "I'll be right back."

He didn't say anything about her still having her purse under her arm, and Maggie didn't feel the need to point it out. Confident that she had distracted him with the pie, she hurried down the hall into the small office.

The printer for the computer was also a scanner and copy machine. She wasted no time in turning it on and, while it warmed up, she pulled the sheaf of papers from her purse.

She had just put the third page in the machine when Sam appeared in the door.

"Clearly, you think I am a moron," he said.

Maggie noted he was still working on his dish of pie. Best to take the offensive.

"Do you always wander around people's houses?" she asked.

"Only when they go to clean up, and I don't hear water running but I do hear the sound of a copy machine," he said. He put his fork on the plate and held out his free hand. "Game over."

Maggie scowled. She handed him the stack of papers.

"The one in the machine and the copies, too," he said.

She lifted the lid with a huff of disgust and handed him all of the papers.

"Thank you," he said.

"What are you going to do with them?" she asked.

"Read them," he said.

He turned and left the office, heading back to the kitchen. Maggie had assumed he'd leave now that he had what he wanted, but instead he passed through the kitchen to the sun porch and took a seat on the wrought-iron furniture.

"What are you doing?" she asked. She knew her tone was unfriendly, but she couldn't help but feel that Sam Collins was getting entirely too comfortable in her house.

"I'm going to read and finish my pie," he said. "Go ahead and clean up. We can talk more when you're done."

Maggie went to run her fingers though her hair and realized that she couldn't. The sundae toppings had hardened. For the first time since the incident, she wondered how bad she looked.

She looked at him suspiciously. He seemed to read her mind.

"I promise I won't move from my seat."

"I don't trust you," she said.

"On my badge," he said. "I swear."

That gave Maggie pause. For however much she knew him to be a big, fat liar, she also knew that he had been an excellent detective in Richmond. Maggie knew he valued his job above all else.

"Okay, then," she said. She turned and left the porch, hurrying to her bedroom, where she shut and locked the door. Her room was done in shades of cobalt blue and white, and it immediately soothed her. She grabbed fresh clothes out of her dresser and headed to the master bathroom.

One glance at her reflection in the full-length mirror and she had to stifle a scream.

Her mascara was smeared, giving her a sunken-eyed look that she was pretty sure would scare off a zombie. Her auburn hair was caked with hot fudge sauce and melted whipped cream. A streak of strawberry ice cream had hardened on one side of her face and a maraschino cherry was stuck in her hair just above her ear.

She looked like she'd had a brawl with the Good Humor ice cream man and had been beaten severely. She sighed and turned the tap in the shower to scalding. She knew she could wash away the remnants of the sundae, but she feared her dignity was forever lost.

Sam was sitting in the same spot on the sun porch, but now he had company. Mr. Tumnus had curled up in his lap, and Sam was gently rubbing his head while the cat purred as loudly as a diesel engine.

"Making friends, I see," Maggie said as she took the seat across from him. She continued to towel dry her hair, hoping that after two washings she'd gotten all of the sticky out.

Sam looked up at her and tipped his head to the side.

"What shampoo is that?" he asked.

"Some generic brand," she said with a shrug.

"It smells like lime and coconut," he said. "It's nice."

Maggie felt her face grow warm, and she rubbed her hair with renewed vigor.

"So, what do you make of the e-mails?" she asked.

"He certainly sounds like he had the potential to commit

murder," Sam said. Then he shook his head. "Who would have thought it of Hugh Simpson?"

"Or of any of them," Maggie added.

"What do you mean?" he asked.

"Well, you know, all of the people who took loans from John Templeton have good reason to want him dead," she said.

Sam's blue gaze sharpened like a laser pointer, and Maggie knew she had just said too much. *Damn it!*

"Maggie, what exactly have you been up to?" he asked.

"Nothing," she said. "Just talking to people."

"Why?" he asked.

"Oh, a smart detective like you already knows, I'm sure," Maggie said. "I'm just trying to gather the facts."

"So, I figured," he said. "But what concerns me is whether you've compromised my investigation or not."

"Oh, be serious. How could my talking to a few townspeople affect your investigation?" she said.

"A few townspeople?" he asked. He sat forward, much to the ire of Mr. Tumnus, who hopped off his lap while casting a dirty look at Maggie as if it were her fault, which she supposed it sort of was. "Maggie, exactly whom have you spoken to about this?"

"No one," she said. "Not really."

"I want to know exactly who you talked to and what was said," he commanded. He had his cop face on, and Maggie knew there would be no playing dumb to get out of this.

"All right, fine," she said. She started from Ginger's list of local businesses that had taken money from Templeton, and then she gave the short version about how they had all picked one of Templeton's clients to question.

"Of course, the e-mail pretty much clinches that Hugh is the one who did it," she said. "I mean, he straight-up says he's going to kill Templeton in those."

Sam was gazing out the window across her backyard while he contemplated all that she had told him. "Not necessarily," he said. "The thrust of the knife indicates it was overhand, which is more common in female assailants."

Maggie gasped. "So, you think it was a woman."

Sam's eyes snapped from the window to her. "I didn't say that. In fact, forget I said anything at all."

"Do you suppose it was Eva?" she asked, completely disregarding what he'd just said.

"I mean, she was so angry that he had dumped her," she said. "And she definitely thinks he dumped her for Claire, which would give her a reason to lure him to the library and kill him there, making it look like it had been Claire."

"Templeton was a womanizer," Sam said. "He didn't have a thing with just Eva, he was also involved with Sum—"

Abruptly he cut himself off, but Maggie latched on to the beginning of the name with a gasp.

"You were going to say *Summer*, weren't you?" she asked. "He had a thing with Summer, too. That means she could be the killer."

"Now, Maggie," he said, holding up his hands as if to slow her down. "I didn't say that. I said *some* as in *somebody else*."

Maggie shot him a look of disgust. "Oh, please, just admit it. He was seeing Summer, too, wasn't he?"

"He was seeing somebody else, but I am not at liberty to say who, and I shouldn't have said as much as I did," he said.

Maggie wanted to growl in frustration. But one look at the stubborn set of Sam's chin, and she knew he wasn't going to give her any more information. *Darn it!*

"Well, I know that Eva was seeing him," she said. "She was very forthcoming about it, which you wouldn't think she would be if she was the killer."

Maggie thought that, maybe if she kept talking, she could get Sam to spill more information. She didn't notice the muscle clenching and unclenching in his cheek as she continued.

"I really thought she'd be more a crime-of-passion type and less premeditated, though, you know?" she asked.

"I understand the crime-of-passion part," Sam said. The sarcasm in his tone brought Maggie's attention back to him.

"Now, listen, Maggie," he said. "The person who killed Templeton is desperate. They tried to frame Claire, and they're obviously capable of murder. You need to butt out of this, for your own good."

"Do you really think the murderer would kill again?" Maggie asked.

"At this point, they have nothing to lose," Sam said. "So, no more asking questions, am I clear? I want you to let it lie."

"But—"

"No!" Sam roared. He stood up and glared down at her, looking as stormy as yesterday's thundercloud. "No buts. You are to stay away from this case and not ask any more questions."

"You don't have to yell," she said. "There's nothing wrong with my hearing."

"Really?" he asked. "Because you seem incapable of following the most basic instructions. Now I want you to back off."

"What if I just happen to find out something relevant?" she asked.

He blew out a stream of breath that sounded like a steam engine releasing pressure.

"Woman, you are the single most infuriating human being I have ever had the misfortune to encounter."

He stuffed the papers into his back pocket and took his plate and his fork into the kitchen and rinsed them in the sink. Maggie followed and, when he was finished, she took them from him and put them in the dishwasher.

When she straightened back up, Sam was watching her with an intensity that left her throat dry.

He reached out his hand and brushed one thick lock of her hair back behind her ear. Then he shook his head in wonder.

"You have been winding me up since I was three years old," he said. "And just like then, I don't know if I want to strangle you or kiss you."

Chapter 31

"Aunt Maggie, we're home," Sandy called as she and Josh tumbled in through the front door.

Maggie ripped her gaze away from Sam's and was surprised the action didn't make a noise like unfastening Velcro. She swallowed, trying to get some moisture in her throat so she could speak.

Thankfully, Josh made a beeline for her on his chubby little legs and threw himself at her. Maggie reached down and scooped him up, propping him on her hip.

"I got wormie," Josh said. His eyes were huge as he tried to impart the enormity of this discovery to Maggie.

"You did, huh?" she asked. Her gaze avoided Sam as she held Josh between them as if he were her personal shield.

"The rain last night must have brought the worms all above ground," Sandy said. She held up a paper cup. "We have a whole bunch of new friends in here."

Josh was staring at Sam. Sam smiled at him, and Josh considered him for a moment before grinning back.

"Worms!" he said to Sam, and Sam chuckled.

"Worms are good," Sam said back.

"In the garden," Maggie added. "Not your room."

Josh heaved a put-upon sigh as if he had expected this response from her. "Okay. Garden, Mommy."

He wiggled in Maggie's arms, and she let him down so he could introduce his friends to their new home. Maggie watched him scramble to the back door. She didn't think she imagined the significant look Sandy gave her as she passed Maggie to follow her son.

"Nice to see you again, Sam," Sandy called as they slipped out the back door.

"You, too," he said.

Not wanting to get sucked into another bout of awkward, Maggie led the way to the front door and held it open for him.

"I'll have your word, Maggie," he said.

"What?"

"Your word that you'll stay away from this investigation," he said.

She got the distinct feeling that he wouldn't leave if she didn't cough up a promise.

With a sigh as deep as Josh's at letting go of his worm friends, she said, "Fine. I promise I won't ask any more questions."

Sam frowned at her as if examining her statement for loopholes. Finally, he gave her a slow nod.

"I'm going to hold you to that," he said. "I don't want to see you hurt, Maggie."

It was on the tip of her tongue to point out the irony of him not wanting to see her hurt when he had crushed her twenty-four years ago, but she didn't. She just nodded and waved him through the door.

"Good-bye, Sam," she said. She did not wait for a reply, instead shutting the door firmly behind him.

Maggie went to visit Claire the next morning. Her preliminary hearing was the next day, and Maggie knew that Claire was getting nervous. She wanted to give her a pep talk. Since they had found so many people with motives to kill Templeton, things were looking up for Claire, even if it didn't feel that way.

"I want a shower," Claire said.

"They haven't let you shower?" Maggie asked. "That's barbaric."

"No, I'm allowed a few minutes to shower," Claire said. "But I'm not allowed a razor, and its harsh soap and shampoo. So, I'm hairy and I don't smell right. Thank God there's no mirror in here."

"You look fine," Maggie lied. "Better than fine, really."

"And that's why you're my friend," Claire said. "You're a terrible liar, but you sure give it a try."

Maggie looked at Claire, her bright and lovely friend, and tried to find something to say that would lift her spirits. But other than the fact that there were some other solid suspects, she had a whole lot of nothing.

"Have you and Max worked out a strategy for court tomorrow?"

"Yeah, he's been great," Claire said. "His brain is

absolutely amazing. I can't believe how well he knows the ins and outs of criminal law in Virginia. Now, so long as he doesn't show up in shorts and a Yoo-hoo T-shirt, I think we might stand a chance."

"Oh, I didn't even think of that," Maggie said. "We need to get him a suit."

"So, change of subject," Claire said. "Are you really going to butt out of the investigation?"

"I said I wouldn't ask questions," Maggie said.

"I can't believe Sam accepted that for a promise."

"Me either. Obviously, the man is a terrible judge of character."

They both chuckled.

"Well, listen, I'm going to get Max and make sure he has the appropriate attire for court tomorrow," Maggie said. "I do think he can argue a good case for your innocence, and we'll figure out how to make it happen. Okay?"

Claire looked doubtful, but she nodded. "Max brought me *Gone with the Wind* to read. So, my mind will remain occupied."

"Good." Maggie reached through the bars and gave Claire's hands a squeeze. "I'll check in later."

Maggie's first stop was Max's house. Thankfully, he didn't have to work this morning, because after yesterday's revelations about Hugh, Maggie was sort of nervous to go to the Frosty Freeze, and she didn't want Max to be anywhere near it either.

Then again, Sam had said that Templeton's chest wound had been overhand, which indicated a female assailant.

Lying in bed last night, Maggie had convinced herself that Summer Phillips could be the killer. Maggie had seen

Summer when she came at her with that sundae, her face twisted with rage. Yes, she could absolutely see Summer as the killer.

That she-devil could have stabbed Templeton and left him in the basement of the library to die. Wasn't Summer the one who had been going around telling everyone that the body had been naked and wearing high heels? It was the perfect cover to be the person spreading misinformation, obviously a ploy to make herself look innocent.

As she walked from the jail to Max's studio apartment above the town garage, Maggie mulled all that she had learned over the past few days. She felt as if she must know who the real killer was, but she had met so many people with a reason to kill Templeton, she was hard-pressed to pick just one.

A rickety set of wooden stairs ran up the back of the brick building to Max's place. His door was weathered and badly in need of a coat of paint. Maggie knocked hard against the door. A moment or two passed before Max pulled the door open.

"Hi, Maggie," he said. He didn't seem surprised to see her. He was wearing his usual cargo shorts and a tie-dyed Grateful Dead T-shirt in vivid shades of blue, red and yellow.

"Max, do you own a suit?" she asked.

Max looked at her in puzzlement.

"Max, you need a suit."

"I owned one once," he said. "I had to wear it when I was valedictorian."

"Well, dig it out so we can be sure it still fits," Maggie said. "You need to look professional for court tomorrow."

"Oh, sure, okay," he said.

He turned and led the way to a dresser that was tucked against the far wall.

Because it was an attic apartment, the ceiling sloped down on both sides, so if you left the central part of the apartment, you had to hunch over or risk smacking your head.

Maggie hunched down and followed Max to the dresser. He squatted as he rifled through the bottom drawer. Finally, he pulled out a charcoal gray suit. It looked promising—until he unfolded it. Aside from the many wrinkles and creases from being stuffed in a dresser, it looked suspiciously short.

"Try it on," Maggie said. "At the very least we need to get it pressed."

"Now?" Max looked at her in horror.

"I'll turn my back," she said.

Max blew out a breath in a way that said *unhappy*, but he didn't protest anymore.

Maggie went and stood at the tiny breakfast bar in the mini kitchen. It was stacked several feet deep in legal paperwork and reference books. His laptop was open, and it appeared he was hard at work on trial prep.

"All right," he said.

Maggie turned around and blinked. Although he was as skinny as he had been when he'd last worn the suit, and the shoulders and the waist fit, the pants were several inches too short, and so were the jacket sleeves. Also, he had the tie-dye on under the suit jacket.

"You've had a growth spurt since you wore that last, yes?"

"I think so. It was six years ago," he said.

"Max, we need to go get you a new one," she said.

He looked horrified.

"Don't worry. I'm paying for it," she said.

"But I don't have time," he said. "I'm in the middle of preparing my closing. I'm working on three different ones, depending upon what the prosecutor throws at me. I can't take time out to go shopping."

"Max, presentation is critical," Maggie said. "Now, we're just going down the street to the second-hand shop. I know they have a ton of suits, and I'm sure we'll find you one. Give me half an hour."

Max looked miserable, but he reluctantly agreed. "But only because I look like Pee-wee Herman in this."

The thrift store My Sister's Closet was in the center of town, nestled between the dry cleaner and a yarn store. Ginger had told Maggie that the store had already done a deal with Templeton and that they were planning to stay open until the end of the summer. She could only hope that was true and that they had some men's suits still in stock.

The window still had mannequins on display and one was wearing a very fetching aqua chemise dress that caused Maggie to slow her pace, wondering if it might be in her size.

"Maggie, focus!" Max said.

"Oh, sorry," she said.

He pulled open the door, allowing her to enter first. Trudi was at the front counter, ringing up a sale to Tyler Fawkes.

"Hi, Maggie," she said. "I'll be right with you."

"No worries," Maggie said. "I'm going to browse suits with Max."

"Help yourself," Trudi said. She peered over her reading glasses at Max. "I think there's a navy blue pinstripe that might fit him."

Max was rifling through the rack of suits. Maggie had to admit that Trudi had some amazing stuff, all sorts of designer labels from high-end shops for a tenth of the price.

"Hey, I like this one," Max said.

Maggie took her eyes off of the rack of dresses behind her and turned to see Max holding up a black suit that had flames shooting up from the cuffs and the hem.

"Do you want the judge to think you're Satan?" she asked.

"You have to admit it's badass," he said.

"You got first part of that right," she said.

Max sighed and put it back. They flipped through the rack together until Maggie came across the pinstripe suit she was sure Trudi had been talking about. She held it up to Max. He looked aggrieved.

"I'll look like an accountant," he said. "A dead one."

Maggie ducked her head to keep from laughing. There was no point in encouraging his whining. She grabbed a dress shirt and a tie and added them to his bundle.

"Go try it on," she said. "The dressing room is right over there."

Max went into the curtained closet, and Maggie decided to kill time by checking out the aqua number in the window. While she fingered the price tag, Trudi joined her.

"I love that little chemise," Trudi said. "It would really compliment your skin tone."

"Thanks," Maggie said. "But I can't afford a Maggy London, even at a resale price."

"Well, keep an eye out," Trudi said. "I have no idea what is going to happen to all of this merchandise now that I am leaving."

"So, you're really going?"

"Yep, Jacob and I bought our little retirement house in Florida, and we're leaving St. Stanley," Trudi said. "I have no idea what Templeton's company will do with my little storefront now that he's dead, but I'm out for sure."

"Good for you," Maggie said. "But I'll miss shopping here."

"Maybe you should buy the store," Trudi said. "If they offer it up for sale, you would be a natural. You're so good at bargain hunting, and selling is the easy part. When you pick out the good stuff for resale, the items just sell themselves."

"I don't know," Maggie said. "I'd have to give up working for Dr. Franklin, and I'm not sure I have the stamina to own my own business."

"The only part that would do you in would be dealing with Summer Phillips," Trudi said. "Since she lost all of her money to her last husband—and her romance with Templeton didn't work out—she positively haunts my shop. She has me put away all of the high-end designer stuff for her, and then she tries to haggle down the prices. What she doesn't know is that I only put away the butt-ugly stuff that I can't sell to anyone else."

"Oh, right there, game over," Maggie said. "I can't have Summer Phillips entering any shop I would own."

Trudi laughed. "Well, if you own it, you could ban her."

"So, is she really broke?" Maggie asked doubtfully. She just couldn't imagine it.

"Yes, her husband cleaned her out."

Maggie felt the world tip a little bit on its axis. This was big news in the Motives to Kill Templeton department. She couldn't help but think that this would certainly give Summer a reason to commit murder, especially if she had thought he was her ticket out of the poorhouse and he reneged.

"It was a nasty divorce," Trudi said. "I heard her husband had photographic evidence of her and the lifeguard at the country club pool doing the breast stroke—but not in the pool, if you get my drift."

"Trudi, I'm shocked!" Maggie teased through her laughter. Then she held up her hand for a high five. "Good one."

Abruptly, the curtain to the dressing room was flung back, and Max stepped out.

For a second, Maggie didn't recognize him. He looked taller and more mature. Then his hair flopped forward and the image was ruined.

"This is going to work," Trudi said. She checked him over. "The pants need to be taken in, but the shoulders are a perfect fit. You know, they can do the tailoring at the dry cleaner next door."

"Perfect," Maggie said. "What do you think, Max?"

He studied himself in the mirror, turning this way and that. Maggie fished a hair band out of her purse and fastened his hair at the nape of his neck. It was the first time she'd ever clearly seen his face. Despite the acne, he had very handsome features. She also redid his tie, which looked more like a square knot than a Windsor knot.

"Not bad," he said.

"Not bad?" Maggie asked. "You look great. You look like Maxwell Button, Esquire, now."

"Thanks." He flushed a bright red.

Maggie looked him over one more time. "Uh, except for the shoes."

All three of them looked down at Max's Converse sneakers.

"Go find a pair of shoes," Maggie ordered. "On the rack over in the corner."

"No sneakers?" he asked. "Really?"

"Really."

He turned and headed toward the back with a put-upon sigh.

"Go for brown, and make sure they fit," Maggie called after him.

"So, he's really going to court tomorrow to represent Claire Freemont?" Trudi asked.

"Yes, unless the killer is caught in the next twenty-four hours."

Trudi lowered her voice, and asked, "Do you think he can handle it?"

"I wouldn't trust this case to anyone else, and neither would Claire," Maggie said.

"Tell Claire I'm pulling for her," Trudi said. "I never believed that she could have murdered Templeton. You know, when I was looking for ways to promote the shop, she gave me loads of books on marketing and introduced me to a small-business mentor."

"She is an amazing librarian," Maggie said. "St. Stanley would certainly feel her loss, but that's not going to happen."

Trudi gave Maggie's arm a squeeze. She wasn't sure if it was in reassurance or agreement, but she patted Trudi's hand all the same.

Max found a pair of Cole Haan brown wingtips with just a small scuff on the heel. They added an inch to his height and, with his hair pulled back, he was barely recognizable.

Maggie paid for the ensemble. A Brooks Brothers suit and Cole Haan shoes for fifty dollars! Trudi said it was because she didn't know anyone else as skinny as Max and she'd never unload the suit, but Maggie suspected this was her way of helping them help Claire.

Max wore the suit out of the shop. Maggie didn't think it was her imagination that he seemed to be walking a tad taller than usual, and it wasn't the shoes either.

"How are you feeling about tomorrow?" she asked.

"Scared to death," he said, and he deflated like a helium balloon having its air sucked out.

"Would you care to try a little experiment?" she asked.

"I really have to get back," he said.

Maggie consulted her watch. "I've only borrowed you for twenty minutes; I have ten left. Come on."

She took him by the arm and led him across the town square to the Perk Up.

"Maggie, the last thing I need is coffee," he said. "I'm already so amped on energy drinks that my heart will probably explode out of my chest."

"Then we'll get you a decaf," she said.

She pulled open the door and pushed him inside ahead of her. The place had a few more people than usual but wasn't exactly the picture of a bustling coffee shop.

She brought him up to the counter at the front and was a little disappointed to find Gwen there. Jay was infinitely friendlier, but no matter.

"Hi, Gwen," she said. "May I have a decaf cup of coffee for my friend and a café latte for me?"

Gwen glanced at her over the counter. "For here or to go?"

"Here, please."

"Do you want cream and sugar in the decaf, Mr. . . . ?" she asked.

Max looked behind him to see who she was talking to, and Maggie nudged him. "She means you."

"Oh, yes please," he said.

"I'm sorry," Maggie said. "Gwen, this is Maxwell. Maxwell, Gwen owns the Perk Up."

"Nice to meet you," Gwen said. "Are you new in town?"

"Me?" he asked. He looked incredulously at Maggie. Gwen didn't recognize him. "Um, I, well, I'm just passing through."

"Maxwell is an attorney. He is helping with Claire's trial."

"Seems to me they ought to throw the book at her," Gwen said. She still didn't recognize Max, and he and Maggie shared a wide-eyed glance while she turned away from them to fuss with their coffees.

"What makes you say that, Gwen?" Max asked. Maggie noticed he'd made his voice sound a bit deeper.

Gwen was scooping the steamed milk onto Maggie's latte and didn't look up.

"It's not brain surgery," she said. "The man was stabbed with her cake knife in her library with her book lying next to him. It seems reasonable to me that the killer has been caught. I don't see why they need to go wasting taxpayer money investigating a case that is closed."

Max frowned at her. "It does seem to be a done deal, doesn't it?"

"Yes, it does," Gwen said. She turned and put the two cups in front of them.

"Maggie," Max's voice cracked with emotion. "I have to get back to the books. I have to study up. I'm supposed to work tonight, and if I'm going to be able to give Claire my best, I have to get to it."

"Relax, Max," Maggie said.

"Max?" Gwen gasped, staring at him in his suit. "You're the kid from the ice cream stand. Oh, my word, so it really is true? You're defending Claire? Oh my God! She's a dead woman walking."

"Gwen!" Maggie snapped. "That was uncalled for."

"Sorry, but how old are you kid? Twelve?" Gwen asked.

"Please put these in cups to go," Maggie said. "I've changed my mind, we're leaving."

Gwen shrugged, and Maggie could see the ghost of a smile on her lips.

"Listen, Max, let's leave the suit at the dry cleaners for tailoring, and then I'll drop it off at the Frosty Freeze tonight when it's ready," she said.

Max looked worse than a deflated balloon now: He looked like he'd been popped, and Maggie had to resist the urge to leap over the counter and kick Gwen's behind.

Gwen handed them paper cups with their coffee, and Maggie paid her.

"Sorry," Gwen said. "I didn't know he was so sensitive."

"No, it's my fault," Maggie said. She had thought not being recognized would give Max a confidence boost, and it had. She just hadn't expected it to backfire so severely.

They stopped at the dry cleaner where Mrs. Kellerman

measured Max and agreed to have the suit ready by the end of the day.

They parted at the steps to his place, and Maggie asked, "Are you going to be all right?"

"Yeah, I'm good, really good." Then he gave her a small smile, and said, "Well, at least I'll *look* good tomorrow."

Maggie gave him a hug, and said, "I'll see you later. Go study, but don't worry. You're going to do just fine."

Max looked like he desperately wanted to believe her, but just didn't.

Chapter 32

Maggie left Max and walked over to the police station. She wanted to tell Claire what she had learned from Trudi, and she also thought it might do her some good to tell Sam about it, too. Surely, he couldn't get mad at her for that. It's not like she had asked Trudi to tell her about Summer's impoverished situation.

Maggie arrived at the sheriff's department to find that the crotchety older deputy, Deputy Crosthwaite, was the only one on duty.

"Hi, I'd like to see Claire Freemont, please."

"No."

"Excuse me?" Maggie said.

Deputy Crosthwaite glanced up from the newspaper he had spread over his desk. "You hard of hearing?" he asked. Then he shouted, "No! No one gets back there. Sheriff's orders."

"But I need to talk to her," Maggie spluttered.

The spindly old man shrugged. Not his problem.

"How about Sheriff Collins?" she asked. "Is he available?"

"Nope, he's out," he said.

It was times like this that Maggie really wished she were the sort of woman who could throw a hissy fit to get what she wanted. It just wasn't in her DNA, however.

"Fine. Can I leave him a note?" she asked. "Will you be certain that he gets it? It's very important."

"Yeah, sure, very important," the deputy muttered.

Maggie dug a pen and paper out of her purse. She had to write on the back of a 20-percent-off coupon from the car wash, which about killed her to give up, but she did it anyway.

She leaned against the desk and tapped the pen against her lips. What to write? That was the question. The simple fact was that she was now sure that Summer Phillips was the killer. Why? Well, she was a woman, so the overhand thrust of the knife fit. Templeton had broken up with her, so there was a crime of passion in the making: a woman scorned and all that. Then there was the location of the crime, something that had always bugged Maggie.

Why had the killer chosen the basement of the library? But then, she realized today, it was a perfect pick for Summer. Why? Because twenty-four years ago when Maggie had her heart cut out of her chest and served up on a platter, it was because Summer Phillips had lured Sam Collins into the basement of the library and seduced him, and Maggie had walked in on them. That had been the evil genius of Summer's plan: She'd had one of Sam's friends tell Maggie that Sam was down there waiting for her and Maggie had gone to find him like a lamb to the slaughter.

Add to the facts that Summer was broke and out to get revenge on both Templeton and the woman she believed he was leaving her for—which would be Claire—and Maggie now had no doubt that Summer had killed Templeton in the library basement. She used Claire's cake knife, and then, probably to make the scene a perfect setup, she had tossed Claire's copy of *The House of Mirth* in as well.

Maggie stared at the paper until she started to see spots. She didn't know how to phrase it. She and Sam had never talked about her walking in on him and Summer. He had come to see her the next day, and she had refused to talk to him. He left for college the day after that, and she had only caught the occasional glimpse of him when he'd come back to visit his parents in St. Stanley. She wondered now if she should have let him explain what had happened.

She shook her head. It didn't matter. It was the past. The only thing that mattered now was getting Claire out of jail and Summer in.

Finally, Maggie decided her best format would be clear, concise bullet points. Once she was done, she folded up the note and handed it to Deputy Crosthwaite.

He grumbled at her, but she saw him put it in what appeared to be the sheriff's inbox. It would have to do.

Maggie lingered as long as she could, but finally she had to leave for home so she could grab her blue paisley coupon holder, Old Blue, and hit the grocery store. Today was triple coupons, and if she didn't get a move on, all the good stuff would be gone.

As she drove home, her mind spun from the high possibility that Summer was Templeton's killer to thinking about what it would be like to own her own resale shop. My Sister's Closet had been an institution in St. Stanley since Trudi had moved here fifteen years ago. It would be such a shame to lose it.

She pictured Summer in the orange jumpsuit Claire had been forced to wear, and she smiled. Then she wondered how different medical billing could be from running a consignment shop.

No, no, she had to stop thinking about it. She liked working for Dr. Franklin, and she liked her life just as it was. Then why did the thought of unlocking the door to a place that was all her own hold so much appeal?

Maggie shook her head. Obviously, the strain of the past few days had wreaked havoc on her nerves. And she was probably having a midlife crisis. It was best just to let it go. Except she didn't.

She had lunch with Sandy and Josh and then went grocery shopping. While standing in the frozen vegetable aisle, she got so lost in thought reconfiguring the shop in her mind—she'd always thought the shoes should be near the front of the store—that she completely forgot what she was doing until a not-very-subtle cough sounded behind her.

"Maggie, are you taking root there?"

Maggie turned to find Bill Parsons leaning on his cart staring at her in irritation.

"Oh, sorry, Bill," she said. She moved to the side to give him access to the bagged broccoli. "Can I ask you something?"

"You can ask," he said.

Bill was a St. Stanley son, born seventy years before in

the county hospital; he had never left St. Stanley, not even for a vacation. He did not like to leave his zip code, as it made him edgy.

Although he was known for being as cantankerous as a rooster after sunrise, Maggie thought he might offer valuable insight into her dilemma. Or, more accurately, there was no one else present to ask.

"Do you think I'd be a good owner of the secondhand store My Sister's Closet? You know the one . . ."

"Yeah, I know it," he interrupted.

He picked out a bag of broccoli and another of spinach and plopped them in his cart. Then he turned and looked Maggie up and down.

"You're not going to raise the prices, are you?"

"No."

"You're not going to sissify it with a lot of pink colors and girly stuff, are you?"

"No."

"You aren't stupid, are you?"

"No."

"Well, then, it should be all right," he said. He pushed his cart away, moving down the aisle in a "this conversation is over" move that Maggie had to admire.

She tossed the quickly defrosting bag of broccoli into her cart and made her way to the checkout. Maggie Gerber, a shop owner. She felt her insides buzzing with an excitement she didn't think she could ignore.

The buzz lasted until she got to the parking lot of Santana's grocery store to find Summer Phillips leaning on her Volvo.

Maggie did a quick check of her canvas tote bags. She

Josie Belle

could slam Summer with the bag of broccoli, but the pot roast probably would have a better impact—although she hated to waste a fine cut of meat that she'd gotten on sale.

"Nice parking job, Gerber." Summer sneered as she pointed out that Maggie's car was almost on the white line that designated the parking spot.

"Really?" Maggie asked. "You're reduced to harassing me about my parking?"

She moved around Summer, opened the back of the Volvo and started loading her bags in. She glanced at Summer's hands. She still had her nails done in a deep crimson, an appropriate color for a killer, and her hands were large, almost man hands. Certainly, they were capable of plunging a cake knife into a man's chest.

"So, tomorrow is the hearing for the poor little librarian," Summer said. "I bet she gets put away for life."

"That would certainly work out well for you, wouldn't it?" Maggie asked. She slammed the back of her Volvo shut and glared at the bleached blonde in front of her.

Summer frowned at her. "What's it got to do with me?"

"With the wrong person in jail, the police won't arrest the real killer—you!" Maggie said.

Summer blinked at her. Then she tipped her head back and laughed. It was a raucous laugh that roared up from her belly and caused other people in the parking lot to turn and stare at them.

"You kill me, Gerber," Summer said. She carefully wiped away the moisture from her eyes, so as not to smear her thick black eyeliner. "Why on earth would I have killed John Templeton?"

"Because you're broke," Maggie said.

Summer's eyes widened, and Maggie continued. "Oh yeah, I know you're busted, and John Templeton was slated for—what are you on now, husband number five or six? I've lost count."

"So what if I was seeing Templeton?" Summer asked. "Your theory is stupid. Not a surprise, because why would I kill off the man I'm planning to have bankroll me? That's just dumb."

"I don't know," Maggie said. "Maybe he rejected you. Maybe he's just not that into fake boobs and big hair, and you snapped and killed him."

Summer's nostrils flared. "The girls are not fake."

"Oh *puleeze*," Maggie said. "You can't defy gravity at forty unless you have an assist."

"Maybe *you* can't," Summer snapped back with a pointed look at Maggie's chest.

"So, did you know that he used to know Claire?" she asked. "Is that why you chose the library? Or did you just have fond memories of the basement and thought you'd like to revisit it with a lover?"

"You're mental," Summer said.

"So, what happened? Did you get down there and he refused you, so you grabbed Claire's knife and got him in the chest? Nice touch leaving Claire's book by his side. Really, I didn't think you had the brains to pull off such a frame up. But, of course, you didn't, because you're about to get caught."

"I always knew you were weird," Summer said. She stepped away from Maggie's car as if she were backing away from a crazy person. "But now you're just plain nuts. I didn't know John knew the book geek, and I'm not a reader. I'm more of a TV gal, so I certainly wouldn't have a copy of one of her books. You know, you might want to have Dr. Franklin check you out, because you are losing it."

She was so smug. Maggie watched her walk away and really wished she had conked her with the slab of beef.

Well, Summer could protest all she wanted, but the truth would come out. The information Maggie had gotten from Trudi that morning confirmed in her mind that Summer was the most likely candidate to have stabbed Templeton.

Maggie rushed home to unload the groceries. While she was there, Mrs. Kellerman from the dry cleaner called to tell her that Max's suit was ready.

Maggie left Sandy to cook dinner while she hurried back into town. She wanted to get Max his suit as soon as possible so he could try it on and make sure it fit. Also, she wanted to stop by the jail and talk to Sam about her suspicions regarding Summer.

Maggie paid Mrs. Kellerman, who had done an amazing job with the tailoring and the cleaning. The suit looked brand new. Then she hung the suit carefully in the back of her car and headed over to the Frosty Freeze.

She didn't see Hugh Simpson's car, which was a relief. She no longer thought his e-mails, although shocking, were proof that he had murdered Templeton—not now that she had Summer Phillips in her sights.

Maggie waved to Max through the front window. There was no one in line for ice cream, so she signaled that she'd meet him by the back door. The door opened, and she handed him the plastic-wrapped suit on the wire hanger.

"Here you go," she said. "Do you have a place to hang it? You don't want it getting wrinkled."

"I think I can hang it on the door to Hugh's office," he said.

Maggie followed him in—not to micromanage, she told herself—just to make sure he did it right.

"So, Max, I found out some news today that I think might help Claire," she said as she followed him down the short hall.

"What?" he asked. His eyes were big beacons of hope.

"I think Summer Phillips may have killed Templeton."

Max rolled his eyes. "Maggie, just because the woman slammed you with a banana split does not mean you can accuse her of murder."

"No, listen. You were in the dressing room when I was talking to Trudi, but she said that Summer is broke and was going after Templeton to be her new sugar daddy."

"Then why kill him?" Max turned the hook part of the wire hanger forty-five degrees and hung it over the top of the door.

Maggie ran her hand over the plastic covering, making sure the suit was smooth.

"Because he rejected her," she said. "She's a vicious, evil woman and probably couldn't stand the rejection."

"I think you're reaching," Max said. "What about the lack of prints on the cake knife? What about Claire's book *The House of Mirth* being found beside the body? That was premeditated, with Claire being the object of the frame. Summer isn't capable of that. I doubt she even reads."

"Well, who do you think murdered Templeton?" Maggie asked.

"Well, I don't know," he said. "I've been busy trying to defend her, not solve the murder. Who is your next best suspect?"

"Whoever Claire loaned *The House of Mirth* to," Maggie said. She sucked in a breath. Just like that it all came into focus. "The key is the book."

"Brilliant deduction, Maggie," a voice said from behind them. "I was wondering how long it would take for you to get there."

Max and Maggie whipped around to find Gwen Morgan standing in the open back door, holding a very large, very lethal looking knife.

Chapter 33

"Gwen," Maggie said. "What are you doing?"

"Sadly, it appears I'm tying up loose ends," she said. "I knew when you were in the Perk Up today that I'd said too much. I knew it as soon as I mentioned the book. Who else would know about the book but the killer?"

"You killed John Templeton," Max said. His voice cracked, and Maggie knew he was as shocked as she was.

Gwen didn't answer him. She didn't have to. Maggie felt so stupid. Her hatred of Summer had blinded her to the real killer. She should have picked up on the fact that Gwen knew about the book. Sam had told her that the killer was probably a woman, and she knew from talking to Jay that Gwen had probably been working with John behind his back.

"Jay doesn't know, does he?" Maggie asked. "You did a deal with Templeton behind his back."

Gwen shrugged. "Jay is a child, a big, lovable child, and the realities of business are beyond him."

"Why?" Maggie asked. "Why did you do it? Why did you frame Claire?"

"I should think it would be obvious," Gwen said. "John demanded payment on the loan, we couldn't afford it, so I did some . . . favors for him, but then even that wasn't enough. He was going to take our shop."

She sagged, looking suddenly very tired.

"So, you were the woman Templeton was fooling around with," Maggie said. "Eva said she found a bra in his car."

"Mine," Gwen admitted. "I had no choice. Then, when Templeton called in the loan, I couldn't tell Jay what I had done or what I had been doing. As for framing Claire, John had told me all about her. I knew when he was killed their past would come out, so I figured it was her or me. She was kind enough to leave her cake knife behind at the library. I used a plastic glove from the restaurant, and between that and the book, my setup was complete."

They were all silent. Max kept opening and closing his mouth as if he couldn't believe what was happening, and Maggie was trying desperately to think of a way out. There was none. Gwen had the knife. Gwen had the power.

"On the upside," Gwen said. "I'm not really up for stabbing anyone again, so you two will just have to suffer an unfortunate accident." Her eyes lit on the door to the walk-in freezer.

"Open it," she said to Max.

He balked. "You can't put us in there. We'll freeze to death."

Gwen gave him a look that said, *"Duh."*

"Wait. Give me your keys," she said to Maggie. "I'm going to need to move your car. I wouldn't want anyone to notice it and get suspicious too soon."

Slowly, trying to buy time and think her way out of this, Maggie held out the keys. Gwen snatched them out of her dangling fingers.

She gestured with the knife for Max to open the door. Frosty air misted out at them when Max opened it.

"Get in," Gwen said.

"No," Maggie said. "Don't do it, Max. She can't stab both of us."

"Can't I?" Gwen asked. She did some complicated twirl thing with the knife, flipping it over the back of her hand, while never breaking eye contact with them. When she got done with her showmanship, the knife appeared a mere centimeter from Maggie's nose.

"I used to work at Benihana," Gwen said.

Maggie gulped, and when Max grabbed her sleeve and pulled her back into the freezer, she went. The door slammed shut behind them with a loud *thunk*.

"I don't like closed-in spaces, Max," Maggie said.

"Don't worry," he said. "There is a safety latch. Even if she locks it on the outside, we can get out. Let's just wait a few minutes until she clears out."

"Okay," Maggie said.

She walked down the narrow aisle to the end of the freezer and back. She counted in her head to try and mark the time. Max, meanwhile, stayed near the door with his head cocked, as if trying to hear what was going on outside the steel door. When she hit the five-minute mark, Maggie was ready. More than ready. The cold was beginning to seep into her bones, and she was shivering uncontrollably

"Let's try to open it," she said.

Max nodded and pressed the safety lever. The door moved, but barely. He tried it again. Nothing. He threw his full body weight against it. Still, it didn't budge.

"Yeah, sorry about that," Gwen called in through the tiny crack. "I know about the safety latch, you see, and I can't have you getting out, so I wedged a broom under the handle. And don't worry, I locked up the Frosty Freeze for the night. You should remain undisturbed."

Max and Maggie strained to listen, but all they heard was the sound of the back door closing.

"Oh my God!" Maggie said. "We're going to freeze to death. She's going to let us freeze to death."

"Calm down, Maggie," Max said. He sounded completely unconcerned. "We'll find a way out of this."

"Do you have a phone on you?" Maggie asked.

"No," he admitted.

"We're going to become human popsicles," she said.

"Relax, it takes a while for hypothermia to set in," Max said. He was running his hands over the tiny crack in the door as if looking for something.

"How long?" Maggie asked.

"That depends," he said. "It sets in faster if you're wet and it's windy, but basically once your core body temperature is below ninety-five, you're in trouble."

Maggie's teeth began to chatter, and she wasn't sure if it was from fear or the freezing cold.

"I think this is all a case of leverage," he said. He glanced around the freezer. "I need something metal and strong."

Maggie looked at the shelves of ice cream cakes and tubs of flavored ice cream. "Like what?"

"A makeshift crowbar," he said. "Here, help me."

Max began to off-load ice cream tubs onto the floor. Maggie helped him. The huge five-gallon tubs were heavy and hard, but once the steel shelf was clear, Max was able to pull it from its fasteners.

He wedged one end into the tiny crack in the door and then began to pull, trying to pry it open. Maggie moved to stand beside him, and together they pulled using all of their body weight.

Maggie grunted, and Max said, "No, no noise. Focus all of your energy on the opening."

"What are you, a labor coach?" she asked.

"On three," he said. "One, two, three."

They pulled, and Maggie could swear she felt the door move, but when she looked, there was no notable difference.

She sagged against the shelf.

"Again," Max ordered.

Maggie let him be bossy, because at least the physical activity was warming her up. They tried again and again. Still, it didn't feel as if they were making any progress.

"Max, there has to be another way," Maggie said. She couldn't feel the tips of her fingers, and she was pretty sure her lips were blue.

"If there is, I can't think of it," he said. "Come on, try again, and this time you can yell and scream all you want."

They stood shoulder to shoulder, and Maggie let out a war whoop as they pulled against the shelf. Even Max let out a few throaty yells, and Maggie echoed them. And suddenly, they weren't pushing against the shelf anymore but

Chapter 34

"Maggie! Max! Are you all right?" he asked as he lifted them to their feet.

He let go of Max, but his arm went around Maggie, pulling her close as he rubbed her bare arms, trying to warm her.

"It's Gwen," Maggie said. "She's the one who killed Templeton."

"I know," Sam said. "In fact, she's outside with Deputy Wilson."

"You mean you caught her?" Max asked.

Sam nodded. "We're taking her in right now. She actually thought she'd get away with it all. Oh, and your client, Claire Freemont, is being processed out as we speak."

"I have to get down there," Max said. "She might need me."

"Come on, I'll give you a ride," Sam said.

"How did you . . . ?" Maggie asked, letting the question dangle.

"Your note," he said. "The note you left with Deputy Crosthwaite put it all together. Come on, I'll explain while we drive."

Outside, a very unhappy-looking Gwen Morgan was sitting in the back of one of the sheriff's squad cars. Deputy Wilson—Dot—had her arms crossed over her chest while she glared at the woman in her car as if daring her to make one false move.

"You ready to roll, Dot?" Sam asked.

"I was born ready," Dot answered, and she climbed into her car.

Sam gestured for Maggie and Max to climb into his car, and they followed Dot all the way back to the jail.

"So, how did you figure out from my note that the killer was Gwen, when I was pretty emphatic that it was Summer?" Maggie asked.

She turned in her seat so that Max, who was in back, could hear her.

"I took the note to Claire," he said. "You know, the book that was left at the scene of the murder—we just assumed it came from the basement. But because you singled it out as having been put there on purpose by Summer, well, it made me rethink. "

"I asked Claire who she loaned the book to, and she—"

"Said Gwen Morgan," Max jumped in.

"No," Sam said. "She said Tyler Fawkes."

"Huh?" Maggie was confused.

"So, then I tracked down Tyler Fawkes," he said. "And he had loaned it to—"

"Gwen Morgan," Max said again.

"No," Sam said. "He loaned it to Alice Franklin, who loaned it to Bill Parsons, who loaned it to Cheryl Kincaid, who used it for third base during a softball game, and then left it in the Perk Up after the game for Gwen Morgan."

"Whoa, talk about your six degrees of separation," Max said.

"Indeed," Sam agreed. "From there it was pretty easy to read the Perk Up's financials and see that Gwen had taken money from Templeton and that they were in trouble."

Sam pulled into the parking lot behind Dot. While Dot escorted Gwen into the building to be processed, Max ran around them to help expedite Claire's release.

Sam opened the car door for Maggie and looked her over when she stood before him. "Are you all right? No frostbite?"

She shook her head. "No, we got lucky. I don't know what would have happened to us if you hadn't gotten there when you did." She placed her hand on his arm while her gaze met his. "Thank you, Sam."

Sam looked like he wanted to say something, but instead he opened his arms and pulled her in for a hug. He held her for a minute without speaking, and then he leaned close to her ear and whispered, "Don't ever scare me like that again, Carrots."

Maggie smiled into his shirt front, surprised that she didn't feel the need to knee him in the privates for use of the abhorred nickname.

Sam must have been surprised, too, because he pulled back to study her face. "Don't tell me we're going to become friends now."

"Why not?" she asked.

"We've been everything else," he said.

"Enemies," she said.

"Lovers," he said.

Maggie felt her face get hot, but she ignored it.

"Maybe being friends will suit us," she said.

"Maybe." But the look he gave her scorched, and Maggie wondered if perhaps he viewed friendship a bit differently than she did.

"There is one thing we need to clear the air on, however," he said.

"What's that?" Maggie asked.

"I was never in the library basement with Summer Phillips," he said. "That was someone else."

"But I saw your football jersey," she said. "Clear as day. The name on the back of it read Collins."

"Yeah, I gave that jersey to Tim Kelly to hang in his bar at the end of the school year," Sam said. "When I was in his bar the other night, he told me Summer Phillips had borrowed it the night before I left town. She told him she was going to have me autograph it. I checked the signature. It isn't mine, but I didn't have the heart to tell Tim that."

"So that wasn't you?" she asked. "She set me up."

Sam nodded. Maggie felt as if she'd been sucker punched. She had a million more questions for him, but she never got the chance to ask them.

Just then the doors to the building burst wide open and

out ran Claire with Max, Ginger and Joanne right behind her. Maggie was enveloped into a group hug that included tears, crusher squeezes and lots of laughter. When she did extricate herself from her peeps to look for Sam, she saw him walking into the building. He didn't look back.

The Good Buy Girls' Top Ten Thrifty Tips

1. Do as Maggie does and sign up for every free customer rewards program you can. Dedicate one e-mail account to these programs, which you can monitor for special savings and deals. Even if you rarely shop at some of these stores, having a rewards card will eventually earn you coupons and discounts.

2. Joanne is the list-maker, and her advice is to write a list before you go shopping—and stick to it. Make a careful plan of what to buy before you go and don't put anything in the cart that's not on the list.

3. Follow Maggie's advice and clean out your closet. If you haven't worn something within the last year, get rid of it. You can have a yard sale or take it to a consignment shop, or even donate it for a tax deduction.

4. Ginger's best tip is to plan your meals around your grocery store's flier. With five men to feed, she can get creative in the kitchen but needs to buy the food that's on sale in the grocery store's flier. You can do the same.

5. Claire recommends doing your holiday shopping right after the holidays. And she doesn't mean just for Christmas—the day after any holiday is an excellent time to stock up. Buy your plastic eggs the day after Easter or your Fourth of July decorations the day after Independence Day, when the prices are usually 50 to 75 percent off.

6. Ginger's tip when shopping for seasonal items, such as children's sports equipment: Start by shopping used. Used items cost so much less than retail and are usually in fine condition.

7. Joanne suggests learning to live by the golden rule of the ten-second pause. When you pick up an item, before you can add it to your cart or take it to the cashier, pause for ten seconds and consider why you're buying it and whether you really need it. If not, put it back.

8. Ginger suggests trying generic brands of items you buy regularly, like vitamins. Instead of sticking to your familiar label, try the store brand or generic version of the item.

9. Claire suggests going to your local library. It's not just for books anymore. Libraries have free computer access, DVDs, CDs, video games, free passes to museums and loads more. Some even have their own cafés.

10. Maggie recommends buying your staples in bulk. If you buy your non-perishables, such as trash bags, detergents, diapers and so on, in bulk, it cuts down on their cost per usage by quite a bit and will save you a nice chunk of change.

A heartless murder for Valentine's Day.

FROM
JENN MCKINLAY

Buttercream Bump Off

A Cupcake Bakery Mystery

Melanie Cooper and Angie DeLaura's Fairy Tale Cupcakes bakery is gearing up for Valentine's Day. Unfortunately someone has iced Baxter Malloy on his first date with Mel's mother. Now she's a suspect, and Mel and Angie need to find time between frosting Kiss Me Cupcakes to dig into Malloy's shady past and discover who served him his just desserts.

PRAISE FOR *SPRINKLE WITH MURDER*

"A tender cozy full of warm and likable characters . . . Readers will look forward to more of McKinlay's tasty concoctions."   —*Publishers Weekly* (starred review)

"A delicious new series!"
—Krista Davis, author of the Domestic Diva Mysteries

INCLUDES SCRUMPTIOUS RECIPES!

JENN MCKINLAY

Death by the Dozen

A Cupcake Bakery Mystery

Melanie Cooper and Angie DeLaura are determined to win the challenge to the chefs to promote their Fairy Tale Cupcakes bakery. Mel's mentor from culinary school, Vic Mazzotta, is one of the judges, but Mel and Angie will have to win fair and square. When Vic's dead body is found inside a freezer truck, Mel and Angie will need to use their best judgment to find the cold-blooded killer who iced Vic, or they may lose more than the contest—they may lose their lives . . .

INCLUDES SCRUMPTIOUS RECIPES!

PRAISE FOR THE CUPCAKE BAKERY MYSTERIES

"A tender cozy full of warm and likable characters . . . Readers will look forward to more of McKinlay's tasty concoctions." —*Publishers Weekly* (starred review)

"Delivers all the ingredients for a winning read."
        —Cleo Coyle, author of the Coffeehouse Mysteries